About the author

Georgia Benvenuti is a young Australian author debuting her first novel, *Raider*. She works as a clinical nurse in a private hospital in Brisbane. Georgia currently lives at home with her family and dog, Lulu.

RAIDER

GEORGIA BENVENUTI

RAIDER

Vanguard Press

Dedication

To my family, who I love. Will you read it now?

Chapter One

Another burning flash of golden light flew across the sky as we drove along the panicked street. Dad swerved the truck to dodge the other cars; some piled up in burning heaps in the mayhem and confusion. I'd never seen so much on fire, except on the TV, but that was in other places where the war was. All the stories they'd tried to keep from us about the children disappearing and those who were left being rounded up by these creatures. I was told I would understand when I was older, but I felt I was grasping the situation pretty quickly at the moment. Mum and Dad had said we were safe here; no one would be able to get us. Perhaps Mum and Dad were wrong? But that couldn't be right.

"Kids! Hold on!" Mum shouted from the front seat.

I looked up at her, seeing more golden lights explode through the night sky outside the windshield. My brothers were quiet by my sides, looking out at the devastation through their windows. Enormous dark ships with gold lights were landing all over the place: on top of houses, in the middle of streets and shopping centres. I didn't dare to look out of the window again after seeing one crash straight through my favourite playground. People ran through the streets, crying and shouting as they watched their homes being destroyed and their loved ones trapped in the wreckages with no chance of help or escape. Some of them came towards the cars, slamming their hands on the doors as we tried to dash through the destruction. It felt bad that we were leaving them behind. I looked up through the sun roof, watching the gold lights come closer and closer. There seemed to be so many of them. I felt the fear run rampant through my mind.

"Does dying hurt?" I mumbled, as we continued to drive recklessly through the streets.

"We're not going to die, Maddy. We just have to make it out of the city. There's a rally point there, and people who can help get us away," Dad said calmly, as he concentrated on the road.

"We're going to die?" Max asked from my right, as he kept looking out of his window. Another gold ship crashed through a two-storey house, and he jumped back towards me in fear.

"Jackson at school said that we go to heaven when we die. But we have to climb a lot of stairs…" I continued mumbling. However, Max's comment seemed to set off my other brother, Jasper.

"Oh, no… No, I don't want to die. Can't we just go home? They can't get us there!" he shouted, distressed.

"Kids – calm down!" Dad shouted now, taking a quick look back at the three of us. His brown eyes were filled with worry. Mum put her hand on his arm and they shared a small moment. It was as if they had a whole conversation just by looking into each other's eyes.

"Kids – remember that summer we spent camping up at the lake? We went on that bushwalk and got horribly, terribly lost?" she said warmly, although I could hear her voice shake as she spoke.

I nodded, but I think the boys were sort of too distracted to answer.

"Well, we walked for hours and hours and it was dark when we made it back to camp, but we made it. Your father knows what he's doing, just like then. We just need to stay calm and stay together, all right?" Mum said kindly, but reaching forwards and giving Max a firm squeeze of his hand.

We drove on for a few more minutes or so, racing past the destruction and into a relatively new neighbourhood that seemed untouched by the ships landing behind us. I felt the truck kick into another gear as we sped off. I looked back up at the night sky through the sun roof, resting my head back against the seat. Mum and Dad were right: we would be safe. Nothing bad could happen to us with them here.

Suddenly, out of nowhere, a mix of golden light flew right over our heads, spinning and gliding through the air before screeching to a halt as it crash-landed on the road in front of us. A jet screamed over our heads as it made a turn back towards the ships, the noise of it rattling the car. Jasper put his hands over his ears, screaming and ducking his head down to his knees.

"No, Jaz – come on," Mum said, reaching back to try to calm him down.

But the real concern was what was ahead of us. We were at a crossroads and there were other cars and trucks heading straight for the wreckage, as well. Dad swerved to get around it and to steer clear of the other traffic, but we were going too fast and there wasn't enough time. The back of the truck began to swing as he hit the brakes as hard as he could, sending us skidding and smashing straight into the dark ship on fire in the middle of the road. The front of the truck crumpled and crushed, making a noise so deafening I thought my head would explode. Mum, who had been turned around in her seat, lifted her head slowly.

"Is everyone all right?" she asked, trying to reach for Jasper again. No one answered, but Jasper made a move for the door handle, taking off his seat belt. He didn't like the car at the best of times.

Suddenly, another pair of lights came from our left and swerved a little before spinning and hitting us hard in our side, tipping the truck over.

I heard a few screams and the frightful, sharp breaths of my family members. As the truck rolled, Max, Jasper and I bumped into each other, yelling out in pain as windows shattered and the glass fell in on us. When the truck finally stopped rolling, everything was dark except for the two flickering lights of the truck that rammed us glowing gloomily outside the broken windows. My head hurt really badly and my tummy was still turning, even though I had stopped. I looked through the smashed sun roof, seeing other cars zooming past the wreckage, as we had done, before. I was lying heavily on Max, held in place by my seat belt, but I couldn't see Jasper anywhere. I looked back up to where he had been sitting next to me just moments ago, but the door was gone.

"Max…" I said, uneasily. "I'll get out. We can get out. I just have to get my seat belt…" I said, trying to be brave, showing that I had a plan. Suddenly, the dark ship sprang to life again, its engine buzzing and the golden lights glaring.

"Mum? Dad?" I called out shakily, as I tried to take my seatbelt off. There was no answer. Feeling panicked by the fact the ship was running again, I moved a lot quicker. I pushed hard on the back of Dad's chair, trying to hold myself up off Max. With a few hard tugs, I finally got free of my belt and clambered over my brother and out through the sun roof.

I scratched my arms as I climbed out, but I didn't care. I turned back to Max, his round face covered with blood.

"Hold on, Max…" I said, trying to be reassuring, but I could hear the panic in my voice.

I reached back in through the sun roof and unclipped his belt. He rolled forwards, with a cry of pain.

"My leg!" he whimpered, his hands moving to hold it, curling up in a ball on the broken glass.

Max was only a couple of years older than me, but he wasn't that big for a twelve-year old. I held out my hands shakily to him. "Come on – we have to get out," I said, looking back at the flashing gold lights.

He took my hands and with much effort, I managed to get him through the sun roof. I pulled him over to the kerb and sat him down on the grass, a little way from the pile-up.

"Wait… Where's Jasper?" Max asked, quietly, looking back at the wreckage. Cars zoomed dangerously past us as we sat on the edge of the road.

"He wasn't in the truck. The door's gone…" I faded off, slowly. "Stay here. I'll help Mum and Dad," I called, as I ran back to the black truck, dodging the cars coming towards me.

"Mum? Dad?" I called loudly as I got back to where Max and I had escaped. Again, there was no answer.

I crawled back inside the truck to where my mother was slumped over, held up only by her seatbelt. I reached out my hands and pulled her head back up, hoping to see her loving eyes open and her warm smile there waiting. But her head just rolled… There were no signs of my warm mother left. My mind started to panic and my heart was racing. I tried to feel for a pulse, like they'd taught us about First Aid in school, but I wasn't sure. My hands wouldn't stop shaking as I held my fingers to her neck.

"Mum?" I asked, quietly, fighting back the tears. Nothing.

I shook away the tears and moved to my father next, hoping he would help me. My strong, sturdy father with his brown hair and brown eyes looked like a ghost in the gold light of the burning ship. I felt for a pulse but there was nothing. He felt so cold. Feeling my strength fading,

I couldn't keep the tears back much longer… I had to find Jasper. He had to be all right.

Suddenly, the flashing gold lights of the ship went solid and I could hear the sound of the hatch door opening. There were a few screams from people who had gathered out on the streets. I froze with fear as I looked through the smashed windscreen. A tall, pale creature emerged from the opening. It was wearing a black suit, but I couldn't see its face. It was too tall. I moved back to Max's seat and looked up through the upturned side of the truck. There, in one small moment, I saw it… A Raider. Its dark, soulless eyes and pale white skin; no sign of emotion. This was what was taking over my world, this thing… This alien.

I ducked down low, praying it hadn't seen me. It took a few steps away from its ship, away from me. I climbed up to Jasper's seat, holding onto the headrests and standing on the console. On my tiptoes, I peered out at the alien. Its strides were so long that it almost looked as though it was gliding across the road. It stopped when it reached a little red car, lying upside down. The people screamed from inside, still trapped in their belts. I could see only one child; a little boy with what must have been his parents. The Raider bent over and looked in at the little family for a moment before picking the car up and putting it upright in one fluid motion. I could hear the confusion from the onlookers… How could an alien, a Raider, help humans in all of this destruction? Their confusion was immediately resolved when the Raider reached out with one long, pale arm, dragging the little boy out of his seat. The child's parents screamed and yelled in fear for their son's life. The boy stayed stiff in the Raider's arms, tears running from his eyes. The Raider held him up, staring into his fearful eyes for a small moment before turning his cold stare into a blood-curdling smile. The Raider kept the boy in his grasp and turned back to the red car. It reached out its ghostly white hand to the father still trapped in the car, grabbing his neck, and with one ear-splitting crack, the man was dead. Chaos seemed to burst from everywhere as people screamed and began to run in all directions, as more of the ships landed over the houses and streets. Gold lights filled the sky, and all of my instincts told me to run as far away as I could, but I had to find my brother. I had to keep us together.

I slid back down to the sun roof, crawling back out onto the street. I took a quick look back at Max: he was still sitting on the curb, his eyes intently watching the Raider. I ducked around the back of the car and peeped out at the Raider still carrying the quiet boy in his arms and ferociously killing all who got in his way. Through all the gold light and small fires burning from the crash, I saw Jasper lying in between the red car and me, on top of the missing door from our truck. With the Raider's back turned, I took my chance, racing forwards, keeping low to the ground. Jasper was scrunched up in a ball and it took a moment for me to loosen his grip on the handle before grabbing his arms and dragging him as fast as I could away from the Raider, still destroying everything in its path. I made it quickly back to the curb where Max was sitting, impatiently.

"Is he all right?" he asked quietly, as I reached him, laying Jasper down in front of us.

"I don't know" I said, wearily, feeling at a loss for words or energy to do anything any more.

Max leaned forward, rolling Jasper's face towards us, his fingers feeling for a pulse in his neck. Jasper's face was covered in scratches and blood, with a few bits of glass still sticking out from his cheek.

"He's okay," Max said, quickly. "What about Mum and Dad?" he asked, turning to me.

I shrugged my shoulders. "I think they're gone. I checked and everything, the way they taught us in school, and they weren't awake or…" I trailed off with my tears.

"Come on, Madds. We've got to get them… We can't be alone," Max urged, holding my hand, his voice cracking a little with the loss. He jogged back across the street, leaving me alone with Jasper for a minute as I watched the Raider taking long strides as it lunged for people.

Max came back swiftly, his face very pale.

"Come on. They'll meet us there," he said, quickly, lifting me back to my feet.

I had a bad feeling he was lying to me, but if there was any hope of them being alive I was going to trust him and cling to it.

A loud buzzing noise fell over the street as what seemed like a wave of golden ships sped towards us. People began to scream and run, dropping everything. I looked at it, watching with horror as the ships began to open fire on the street, letting loose golden fireballs that rolled and smashed through everything in their path, burning tunnels into the ground.

I squeezed Max's hand tightly, feeling the heat as the fireballs made their way towards us.

"Off the road," Max said, loudly, pulling Jasper over to the closest house.

"Mum and Dad will just have to find us later, Maddy. Dad said there was a rally point… Must be at the border," he said, quietly, looking back up the road we had been travelling on. He talked mostly to himself, deciding for the three of us.

I looked around for anyone who could help us, but they were all running in different directions.

"How, Max? Jasper's hurt and we can't drag him all the way," I replied, still looking for something; someone.

"Someone's got to have a wheelbarrow around here…" he trailed off. "Come on," he said, quickly, before grabbing Jasper's arms and pulling him to the side of the house, dodging the fireball ripping right past us.

More Raiders were getting out of their gold ships now, their pale figures gliding across the ground. They seemed so much faster than all the humans running away from them, and effortlessly reached them to snatch the children and kill the parents. Jasper stirred from his place on the ground in the semi-darkness at the side of the house, mumbling a few bits of words I couldn't understand.

"Maddy, I got one!" I heard Max call back from the side of the house as he ran towards us. We both lifted the heavy Jasper into the red wheelbarrow. His lanky body kind of fitted in it and his arms slumped and swung over the edges as we ran through the rest of the street.

We took the first left and ran halfway down the street, where we found a small lane that cut in between the houses.

"Okay, let's go down there. It doesn't seem too dangerous," Max muttered, quietly. I followed close beside him, terrified of the dark little lane.

We ran through the lane to the next street, where it connected to the next and next. The only light we could see were from the flames of the burning houses on either side, where we could hear the buzzing of the Raider ships and their relentless firing. My heart raced with fear, and I helped push the wheelbarrow as much as I could.

Suddenly, we reached a cross section, with a huge black fence, lined with bright lights stretching as far as we could see in both directions. There were a few helicopters buzzing low over the area beyond the gate, with the traffic of people in cars and on foot bottle-necking at the entrance.

"We made it, Maddy," Max said happily, with a smile. "We're going to make it," he stated encouragingly to me, repeating it over and over.

We crossed the street and half-jogged to the gate. Everyone seemed panicked, and a lot of people looked hurt. Through the holes in the fence I could see trucks and buses lined up, filling with people. Other people were sitting in small groups, crying, and there were a lot of people screaming the names of those they had lost. I took a deep breath, hoping Mum and Dad were right to bring us here; hoping that when we got through we'd be safe.

We shuffled along in a big line. I stayed close to Max, holding the wheelbarrow like I did with Mum's shopping trolley. When we reached the front of the line, there were people shouting lots of different orders.

"Over here for injured people! Children this way! Families stay together!"

There was a very tall man in a dark uniform with a stressed look on his face. He looked straight at the three of us. "Ok, kids, you go that way and your injured friend will go to that truck over there," he said, quickly, pointing in different directions.

"We're not splitting up," Max responded, defiantly, putting down the wheelbarrow in a huff.

Before the soldier could answer, a huge explosion went off, not far from us. I could see the reflection of the bright fiery blast in his eyes. His arms kind of slumped to his sides and he dropped his clipboard into the dust. I picked it up for him, trying to give it back, but he was stunned. I turned to look back, and really wished I hadn't. Another wave of golden

Raider ships burst through the tall flames, shooting gold fireballs at the houses and making their way straight for us.

"Max…" I gasped, breathlessly.

The soldier continued to stare at the approaching ships. Panic was all over his face as he was stood, frozen with fear, his thoughts stalling. Max quickly looked at me, determination on his face, and picked up the wheelbarrow, rolling swiftly past the frozen soldier. I tried once more to give him back his clipboard, and he took it slowly, his lip shaking.

We ran through the gates and towards the trucks for the injured. There didn't seem to be many left and lots of people were running and getting onto any truck they could see. We ran as fast as we could, pushing Jasper in the wheelbarrow, but everyone was overtaking us, pushing and bumping us along. I hated being so small: I couldn't see where anything was. All that was visible was a wall of bodies and flashing lights.

The truck we reached filled with people and took off, then another and another. I felt the hopelessness sinking in, but Max kept on pushing harder and harder. Finally, we made it to a big school bus. It looked almost full but we were towards the front of the line. There was a woman by the door letting people in and turning others away. She was stocky and short with dark hair. She looked worried when she saw us, pushing the wheelbarrow to the door.

"No, no…" she began. "You need to go to the medical trucks," she insisted, shaking her head.

"But they're all gone," Max said, wearily. "Please let us on. We'll all stack on top of each other and we won't be any trouble…" he pleaded.

People shoved past us to the front of the line, pushing their children ahead of us.

Max stopped and pulled Jasper out of the wheelbarrow, leaning him against his side. "Maddy – push to the front. We have to get on the bus…" he ordered, sternly.

I nodded, and pushed aside other kids, making our way back to the woman standing by the bus door.

"Fine. Get him on," she said, annoyed, throwing her arms in the air.

I stood aside as Max carried Jasper up the stairs. A couple of other kids helped and more people made it onto the bus.

More blasts erupted from the already chaotic scene, as helicopters from our side of the fence took off and more trucks went away. Everyone panicked at that moment. The bus engine turned on, kicking into gear as it slowly began to roll.

"Maddy!" I heard Max shout from inside the bus.

My heart jumped into my throat as I realised I had to get on now, but the long line of people bustled past me, and I got knocked over and pushed aside. The soldier woman pulled me towards her, picking me up off the ground.

"Don't worry. They said there'll be another bus," she said, assuredly, but I didn't believe her.

As the bus driver panicked, the doors of the packed vehicle closed suddenly, even with people still trying to get on, and it jerked away in a hurry, kicking up a cloud of dust behind it.

For one moment, my world slowed down. The screams of my brother faded into the background as my heart pumped louder and louder.

The next bus never came. Raiders and their ships surrounded us on all sides and I watched the headlights of the last rescue vehicles fade into the black night. I held on tightly to the woman I had only just met, but she was the only one I knew in the sea of lost faces. That was the last time I saw my brothers, and the last time I was ever really me.

Four Years Later

The hot metal poured through my back, burning its way along my spine. I could feel my insides cooking. There was a smell of burning flesh and the screams escaped my mouth as I tried desperately to relieve the pain. The hand of the pale Raider grasped mine tightly, as if it was trying to comfort me, but I didn't understand. She spoke kindly to me, telling me I was going to be all right, that she was my new home now. But I didn't want a new home: I wanted to see my brothers and my parents, but they were gone now. I was the one in danger, the one who got caught. The metal burned its way through my body, moving to every part, covering my bones and stretching out to my muscles and skin. I could feel it taking over, like a living thing. It took my body. I screamed out for help, begging for the pain to stop, as the last of the metal slowly stretched up to my mind. I wasn't afraid any more. The pain stopped and my body felt different, the cold hand grasping mine was comforting… with a flick of a switch I felt nothing, but now I belonged.

I woke up. I always have the same nightmare. But the result was always the same: I didn't feel sad about what had happened and I didn't miss my family. I sat up in my bunk and ran my hands through my long, strawberry-blonde hair. I was told not to be afraid and that humans who are against us are against everything good in the world. The Gouteszi, or what we call Raiders, didn't want to hurt us: they simply came back to Earth to take what was rightfully theirs. I looked around at the other sleeping kids in my dorm. They seemed untroubled in their dreams. Somehow, it was always me who was cursed with these flashing images running through my mind, interrupting my sleep.

Orders are that no one is allowed out of bed until dawn, but I desperately wanted to go for a walk to feel the cool night air on my skin. It went against every fibre in my body, but I managed to get up, put on my boots and walk to the end of the corridor. I could hear the synchronisation of hearts beating peacefully as the other kids slept:

everyone was made the same here. Knowing that no one was watching me from inside, I leant up against the door and listened out to the courtyard for the patrol. Like clockwork, the two Raider guards walked around the corner of our dormitory, passed the door and continued on. I couldn't hear anyone else out there, so I made my escape, quickly unlatching the door and running out to the courtyard. Peering around the corner of the dorm, I saw the two guards disappear around the other end, so I walked out across the courtyard and to the many rows of tents of sleeping Raiders. I knew the routine here; when the guards would come around and when we would be woken up. I walked quietly through the camp, avoiding all Raider eyes and keeping out of the guards' earshot. I always liked to do this; walk around the camp to stretch my legs before going back to the boring routine of being a solider. I could never understand how everyone else fell in line so obediently.

I made my way to the edge of camp, glad to see the beautiful trees the Raiders had planted. They glowed different colours: green and yellow, blue, purple and red, like veins along their dark shadowy trunks. The leaves glowed, as well, and some broke off from their branches as the wind rustled through. The trees were all connected through dark red veins of pulsing light under the ground. The further out the Raiders conquered, the more the trees began to flourish and spread, taking over the land in their own way. I loved being out here. No one ever came here at this time and it was like my own little forest of glowing night lights. I made it to the border of the camp, looking out at the free world. I could escape, I knew I could do it, but why? I had everything I needed and would ever want here with the Raiders. Besides, there were Rebels out there, hiding in their bases.

I could feel the change in the air as it began to warm: a sign that dawn was fast approaching. Begrudgingly, I turned away from the trees and made my way back to the dorm with ease, walking without fear as the guards went about their patrols, and slipping back into the dark room with the other kids still sleeping soundly. I quietly got back into bed and waited for dawn to come.

My brothers' faces always flashed in my mind, like they were still calling for me to get on the bus. I always viewed my past like a movie, not really invested and you know what you should be feeling, but it always ended up being distant. The Raiders broke through the barrier of the city and surrounded all of us who were left behind. At first there was some confusion, but when they began to separate the young from the old, the weak from the strong, it was quite clear there was some intention for us. Many people wept as they were torn apart from their loved ones. I don't remember crying. There was widespread fear and anger. I remembered being very cold as I was pushed into a carrier ship with other children, and sent to a large warehouse. The one thing I remembered being unsettled about were the screams: hundreds of children yelling and crying, whimpering as they were turned into the Raiders' soldiers. My mind wandered through my memories like a clear timeline printed on a page: everything was set out neatly, all my questions were answered and I had everything I needed. My brothers were bad for trying to run away from the Raiders; there is no such thing as love, only selfishness… Lines were drilled into my mind; all the things I was told about my life that I had to accept. I don't know if I can accept them like everyone else did.

I heard the shuffling of heavy footsteps on the dusty ground outside the dorm. I listened hard to the world outside and heard the quickening heartbeats of the waking Raiders in their tents. I waited patiently for the squad leader to begin our day.

Three… two… one.

***

"Children, wake up," chimed Kartiia, as she entered the room.

She was like all the other Raiders: pale skin with dark eyes, except she had faded black marks across her skin. She was a Class-Three Raider. She was still, of course, super tall and terrifying but didn't seem to glide as smoothly as the others. Class Threes were pretty much the runts of the Raiders, their DNA marred by the endless copying and printing to add to their numbers. The more they made, the further they got away from being proper Raiders. Besides that, Kartiia always made me feel stronger: with every word, she made things seem more hopeful. She was the one, after all, who was in my dreams, telling me I was going to be all right and holding my hand when they had changed me. I think all the squad leaders had this effect on their squads. I once heard about one squad who lost their Raider leader, and they all died. It was as if their bodies didn't want to live any more. But that was just talk I'd overheard from a few guards.

Like machines, we all sat up in our beds, as if we had all been lying awake waiting for her call, but that was never the case. The Raiders always managed to control us, to make us behave and be good little soldiers. I'm just glad I'm a good liar.

We all moved simultaneously to the ends of our beds, putting on our black jackets and boots. We always slept in our uniforms: that way we were ready for a fight at all times.

"Everyone line up. General Carterra is holding an assembly," Kartiia said, happily, checking each of our uniforms as we walked past.

I stepped out of the doorway, glad to see the rising sun and the pink and orange colours it made in the sky. I didn't look too long, otherwise Raiders would notice me. I followed the line, marching out into the courtyard with my eyes forward. The courtyard was a large area, with the bright green grass beneath our feet and no roof above our heads. There were some silvery metallic veins that stretched under our feet; like the trees, they glowed different colours. I wasn't sure what they did, but they were quite mesmerising, nevertheless. I watched as other kids filed out of their dormitories across from us. We all walked in our lines to the front, filing along to make a perfect formation. No one taught us how to do this: it was just always in our heads. We knew where they wanted us to stand.

It took only a minute before we were all out and in lines. I could see most of the Eastern side of the camp. Hundreds of tents stretched out in front of me. Mixed in with them were larger open spaces used as dining areas. The main building, Headquarters, was to my left. It was as though a huge, grey box had been plonked down in the middle of a field. We had other larger buildings: to the west were the Hornet Hangers; to the north, the supplies; the south comprised the main training facility and another supply building, and to the east was the Armoury. The Armoury building wasn't very high, but it was spectacular underground. When the main-carrier Raider ships landed, they drilled into the ground. Like a ready-to-go civilisation. The base was made of three of these ships: huge, black, spiky-looking things. From the surface, they looked like a circle of daggers pointing dangerously out of the ground surrounding HQ, the

Armoury and one of the supply buildings. Other buildings had been built after the Raiders got here. The metallic veins stretched out from the ships, changing the ground and working in the Raiders' own ecosystem, mixed in with the camp.

General Carterra marched out from the doors of Headquarters, followed by a few other Raiders. He was stocky for a Raider, but was still just as tall and just as pale; his eyes were soulless, black holes. He was Class Two, the closest you could get to being a real Raider, without being in the royal family, that is. He was very intent on making sure Classes were separated, that everyone knew their place. We human soldiers, we were at the very bottom.

I stood in the front of the line as the general walked past, keeping my head held high and my eyes forward, trying hard to not get distracted by my surroundings.

"You have all come a long way," the general spoke, proudly, as he came to a stop in the middle of the courtyard. "Many of you have lost much, but now, in this new-found life, you have gained a new way to live." He walked along the lines of us, standing in our black uniforms. "Great is the mercy of the Gouteszi and our mercy has led to the victory of your race. We have brought peace. But there are those who will stand against us; those who believe we claim no right to this world. As children of Earth, and now heroes of the Gouteszi, you will prove them wrong. You will infiltrate and capture the humans who do not believe in our cause, and together, my dear children, we shall put an end to these rebels, and bring peace to our home."

The general looked back up and down the line, his eyes hungry for war. "You will receive your orders immediately, and set off into the night. Good luck, my dear children. I know you will make us proud," he added, with a smile, before striding back up to Headquarters, followed again by the other Raiders.

We stood there for another few moments as our Team Leaders talked quietly amongst each other. They were all Class Threes. I felt almost excited at the chance of leaving the camp, by going out and causing some damage.

Minutes later, we were all marched to the east, to the Armoury. Each dormitory was a team; a squad of its own. Each had ten boys and ten girls. Out in the field, we would have a leader chosen by Kartiia. Usually, it was Wade – one of the older boys. We walked in through the grey, guarded doors of the Armoury and into the cool building. The Armoury was like all the other buildings: high ceilings, cool dark metal walls and concrete floors… Nothing spectacular. Guards stood outside each door along the long-stretching hallways.

We all walked down the first hallway to the left, keeping our eyes forward, stepping confidently past the guards' careful watch. When we reached the end of the corridor, we each walked through the last door, down a staircase and into the first of the lower levels of the Armoury. The first level was twice the size of the building above the ground. We all filed out to the edge of the terrace, peering down at the bustling world beneath. There were many floors to the Armoury, with the staircase circling down to each one leaving a big, open hole stretching all the way down to the last floor. I could see the many Raiders testing strange weapons and running and leaping over blocks, jumping out from walls and the floors.

Suddenly, there was a huge burst of golden light coming from the bottom floor. The light rose increasingly quickly and a large gust of hot air shot upwards, thick with the smell of burning toast. Some of the kids by my side jumped back as the lights rose higher and higher, but I stood my ground, fascinated by the buzzing thing climbing up through the air. The gold lights came to a stop right in front of us. Hovering in the air was a Hornet. I had never seen one so up-close before; not since the night my parents died. It waited there for a moment before a bright light opened in front of it, leading to a large hangar. Inside were heaps of Hornets, their bright, gold lights filled the empty space, all buzzing in harmony as if they were alive. Hornets are not the biggest ship the Raiders have, but are still pretty capable of some scary damage. They are made out of a dark onyx metal that shines like the sun and its body is the size of a couple of trucks. Hornets are torpedo-shaped, widening towards the tail which has two vertically standing fins. They have two sets of wings, the first pointing forwards, and each with two golden orbs that are the power source for the ship. The second pair of wings point backwards, acting as stabilisers. The Hornets have barb-like spikes extending from the ships' golden-glowing spine. As for the deadly parts, Hornets have two sets of high-energy blasters that let off huge fireballs that can rip and burn through anything.

'I want one,' was all I could think as I watched the Hornet move through and find a place to land with the rest of them.

"This way, children," called a voice from the front of the line, breaking through my selfish thoughts.

We reformed our lines and marched along the last of the terraces and down the stairs to the next floor. A Raider waited, patiently, behind a desk. She had light-brown hair and dark eyes, but something about her movement made her seem almost caring, motherly. She had a dark patch of skin on the side of her neck, and she seemed quite a lot smaller than the Class Twos. On either side of her, conveyer belts disappeared into the wall behind her.

We all waited in line as she took a pack from the conveyer belt on her left and weapons from the right. She was very quick at her job and before I knew it, it was my turn.

"Hello. Please place your wrist inside the scanner," she ordered happily, as she pointed to the opening sticking out from her desk.

Without hesitation I shoved my hand in and felt the quick burn from the scanner. There were too many of us kids to know by name, so to keep track of us all we each had to have a blood test to be sure of who we were. The metal in our bodies made it a lot easier to identify us, and the scanners only had to make one little slice across our wrist, which healed immediately afterwards, anyway.

"Maddy," she announced, with a smile. She quickly entered something into the machine on her desk. "Please put your hand back in for your orders."

I obeyed and felt a small pin prick in my wrist. My mind filled with schematics, time logs and a mission report. It felt like I had sat on my bed and read through all of these things, studying them long enough for them to be imprinted on my mind.

She turned back to pull my pack and weapons from the conveyer belts. "I bet you must be excited to get out of here?" she asked, smiling.

"I go where I am told, ma'am," I replied, flatly.

"Good girl. Here is your pack," she said, as she handed me my black pack. "And your weapons."

I eagerly took my two swords, dagger and fire-blaster. My weapons and I had been through a lot together, and they had gotten me out of a few sticky situations with the rebels. I always felt a bit lost and pathetic without my weapons, but everyone knows I was pretty hard to beat, even on my own.

I chucked on my pack and weapons and moved back to re-join the line returning to the surface. Every kid had their own preference when it came to weapons: no matter how hard the Raiders tried, we were still all unique. Most of the kids had guns and a dagger: me, I preferred looking in the eyes of the people I killed. That fact may have brought me some unwanted attention from both the Raiders and the Rebels.

We all made it back to our dorms and went on with our daily jobs around the base. I was on the building detail, mainly on housing, for the Raiders. Apparently there were more coming so we had to get the place ready to be sustainable for a larger number. I liked getting to work: it definitely helped to keep my mind off my past. I carried planks of wood and this Raider material, which was like a woven cover but completely waterproof and insulated, perfect for roofing houses. At night, you could see the sky through it, if you wanted to. On my fiftieth run back, carrying a few planks over my shoulder, I came across a not-so-good sight. A Class-Three Raider was getting absolutely beaten to a pulp in an alleyway by a few Raider soldiers, pushing her up against the wall, and laughing slyly as she fell to the ground, spitting out black blood onto the green grass. I didn't realise I had paused, and when the soldiers looked over at me with anger in their eyes, I got back to it as quick as I could. Stuff like that would happen a lot here. Generally, if you did your job right and didn't annoy any of the Class Twos, you'd be sweet, but for some of the Class Threes, going about your day uninterrupted was highly unlikely.

Once the day was done, we all made our way back to our dorms. As we waited until night fell, we went over the things in our packs and re-read the orders in our minds. Basically, because I'd stopped moving, I was filled with boredom, but I was glad I had snuck in a walk to stretch my legs that morning: at least I got some time to myself.

I looked around at the other kids in my squad. We were an odd bunch, all thrown together without much care or thought. Then again, we'd never talked that much until we were out on missions, and that was only talk about the task at hand. Some kids, like Wade, Aiden and Loren, were older; about sixteen I'm guessing. They were taller and the boys were definitely stronger. Me, I was one of the youngest, at fourteen. I am definitely one of the smallest, by far, but that never stopped me making the most out of what the Raiders had turned me into. I hate that my nightmares actually happened, but I can only make the most of my situation right now. We each had our own traits and qualities that made us different. Aiden was really fast; Wade was really strong; and Charlie was smart. Emily was calm under pressure… Me, well – I was good at everything; not to brag or anything. Anyway, once we were out in the field doing what we were made to do, our squad worked well together, despite our differences. We'd been doing this for the last few years and had gotten pretty good at holding back the human Rebels, crushing them down and making them hole-up inside their bases.

When night came, we were all geared up and ready to go. Kartiia bustled into our dorm. Sometimes, I felt like she didn't really care that not all of us would come back; like we were just some expendable kids fighting the Raider war for them.

"All right, let's get you all moving," she said, cheerfully, as she walked from one end of the dorm to the other, checking uniforms, packs and weapons.

Like clockwork, we were led out of the dorms, through the camp, past the northern supply building and to the small Raider forest that glowed on the edge of camp.

"Now children, you all have your walkies, so make sure you use them and keep in touch with each other. Wade, you're squad leader, so we will need regular check-ins from you after each check point. I do hope you all come back. Good luck," Kartiia said, carelessly, as she turned on her heels and walked away without another word.

We all looked around at each other for a moment. This was always the time the other kids would come out of their shells and actually talk. I hadn't spoken to any of them since our last mission a few weeks back, so I was glad of the chance for them to act like anything other than robots.

We stood inside the tree line, the glowing light showing nothing of the dark, untamed world beyond which our mission awaited.

I waited, in anticipation, before looking to Wade as he worked up the courage to say something. Normally, at camp, we would have our scripted lines that were drilled into us after we first got here. Now it was hard for anyone to say anything original.

"We have a lot of ground to cover tonight," Wade started, slowly. "According to the map, we should make it to the target in two days. If you can't keep up, then you're on night duty for the entire mission," he added threateningly. No one wanted to be on night duty: it was most likely the most boring job out of all the cool stuff we got to do on missions.

"Are there any questions before we head out?" he asked as he looked around, getting back to his normal leader self again.

With no answer to his question, that was that. I could feel the excitement start to bubble up from inside my chest. Although I couldn't show it, I felt freer than I had in a while: the field was where I belonged. Starting our long journey, I took in the sights and sounds of the world around me as we ran along through the night; running towards our possible demise but with our purpose being fulfilled. I couldn't think of anything better.

Chapter Two

In one forceful swing, I struck my sword across his back, watching the Rebel gasp in pain as he fell to the ground. Finishing the job, I plunged my sword into his chest. I watched as the life quickly fled from his eyes. I searched his body. Finding nothing interesting, I moved on.

"Sorry, mate," I said cheerfully, with a smile, as I dragged his body behind a blue sedan to hide it. I took another look back up at the giant stadium, its huge walls arcing up hundreds of meters above my head, like a fishbowl. From the top of the large black walls sprung out the one thing Raiders could never get their hands on: force fields. They were blue, like a net that covered over the entire stadium, making it impossible for Raiders to get their Hornets in to bomb the place. That's why we kids were their best weapon: small, fast and trained to kill. That, and we were disposable.

Rebels could never make a move to kill us kids: whether they wanted to or not, it was wrong. Perhaps they still believed there was some hope for us. Then again, we'd made it known just how deadly we were: this was the third base we were taking out this year. I loved the feeling of adrenaline pumping through my body, spurring me on. I dashed forwards, running across the jungle of a car park, taking cover behind an old truck. I peered towards the first main gate to the stadium. There were a few guards out on patrol and others standing by the doors with some heavy looking artillery on either side. I saw Wade and Charlie off to my left, a little way ahead of me. Staying low, I jogged up to them.

"I have a plan to get in, if you want to hear it?" I said, happily, with a smile.

"Maddy? What are you doing here? You're on with Aiden and Loren. Jack and Chloe are supposed to be here," Wade said, frustrated.

"I didn't want to be with them. Besides, Jack and Chloe can't do anything as good as I can," I retorted, defiantly.

"But we all have orders," Wade said, angrily. "Why didn't you listen to me?"

"Maybe my orders are different to yours," I suggested to him, although it was a big lie. I must be defective or something to have my own mind to myself. I just shrugged my shoulders at his annoyed look.

"Look, do you want to listen to me or not?" I asked, looking from Charlie to Wade. "You split us all up to find a way in… I have a way in."

"What is it, kid?" Charlie said, in a hushed voice.

Wade took another quick look over at the five guards standing watch at the gate, before turning his attention to me. Knowing I had their attention, I quickly whipped off my pack and my jacket, untucking my shirt and pulling my hair out of its long braids.

"What are you doing?" Wade said, uncomfortably.

"Watch this," I said with a smile, as I went for my dagger. With a deep breath, I plunged the dagger into my stomach. I fought back the tears and the cries. It really hurt, but I could already feel my body healing.

"That's so wrong," Charlie said, looking away.

"You're going to get us in trouble. Now what, Genius?" Wade said, flatly.

"I'll draw most of them away; you get in there and take the gate. Try not to draw any attention to yourselves, otherwise you'll set off the entire base," I said, quickly. "Now both of you split up and get ready to take out whoever stays to guard the gate."

They seemed to feel okay with my little plan, and both ran in opposite directions, edging their way around as close as they could to the gate. I stood up slowly and began shuffling towards the main gate. I pretended to cry as I clawed at my open wound in my stomach like some pathetic child, but I held onto my dagger, keeping it close by my side.

"Help me!" I cried loudly, using my baby voice. "Please… help me!"

The guards seemed hesitant at first, but like all humans, they gave in to their human emotions and ran towards me. Once I knew I had their attention, I fell heavily to the ground.

"Oh no! What happened? Are you all right?!" one man called, as he reached me.

"Where did you come from? There's no other bases around here for miles," another joined in.

I took a quick peek behind and watched as both Wade and Charlie ducked out of the shadows, ready to take the last two guards defending the gate.

Devilishly, I sniffed my nose and gave a little laugh. "Yeah, I'm all right."

They were taken aback by my change in tone, before looking back at the gate. Charlie and Wade stood there, holding their guns, the two guards dead at their feet.

In their confusion, I lunged forward, stabbing the guard kneeling beside me in the neck, before tackling the other to the ground, plunging my dagger into his frantically beating heart. The last Rebel began to run towards the next gate, a hundred meters round the bend, reaching for his walkie for back-up. But I was too fast. I ran around a few cars, and once I had him in my sights, ran up the back of a black car, pulling my dagger down straight into the base of his neck, cutting out his voice just before he spoke into the radio.

I didn't really feel bad. They're resisting the help of the Raiders. That was their decision, not mine.

I left his body there. We'd make quick work of it now, and I made my way back to the boys. Charlie handed me my stuff, and they opened the gate with the guards' swipe cards, as I put myself back together. I hated getting blood all over my clothes, but my stab wound was already healed… Room for more damage.

We stood on either side of the gate as it slowly opened upwards. Peeking out to look up the ramp leading to the main stadium, I could see no one. Granted it was about three in the morning, but the ramp was dark and I couldn't hear any Rebel heartbeats close by. I took a look back at Wade, who shrugged his shoulders and stepped onto the ramp, walking slowly towards the top end. Charlie and I fell in behind him, the gate closing slowly behind us. We all stopped and got down low, pressed up against the walls as we peered out at the stadium.

"This is Wade. We're in," Wade radioed in on his walkie to the rest of the squad.

We looked out at the massive stadium. It *was* like a giant fishbowl, with seats climbing higher and higher around the field. I wasn't ever really into sports back when I was a kid, but I could see the fascination that captured the humans. This place seemed magical. Bright lights shone onto the field; the seats were in complete darkness. On the field, were people running this way and that, from Hangjets to buildings, and disappearing underground to other places below.

"What now?" I asked, in a whisper, keeping my eyes fixed on the action below.

"According to the schematics, the main control panel for the force field is located underground on the fifth level," Charlie said quietly, closing his eyes to remember the plans in his mind.

"We're in now, too, Wade," crackled Aiden's voice over the walkie. "I've got Loren, Ben and Emily with me."

Wade reached back for his walkie. "Where are you?" he asked, as he looked around.

"We are up next to the VIP area; the one with the glass boxes," Aiden said, quietly.

Our heads turned to the sixteen glass boxes all lined up at the southern end of the field. "Okay," Wade began. "We'll go for the main control panel, and you guys get the rest of the squad in and create a diversion up here. Just give us a few minutes to get down there before this place swarms with Rebels."

"Got it. Over and out," Aiden declared, confidently.

Wade turned to look at Charlie and me. "You two are not the ones I would like to have with me, but I guess you'll do. Just stay close and quiet and follow my lead," he ordered, with his standard annoyed face.

I just shrugged my shoulders in compliance. I didn't really feel hurt by his comment. Anything was better than sitting around at base camp.

We slowly crept forward, staying low behind a row of seats, edging along until we found the top of a staircase leading down to the lower levels. The entrance to the staircase was covered by a heavy-looking door. Wade swiped one of the cards from the guards in the slot and it began to open up, slowly.

We had a pretty good run of it. No Rebels came up the stairs and we managed to make it to the fifth floor with ease. It made sense that they wouldn't use the outer staircases, unless for emergency. There was already a main staircase and elevators in the centre of the stadium, leading up to just below the field. The fifth floor felt really small and it was colder than the air outside. It was dimly lit and looked like it hadn't seen much change since the war began. There were rows of desks, each with fancy computers and comfy chairs, all facing towards one massive screen on the wall to our left. We stopped right before entering the room, waiting and watching to scope the place out. There were a lot of people in the room, but none of them seemed to carry weapons or look tough at all. There were guards, however, at every door, watching the room, but they were facing inwards as if to keep everyone on the inside in check and not really worrying about intruders from the outside. With their force fields up, why would they?

I looked back over to Wade and Charlie as they looked out at the room full of people.

"Charlie – you bring the field down, and Maddy and I will take care of the guards," Wade said quietly, as he continued to look out at the room. He then turned to face me. "Maddy, let's try not to kill everyone, okay?" he suggested, with a hint of a joking tone. I'd never heard Wade joke before.

I smiled back, and whispered, "I'll take the right, and you've got the left."

"We'll need a diversion in about thirty seconds, Aiden. Over and out," Wade said confidently, before turning back to me. "Let's go."

We jumped to action. I ran forward out of the staircase, completely taking the guard standing there by surprise. With one swift movement, I punched him square in the face, smashing his head into the brick wall. I could hear some of it crack and crumble as it hit. Or maybe that was just his head.

I ran around, dodging the guards' bullets and taking them out without hesitating. Before I knew it, I had brought down all the guards on my side with time to spare.

"We need help!" shouted a man from his desk in the middle of the room. Before he could shout again, Charlie kicked him hard in the leg. With a deafening crack, he fell to the ground in agony. All the people in the room seemed to fall together in one big huddle around a raised platform in the centre of the room.

I pulled my fire-blaster from my shoulder, holding it up to the group of people, trying to be as menacing as I could.

"Everyone against the wall!" Wade shouted, in a loud and terrifying voice.

They obeyed and walked up to the large screen at the top end of the room. I could hear some women sobbing softly as they all clung together against the screen.

Charlie jumped up to the platform and got to work, figuring out how to bring down the force field. Wade and I stood by each other's side, holding up our weapons against the group of frightened people. Wade looked at his watch and like clockwork, the thirty seconds were up. Suddenly, loud bangs and explosions crackled over our heads on the field above us.

"How's it looking, Charlie?" Wade asked, expectantly, looking back at Charlie working furiously at the panel.

"Nearly there…" he trailed off, as he continued to mash the buttons.

"Why would you do this to us? We're your people, we're all human. Why fight for them?" asked a small man with dark hair, as he stepped bravely to the front of the group.

I used to try to answer their questions: I guess it was one right they deserved before they died, but I'd had enough of humans and all of their little questions. Without a thought, I turned my fire-blaster on the man and fired. I watched in awe as the fireball wrapped and warped around his body, burning him from the inside out. All of the people screamed out as they watched him melt before their eyes.

"Because you're all pathetic," I said quietly. "It was never your world in the first place."

Their eyes turned to a mixture of fear and anger. I just stared blankly back at them, but a few caught my eye. Two young boys and an older man were talking amongst themselves at the back of the huddled group. I turned my head to focus in on what they were saying.

"This is a good thing. We'll get inside, just keep your heads down and we can all get out of this…" the old man spoke quickly but very calmly.

"But sir," began the boy with brown hair. "Gabe and I can't hack their alien tech. It's too advanced."

"I think I can…" answered Gabe. "As long as those kids don't kill us right now, I'm sure the Raiders will find a use for us. We just have to stay alive long enough to get our people out of there and back to the Lifeline…"

I was intrigued by their planning, and I watched them intently as they continued to talk without fear of me blasting them to a crisp.

"It's done," Charlie called, bursting through my thoughts. He jumped down happily from the platform and joined us in front of the group of people.

Wade nodded and went for his walkie, changing the frequency to the Raiders. "The force field is down. You're free to move in."

Chapter Three

The whole landscape of our beautiful home had changed since the Raiders arrived. There is a rainforest where there was once a desert, and the rainforests have turned into snowy rivers and freezing mountains. I liked that it had changed. I mean – come on: who's going to go for an adventure in the desert? Rainforests are much more interesting. The cities and places the humans had been building for centuries had slowly started to disappear under trees and vines. It was cool to see Mother Nature taking control again.

What was left of our squad sat up in the stadium seats as we watched the Raiders move in and march the Rebels onto their larger carrier ships: we call them Crows, mainly because they come in and take whatever's left once our squad has finished with them. They were big black ships, three times the size of the human Hangjets, but more slow-moving and Hornets had to fly around and protect them. Where Hornets have golden lights, Crows have green ones, edging along their backs and along their wings. The only time I'd been in one was on my way to the warehouse to become a soldier, and it was a journey I did not like to remember too fondly.

"Well done, children," General Carterra said, proudly, as he effortlessly glided along the passageway in front of us.

We all stood up like clockwork, keeping our eyes forward. We must have looked a little dishevelled. I know that I did: my hair was still out of its braids and I had dried blood all over my shirt.

"How many did we lose this time?" Carterra asked, as he came to a stop in front of Wade, looking up and down our line.

"Two, General," Wade answered, without emotion.

Carterra gave a small huff. "May I ask how?" The general's tone was a little sterner now, leaning in towards Wade.

"The Rebels fought back, sir. Jack and Chloe were caught in a crossfire, their injuries too sudden and too hard to heal," Wade answered, keeping calm and holding his position.

My stomach began to fill with butterflies. It was kind of my fault they were dead. I kept my head held high as I prepared for what Wade would say next.

"Is there anything that could have been done to prevent their deaths?" Carterra asked, looking up and down our line once again.

"Yes, sir. All squad members should receive the same orders as each other. That way everyone is on the same page," Wade said slowly.

General Carterra took a step back, taking a look at us all with a concerned face. "Who wasn't following orders?" he asked, as he began to walk slowly down the line.

We were standing in height order, and there were two empty spaces where Jack and Chloe were supposed to be. He paused at their empty spaces, flashes of anger escaping from his dark eyes.

I did not speak, but confidently took a step out from the line. I, of course, was the smallest one there and it felt strange stepping out into the middle of nowhere with no one by my side.

"You, little one?" Carterra asked, interestedly, as he knelt down to look me in the eyes. "Why would you have any reason to not follow my orders?"

I took in a deep breath. "I didn't want to preserve the Rebel's lives. I wanted to make them afraid. Swapping places with Jack and Chloe ensured that, sir," I said softly, as I began to trail off.

His eyes terrified me, reminding me of a time when I used to feel fear, when I used to hide from the monsters under my bed. He made me feel like a child.

He didn't say anything, but stood up slowly, placing a heavy, cold hand on my shoulder.

"Step back in line, child," he said sternly, as he removed his hand from my shoulder. "Children, you will go back to base and resume your duties. And for your punishment, no food for three days," he said threateningly, before marching away towards the field.

All of a sudden, I could feel seventeen pairs of eyes on me at once. I didn't look back at my squad members, but I didn't feel very bad. They would all go back into their robotic mode, soon enough, and I'd be left alone again, inside my head.

We ran the whole way back to base. I stayed at the back of the pack the entire time: that way I was out of sight, out of mind. Although we hadn't really eaten anything for the last few days, I could feel that, by the end of this hunger strike, they would all be a bit more vocal about how much they hated me.

Things trailed on as normal, except for the not-eating parts, where we all just sat in silence while the other squads of kids ate. I liked hearing Kartiia's footsteps bustle around in the morning, when she would come to get us all up. It was like an alarm clock for my day to begin. Our entire squad kept their heads down and didn't say a word at any time, nor did General Carterra have me summoned. I honestly would have thought there'd be a punishment for just me.

On the morning we were allowed to eat again – although who would want to eat all of the disgusting alien juice mush – a huge Crow rumbled into base, dropping off its passengers before running back to wherever they all came from. I was out in the main courtyard, hauling planks of wood from a stock pile back to the new street we were building, a few hundred meters over. I slowed down a bit, just so I could see what was going on. I watched as tall Raiders pushed and shoved a bunch of human prisoners towards HQ. There was no obvious reason why they would be here: they were of different ages, heights and races, and all seemed to show different types of emotions.

Bored by it all, I picked up a whole pallet of wood planks and began to carry it towards the houses. Some of the prisoners looked at me in awe, whispering under their breath. One prisoner caught my eye: he had brown hair and brown eyes; kind of stocky but buff for his young age. Gabe, I think his name was. I looked at him intently as he passed me by.

"They're not children. They're just made to look like that to freak us out…" whispered his friend, from his side.

"Are you sure? They don't look too scary…" the other boy said, slowly.

"Gabe, for goodness sake! That one right there was at the attack on Saigo, and I could have sworn they'd said she was the one who looked ten-years old and was murdering an entire Defence Force Unit," the boy said quickly back at Gabe, with a disgusted look on his face as he spoke in my direction.

They disappeared into the building, I was glad that at least someone had recognised my hard work and I immediately lost interest in my building plans for the day. I hated that I couldn't keep focused on one task at a time. This felt personal to me, now. I hurried the pallet to the houses, and ran back to get the next. I listened as hard as I could to what was going on inside Headquarters, praying that the Raiders would keep their cards close to their chests and not let the humans see the whole underground side of the base. I was thankful that I guessed right, hearing the frantic heartbeats from humans coming from the inside of the above ground rooms of HQ.

"I'm sure you're all very frightened and are wondering why you're here," General Carterra's strong voice boomed around the room. "Don't worry. You're all safe for now, as long as you continue to have use. You are all very valuable in your areas of expertise. Agriculture, community planning, engineering, military…" he trailed off. "Well, what I want to know is if you would be of any help to us here?" he enquired, slowly.

There seemed to be no answer from the humans, so he continued. "What I need is for you to work for me, and I will ensure you and your family's safety from the Gouteszi. All I need is to know where the Lifeline Bases are, their capabilities, and how you little humans managed to create your force fields, and then you can all go on your way."

I hadn't moved for about thirty seconds, wrapped up in the interesting conversation unfolding only a hundred meters away, but I was starting to draw attention to myself. I quickly jumped up, picked up the next pallet and moved as quickly as I could back to the houses. I slowed down on my way back past HQ, hoping to catch a bit more.

"There's no way any of us would risk the lives of those in the bases!" shouted an older woman's voice. "You will never get what you want, as long as there is a human alive, you will never win–" Her voice cut out with a deafening crack.

There were some sharp breaths of surprise and a couple of whimpers, but no one else seemed to step up to the plate and join their dead human friend.

"I didn't have to do that. I, actually, wish to preserve human life. You're all so unique and creative. It's really quite fascinating and I would hate to lose that from this world," Carterra laughed, softly.

"What about your little soldiers then?" asked an unfamiliar voice, an older man's tone this time. "In all my years of serving in the military, we only ever see child soldiers as a distraction to what the real soldiers are doing."

"Oh, the children are merely an expendable product of your race. You have plenty of them and you can always make more. They're the only ones we can completely control. They are like a clean slate. A blank canvas, you would say…" Carterra laughed before his voice became softer and stern. "Do not stall me, old man. I will always get what I want. If any of you will not join me and choose to stand in my way, then I have no qualms about sending you back to that horrendous hovel you came from."

"Soldier!" a Raider called from behind me, snapping me out of my daze. He gave me a hard shove, pushing me to the ground. "Get back to work," he snapped, as he waited expectantly by my side.

I quickly got up to my feet and picked up the pallet, hoping I had not caused too big a scene. All I needed right now was more attention.

I worked on and on through the day, but was disappointed when there were no more conversations to be heard. I mulled over the things I had heard… What were the Lifeline Bases and how did Raiders not know how to create force fields? I mean they travelled through space, for goodness sake. I wondered whether any of the humans had cracked under the pressure and given in to Carterra's demands, but I was especially hurt to hear him say we were expendable. It made sense, and I guess I always knew that we were, but I wanted more than that. I wanted someone to be proud of me and my efforts to bring down the Rebels.

That night I lay awake, still listening for any sound of a human heartbeat, trying to make sense of the questions I had in my head. I couldn't understand why I was different; why my mind wouldn't just fall in line like the rest of the squad. It was a cool night and the moonlight shone in onto my face, keeping me awake. It was pretty quiet out, and I could have sworn some of the patrols were getting a bit slack with their job. I hadn't heard anyone come around for a little while.

I rolled over and sat up, looking up at the night sky. It was a full moon tonight. It always used to remind me of my father telling me heaps of stories about the first moon-landing and how many people had been there in the whole entire world. I could still see his face, even now, lighting up in a theatrical way as he would tell his stories. In a huff, I turned back around and lay down again. I didn't understand why I could remember feeling happy about my human life: my father wasn't a monster. I kept getting confused between the truth and what the Raiders had put into my head. I closed my eyes again, hoping sleep would come and let me shelve my feelings for another day.

Suddenly, as if I had dreamed it, a shadow dashed across the sky, blocking out the moonlight for a split second. Confused, I hopped up again to take another look at the sky. Nothing.

"Go to sleep," I ordered myself, as I rubbed my eyes.

There it was again: another shadow. This time, I was convinced something was up. I kneeled at the top of my bed watching, waiting. Suddenly, a black shape zoomed across the sky.

"Hangjets," I whispered under my breath.

I got a sinking feeling in the pit of my stomach, remembering back to what the human boy, Gabe, had said about staying alive long enough to get into our base. They planned something.

I listened hard to the world outside, searching desperately for any Raider who may have noticed the Hangjets flying around the sky, but none were stirring. I couldn't even hear the patrol Raiders walking around. Frustrated now, I jumped out of bed and got dressed as quickly as I could. I considered waking up the rest of my squad for a moment, but thought against it. If I was going to get into trouble again, it would just be me.

I couldn't hear anyone outside, so I opened the door and dashed out into the courtyard, looking up at the night sky. Already, I could smell the jet fuel being carried on the cool breeze.

'What now?' I thought to myself, angrily, torn between the possibility of getting into a whole lot of trouble, or losing the base.

I jogged over to the patrol station where the Raider guards would come and drop off their equipment. A shift change was due at any moment but I couldn't hear anything. I quickly ducked across the courtyard and onto the path one of the patrols would normally take. I followed it for a few seconds before I came across a small pool of black blood in the middle of the street. A Raider was hurt… but how? I followed the drops of blood, leading to a tent. I couldn't hear anyone inside so I decided I'd take a quick peek. I pulled back the navy blue material and nearly shouted out in surprise when I saw the pile of pale Raider patrol bodies. Feeling the panic now, I made my way back towards the dorm. Racing up and through the stairs, I ran over to Wade, who was lying peacefully in his bed.

"Wade… Wade, wake up," I whispered, as I shoved him forcefully.

"Maddy?" he muttered, in a confused daze. "I have to report you. You're out of bed. How do you keep on disobeying orders?" he began, annoyed.

"I know, I know. You can tell on me in the morning, but something's wrong. The patrols are dead, everyone else is asleep and there are Hangjets flying around outside," I whispered, panicked.

Wade jumped to life then, his brown eyes sparking with energy in the darkness. "Okay – then we need to tell a Class Two," he said, slowly.

"What?" I almost yelled at him. "No, we need to jump to action; start killing people," I said, walking back to the dorm door.

"Only if we get ordered to fight," he said, as he stood up. Even in the darkness, his huge, muscular figure was very… muscular.

He got dressed and ran over to the door, peering up at the sky. Every few seconds, another Hangjet would fly by.

"Maybe we can tell the other squads?" I suggested.

Wade jumped out into the courtyard and ran over to the next dorm, waking up the squad leader inside. I could hear them whispering about orders and rights and wrongs, but I couldn't wait any longer.

I ran past the dorms and towards HQ, loudly bursting through the doors. The guards, who normally stood watch, were all pulled up into a pile in the hallway, their black blood pooling out, covering the whole floor. I nearly turned back to tell Wade, but something caught my eye. Footprints led away from the blood, up to the end of the corridor. The thing was that they only went one way. Whoever was doing this was still here.

I listened hard for any sign of life as I walked towards the dead Raiders, taking a gun and a dagger from one of them. I walked across the bloody floor, following the footsteps to the end of the corridor, before coming to a stop at the end door. Suddenly, I could hear a heart beating, pumping loudly through the thin walls. It was joined by several others, all human, but not as many as the prisoners who were dragged in here the day before.

"Maddy?" called Wade from further up the hallway, in a whispered yell.

I looked up at him, signalling to stay quiet, but beckoned him to come and join me.

"Get the squads all ready for a fight. Wake up the Raiders," Wade ordered the other kid, Callum, at his side, who then disappeared quickly back to the courtyard.

Wade grabbed a Raider's gun and quietly made his way to my side. When we were ready, I opened the door and burst inside the room.

Several human Rebels, dressed in black, pointed their guns at me, surprise and fear in their eyes – although that's what I thought I saw: their faces had been painted as dark as night, and their eyes peered out like little white lights underneath their caps. Behind them were about ten humans, all huddled together, distributing weapons and gearing up.

"How did you–" one of the Rebels began, but was cut off.

"Doesn't matter," Wade said. "What are you planning?" he asked, raising his gun to the man.

The man didn't move, but kept his gun trained on us. "It's already done, we all have…" he checked his watch, "seven minutes left to get out of this place before it goes up in flames." He had dark, piercing eyes that watched us all with curiosity, more than fear.

I looked around at the group of people, spotting Gabe, cowering at the back. "You," I said quietly, taking a few steps forwards, before the Rebels closed ranks and blocked my path. "Gabe, is it? You did this, didn't you?" I said, quietly.

He nodded, his heart beating like a drum, I could have sworn it was going to burst. He looked guiltily down at a small black device, flashing red, in his hands.

"We can all make it out of here together. You can come back with us. You don't have to be prisoners here any more. We've found a way to fix you," the man began again, but some of the other humans gave him very serious looks.

"Hell, no," Wade responded, quietly.

"Then why are you whispering? Why haven't you told the Raiders yet?" the man pushed.

"We have. Or, at least, we will…" Wade stumbled over his words, becoming confused. There were no orders for situations like this.

"Six minutes," the man said again, checking his watch.

I turned back to face him, raising my gun to him. "Why would we ever let you go?" I said, quietly.

"What's your name?" he asked softly, carefully watching me.

"My name? It's… Maddy," I answered slowly, confused by where he was taking the conversation.

"You're just another number here, Maddy. You're expendable. They'd be glad to see you dead. They were even planning on it. You're the one breaking the rules; acting out."

"So what if I am? I've served my purpose. You're on the wrong side, not us," I defended, taking a step forwards, feeling the other Rebels tense up beside me.

"They're inside your heads. The Raiders aren't allowing you to think straight…"

Wade had had enough of the talking that was going nowhere. "The Raiders are waking up now. We still have time to get the Hornets out and stop the attack," he said to the man, defiantly.

The man smiled and shook his head. Suddenly, he jumped forward, pushing the gun out of my grip. That set me off, making me angry most of all. I lunged forward, punching him in the gut, before pulling his head hard down to the floor. The other humans in the room moved fast to action.

I cried out in pain as one stabbed me in the back, pulling me off the man. I threw the Rebel across the room in my pain and anger, smashing the glass window with a crack. Wade and I fought them off and managed to regain control of the situation before we heard a yell from outside.

"Wade! Maddy!" called Callum, frantically.

Wade and I jumped up and ran back out of the room and into the dark corridor, me pulling the dagger from my back as I ran. We could hear them now. The loud whirring sound and vibrations filled the air, shaking the glass in the windows of the corridor. The Rebels dashed beside us and back out to the courtyard, still hoping for an escape. Wade and I followed furiously, but got side-tracked as we looked up at the night sky. What was once a clear night had turned into a mottled-black colour, blocking out the light from the moon. More Raiders began to wake from their sleep, running past us into HQ and others to the Armoury. Squad leaders came dashing to the dorms, bringing the squad kids into the courtyard.

"Get to the Armoury!" Kartiia yelled at Wade and me. We had been standing there, watching the commotion.

Like the flip of a switch, the Rebels were forgotten, and Wade and I ran towards the Armoury. Along with the other squad kids, we burst into the Armoury, jumping over the pile of dead Raider guards at the entrance. We ran through, back to where our weapons would come through the conveyer belts. Charlie joined us now and led the way to another door, where our weapons and packs were.

"What? Am I the only one who holds onto the Orientation to the Raider Base Manual?" he said, sarcastically.

I gave him a small smile as we all ran along the rows of stacked cabinets glowing in the darkness, searching for our identification numbers. I was filled with relief when I held my swords, but felt even better when I had all of my stuff and was geared up, ready to go.

"Everyone back to Headquarters, and await further orders!" Wade shouted loudly over the many chattering voices of us kids.

Like clockwork, our entire squad managed to get together. Now we were working like a team. We ran straight back to HQ, forming our lines in the courtyard as a dishevelled General Carterra came marching out to meet us.

"Where are the prisoners? What is going on?!" he shouted furiously to the Raiders trailing anxiously behind him. "Get the Hornets in the air!" he shouted, even angrier. "Children – out to the camp borders, defend us from any ground attack. Their Hangjets won't be enough to take this camp. There must be a larger force waiting. Go, now!" he shouted, straightening up as he walked down our lines.

He waved his hands in the air, signalling to the shadowy trees, glowing as they stood all around. "Go, cover and protect us!" he shouted to them. The glowing colours surged brighter through their trunks, until they got larger and larger; the trees growing, spreading out until their canopies were covering our heads in the courtyard. I watched in wonder as the leaves, flattened and stretched, made a glowing patchwork blanket across the sky.

I looked down the line at Wade, who stood with what looked like fear on his face as he stared up at the mixture of Hangjets and Hornets crashing into a battle in the sky as the final few leaves joined up.

"You, Maddy!" General Carterra's huge shadow blocked my view of everything, and I looked back up into those terrible eyes. "You follow orders or else you'll be having a new home, six feet under. Have I made myself clear?" he threatened.

"Yes, sir," I replied in as confident a voice as I could muster.

He nodded, and continued on through the camp.

I shuddered to think what he was going to do, but was interrupted by Wade, who began to lead our squad to the northern side of the camp. We all ran as hard as we could, making good ground until suddenly, a mix of bright blue and golden lights filled the sky. For a moment, I was mesmerised by them, as I watched them fall, but quickly whipped back into action as soon as the first one came hurtling towards the ground, crashing through a few of the smaller trees, blowing up like a huge, fiery ball. It was like rain after that, and the protective blanket the trees provided were not as strong as the Rebels' force fields. The fiery balls that came towards us broke through the covering, each drop making holes in the ground the size of a swimming pool. Our squad ran as fast as we could, dodging the golden fireballs and sprinting hard to keep ahead of them. Here and there we would have to get out of the way of a falling ship, but the worst part was how big the base was. I'd never realised it until now, when I was desperate to leave. We lost a few members, as the fire reached forwards, swallowing them up into the destruction, but eventually, most of us made it out beyond the wall of trees at the edge of the camp.

We turned back, huffing and puffing, looking at the destruction the Hangjets had created.

"What now?" I panted to Wade, looking up at his face.

"Everyone – arc a line around the camp. Keep at least ten meters apart. Keep your eyes out for any movement. Use your walkie if you see anything," Wade said, breathlessly.

We all followed his orders, peering out into the darkness as we stood guard. Apart from the sounds of the burning camp and the crackling of wood, the field that stretched before us seemed quiet and calm. The grass swayed gently in the hot breeze, brushing against my legs as I watched, silent and still. All of a sudden, the sound of running footsteps reached my ears. Instinctively, I grabbed my swords and ducked down low in the long grass. Closer and closer they came, but there wasn't anything I could see, just yet. I remembered what the Rebels had been wearing when they came inside our camp and knew that, out here, I was going to have to take them as they came. There was no way I was going to see them if they were in all black.

All of a sudden, a black figure burst through the grass by my side. Eagerly, I jumped up from the grass and plunged my swords into the Rebel's back. He cried out in pain as he fell to the ground, but I couldn't finish him off, as more black figures came running at me now.

"Here we go…" I said to myself, ready for the fight. No one was going to get past me: not if I could help it.

I fought on and on through the night as the Rebels charged the perimeter, trying to break through to get to the camp. They knew there was a lot more than what was on the surface: the giant ends of the ships sticking out of the ground like black daggers was a dead giveaway, but I thought it was pretty stupid of them to attack without knowing how many Raiders we really had. The golden fireballs from the Hangjets and Hornets continued to shoot out in all directions, making things especially interesting when one decided to crash land into the field before me. The fire was helpful though, lighting up the Rebels as they ran forwards, the light catching their white eyes behind the paint.

I prayed for morning to come quickly. Everything was always better in the morning, my mum always said… Why was I thinking about Mum at a time like this? I cut down another Rebel as he lunged towards me, his gun at the ready. He got a few shots off first, one going straight through my leg, but I didn't cry out in pain. I wasn't going to give him the satisfaction of knowing he'd hit me. I had a small pang of worry as I looked down at the Rebel I had just killed. A small part of me hoped it was not Max or Jasper; that I hadn't just killed one of my brothers. The rest of me, however, was remembering General Carterra's warning.

"Raider's good; Rebel's bad... Raider's good; Rebel's bad..." I repeated in my head, over and over, as I continued to fight. "You're doing the right thing, Maddy. They'll be proud," I assured myself, but it was beginning to not be enough anymore. I wondered how much longer I'd have before they all saw through me.

Chapter Four

The beginning of a new day would always make me happy, but today the soft pink and melting orange-yellow colours of the rising sun weren't making me feel any such way. Hornets buzzed furiously over our heads as we stood guard at the northern border of the camp. Thick, black smoke rose high into the air, making visibility a little harder, but we had managed to fight off the Rebels in the pitch black night: a little smoke wasn't going to hold us back. Hundreds of dead Rebels lay in the fields stretching before us: it had been a long night. The Raiders came and took to opening fire at the Rebels and their tanks and trucks. None got close to the base though, which I was quite proud of. It seems that our stand in the air and on the ground had deterred them from entering any more people into a losing battle.

I looked over at Wade, who had been at my right side through the night. He looked completely exhausted; his shoulders slumped and his head began to droop as he tried desperately to keep his eyes open and look for any more Rebels. The base hadn't been taken, but the Rebels had made a very good go of it. The downside to being on the Raider side was that everything they did was like clockwork: everything was mapped out and planned for, but they lacked the creativity or flexibility to take things as they came. I felt somewhat proud of my inability to follow orders. If it weren't for me, we'd all be toast.

Footsteps came trudging up behind me from my left. Raising my gun (I was too tired to swing my swords around after all that), I turned to see a dishevelled Kartiia emerge from the camp. Her dark hair was matted with black blood; her pale skin darkened by the smoke.

"Come, children," she said, quietly. Other Raiders came out from the camp behind her, carrying weapons and taking our places as watchers. Hearing Kartiia's voice filled me with strength and hope: at least someone was alive and around to give orders.

We all followed, lumbering our way over bodies and debris, our boots crunching on the charcoaled ground. I had a huge jolt of annoyance as I saw, in the distance, the still-burning houses we had been spending the last few days building. Rebels always ruined everything. The trees had shrunk back down now, and their numbers were greatly diminished, but the glowing veins in the ground beneath our feet glowed brighter, beginning to heal the land inside the camp.

"Imagine if you weren't defective, Maddy," Charlie said softly, as he came to walk beside me. "We'd have all died and never even known something was wrong." He looked a bit of a mess, with dirt and blood all through his wavy, blond hair.

"Thanks – I guess," I said, a little confused, as I jumped up over a crashed Hangjet. It was odd to hear someone compliment me. Normally I was the only one who did that.

We made it back to what was left of the dorms, and all re-formed our lines in the courtyard. The western and southern squads were already there, and looked just as battered as we did. It was hard to line up, now finally seeing who had not made it through the night. We had lost another five members, whether it was in the firestorm battle the Hangjets and Hornets had created or from the ground attack. I stood alone at the end of our line, with four empty spaces beside me. I didn't like feeling this out in the open.

Kartiia stood with the other squad leaders, only meters from me. I listened hard to what they were saying, trying to catch anything of what had happened.

"How did they even know where it was?" one said, her voice rushed with what could have been panic – it was the western squad leader, I think. "I mean, how would they get the information about where it was, let alone how to get to it?"

"I don't understand why the General didn't just kill them all when he had the chance. There was no reason to keep them alive–"

"There was every reason to keep them alive," Kartiia cut in. "Their capabilities are unique. Each one had something different to offer."

"But why take them from the Pit?" the southern squad leader asked, shaking her head in disapproval.

"Well, that I cannot answer. But the humans are continuing to surprise us. Maybe they know how powerful it can be in their hands," Kartiia answered, softly.

"The children are our main line of defence, especially until our reinforcements get here. If they take them…" the Western squad leader trailed off, looking wearily at her own squad. I could have sworn I saw more than worry for herself; that maybe she felt something for the ones who followed her. Then again, she was Class Three and emotions were a bit mottled with these ones.

"They won't. They can't. The children don't have their own minds: we made sure of that when we changed them. It's one thing to take the children, but to get them to change sides… To get them to fight…" Kartiia shook her head with a smile. "They would tear the Rebels apart."

A large group of Raiders came stomping towards the courtyard, the three squad leaders falling back to the top end of their lines. I kept my eyes to the front, confused by what I'd heard. What machine? What did Kartiia mean by us not having our own minds?

"General Carterra has asked that the children begin working immediately on clearing away the dead," said one of the soldiers, as he came to stand in front of Kartiia. Speaking softly, he leaned in even closer. "After that, they can start running the perimeter. They're the expendable ones, not us." He smiled a toothy grin, nodding his head at Kartiia before walking on with the other Raiders, who headed in to the charred HQ.

"We'll each take our quarters," Kartiia said, softly, to the other two squad leaders. "I'll go check on the east squad, see if Malia needs any help. Off you go, children. Don't stop until the work is done." She gave us a small smile, before walking quickly towards the east.

It was a long day, but it was good we were strong. Each of us would take two bodies at a time and drag them away to the edge of camp, where Raiders were loading them onto Crows and taking them away. Inside the camp there were only Raiders, some who were still inside their tents, and others who had been cut to pieces as they crash-landed inside their Hornets. But outside the camp were hundreds of dead Rebels. All of them seemed to be pretty young; boys and girls alike. Their faces etched into my mind as I dragged them towards the waiting Crows, wondering what their names were, and where they had all come from.

The sun beat down pretty hard but by mid-afternoon, the clouds began to blacken and rain broke through the heat. I was glad of the cool drops of water pouring down on my face. No one said anything, but I liked having a whole day to myself just to be stuck inside my own head. I had remembered hearing about the pit a few months after I had been changed. The closest one was a few days away, and it was where they would drop all the humans off until they were sorted or slaughtered, based on what they could offer to the New World. I didn't think there were many humans left to even have use of the pit, but it was where the Crows constantly came and went from, and I was adamant that I never wanted to see it.

Kartiia returned after a few hours, looking even worse than when she had left in the morning. Turns out the eastern squad had chased the Rebels all the way down to a valley a few kilometres from the base. Their night sounded a whole lot more interesting than ours, but I was glad I wasn't in their shoes. They had not covered the entire perimeter and had let a few (more like a hundred) Rebels slip through; something General Carterra was making them pay for dearly. I overheard Kartiia speaking with the Raiders keeping watch about something being taken, and that the Rebels knew exactly where to go to get it. My mind ticked over furiously, wondering what on earth this machine was and why I'd never heard anything about it before. What I also couldn't get out of my mind were the humans Wade and I had found inside HQ, and whether or not the other squads were dragging their burnt bodies out to the Crows, or whether they had all made it out.

As Aiden dropped the last burnt body into the Crow, we all turned to look at each other in the pouring rain.

"I'll starting making tracks and run along our quarter," Aiden shouted through the rain, turning to Wade who was watching the Crow fly away.

"Okay. Maddy, Charlie and Loren – you guys go out further and start on another perimeter line to join up with other squads. It'll be more ground to cover, but it gives us some more room to make a better defensive line. Everyone else, spread out and we'll keep an eye on the horizon." Wade nodded towards us all. "We'll take it in hour-long turns."

It was a horrible slog, pushing out through the long grass and running tracks into the ground. For a long time, all I could hear was the squishing sounds my boots made into the ground, and my breath as I ran a muddy track around our part of the base. When I reached each end, I would see another squad kid doing the exact same thing as me. At least we were all being consistent.

The rain slowed by nightfall and the squad got into the routine, although we were all wet and the cold chill of the night was not helping. I wasn't so sure how long we would keep this up without a break, or food or water (although the rain had been nice), but surely the Raiders wouldn't leave us out here forever…

A group of about forty Raiders came to relieve us just before dawn. It was almost impossible to not give the rest of my squad members a smile when the Raiders came trumping out to us to swap positions. Kartiia led us all back to the Armoury, past countless Raider patrols and workforces tasked with cleaning up and rebuilding the base. I could completely understand why General Carterra wanted to keep the Rebel prisoners alive. If there was any chance that they'd spill the beans, protection from the air with a force field was something worth risking lives for.

As the sun began to rise slowly over the base, I wished the warmth would reach us inside the Armoury: its cool, dark, metal walls and concrete floors made me shiver. We trailed on, walking down the hallway and down the staircase. Instead of stopping at the second floor to drop off our packs and weapons, we continued, lower and lower, onto the fifth floor. We'd never been down this far before, and I could see why not. Heaps of Raiders quickly glided along around us, going about their busy work. There were rooms full of large round discs with glowing lights and flashes sparking out here and there. This must be where the real magic happens, where orders come from and where all the information was. I let my mind wander with curiosity as I tried to take in all the sights and sounds. I peered in through one door left slightly ajar, large flashes of light catching my attention. I slowed to the back of the group, looking in through the crack. There, inside the room, were several

Raiders and a machine in the centre. It looked like a large, rocky archway, and as a Raider walked in, lights would flash and zap him, and when he then exited, he had changed: he had turned into a Rebel.

"Maddy, come away from there," Kartiia whispered quietly to me, pulling me by the arm back to the group.

My mind wandered. They'd found a way to look like Rebels and I wondered how long the image kept up, and whether they were still strong, like themselves, or if it was a permanent change. Surely, that's not the machine they were speaking of… It's still here: the Rebels didn't get it. We finally stopped at the end of the hallway on the fifth floor, the lights on the walls flickering ominously. Kartiia opened a door to her left and led us through.

We were greeted by the tired and bloody faces of the other squads, all sitting at tables around the room.

"Take a seat, have something to eat and get some rest. I'll be back at nightfall with new orders." Kartiia nodded towards an empty table with a tray laden with food packs, and the usual juice mush we were given.

We each swung our legs over the long chairs and sat down, but no one seemed quite so eager to eat or do anything. Admittedly, I was a little ashamed of the rumblings in my tummy, but with a sigh I reached out and took one of the silvery food packs and a juice from the middle of the table. Wade watched me interestedly, as I began to open my pack and eat the wheat biscuits inside.

"What?" I said defensively, shrugging my shoulders at him.

"Nothing… Come on, guys. Who knows when the next time is we'll get food?" Wade said, looking around at the rest of the squad.

After stuffing as much of the disgusting food into my body as I could, I got up and went to sit in the corner of the room, leaning against my pack, using it like a pillow. Wade and Charlie came and joined me, and the rest of the squads dispersed around the room.

"So I guess we'll be getting new squad members soon?" I said, quietly, leaning my head back against the cold wall.

"I guess so," Charlie said, even more quietly. "But it'll take ages right? Who did we even lose?" he said, looking around at our squad sleeping on the floor.

Wade shrugged his shoulders, "Sarah, Matthew… ah… um… Luke and…" he trailed off, slowly. "You know, I'm not really sure who it was."

"We three have been here from the beginning. All these new replacements just make everything so confusing," Charlie said, shaking his head.

"I can't believe we let those Rebels get away, Wade," I said quietly, looking sternly into his big brown eyes.

"Me neither. I was just about to chase after them, but when Kartiia spoke, I completely forgot to."

"Are we robots?" I asked, softly, looking up at the lights in the ceiling. "My brothers used to play video games with robots in them…"

"Brothers? What are video games?" Charlie said, confusedly.

"Never mind… I must have heard one of the Rebels talking about it a few missions ago. Let's just get some sleep," I said quickly, closing my eyes.

"You really are defective, aren't you, Maddy?" Charlie muttered quietly, as he rolled over onto his side.

I laid awake for a little while longer, thinking about whether I was defective. It was a big risk trying to see what the boys could remember from their human lives. Every boy had video games when they were growing up, and if they couldn't remember what family was, then they were still pretty robotic to me. I wondered whether they felt wrong too.

My dreams faded in and out, from giant robots trying to jump to the moon to my brothers' faces full of excitement and energy as they played their video games in the living room. I hoped I wouldn't have to wait too much longer for Wade and Charlie to start to remember things again. I hoped that someone would be able to join me in my defectiveness, otherwise I was going to burst.

Chapter Five

General Carterra stood tall and menacing at the front of the room, as we all sat at our tables having just finished dinner. We had cleaned ourselves up, my leg was already healed, and we were no longer tired but ready for the next round of orders.

"To the north, south and western squads, well done," he nodded in our direction. "You successfully maintained a strong defensive perimeter around the base, giving my soldiers the chance to reclaim the air and ground. As you can see, much of our underground levels have remained intact, and what is on the surface can and will be rebuilt. We suffered some losses, but the Rebels took the harder hit. However…" He paused for a moment, taking a long, stern look at the eastern squad. "The eastern squad has let you down. In the Rebel attack, they got carried away and were led into a trap, leaving the base wide open. You have already received your punishment; one that I hope will stay with you for a long time." He spoke condescendingly. I heard the heartbeats of the eastern squad quicken with fear as the General looked at them. He smiled a small smile: he must have heard their heartbeats, too.

"Now, I do not need to explain myself to you," he went on. "But I will, however, give you all just one piece of advice: there is no place for you outside our ranks. There is no life for you anywhere else but here. Our reinforcements are on their way and do not think, for a second, that your work will be done once they get here." He smiled again, although this time looking towards me. I felt his cold, dark eyes begin to burn into mine, but thankfully he moved on. "Continue to prove your use and there will always be a purpose for you. Maddy, you will stay back. I would like to have a word with you. The rest of you, back up to level two and await further instruction from your squad leader."

My heart sank in fear. Everyone shot uneasy glances in my direction as they got up and moved back out. I stood up, slowly, and walked towards General Carterra, trying desperately to keep my own heartbeat in check.

"Follow me," he said quietly, as he glided out through the door.

I obeyed and moved quickly to keep up with him. Two Raider guards stayed close behind me, watching me carefully, with their guns at the ready. I half-jogged to keep up with the General as he led the way further down into the Armoury. My mind dashed through everything I'd said and done from his last warning. Definitely, the conversation Wade, Charlie and I had had early this morning was something to get into trouble for, but how he could have heard it was beyond me. No – it had to be something else. I had fought bravely and to the best of my ability, making sure no Rebel got past me. The further down we went, the more weighed down I felt. I began to take in all the sights around me as the Armoury turned from being like a huge underground building to a more winding, dark, black hole. Red lights glowed from veins in the dark walls, the air getting colder, and the Raider's skin glowing just a little paler in the dark light. We finally came to the bottom of the staircase, which rounded a corner to a big open space, where about ten glowing Hornets sat on a raised platform. Looking up, I could see the staircase and all the floors stretching up to the surface. If I wasn't so cold and scared, I would have marvelled at the sight. The entire place looked like a buzzing hive filled with workers and soldiers, all going about their duties.

"This way, child," General Carterra said, softly, as he turned to walk around the Hornets. He stopped by the side of the platform and opened a large hatch in the floor.

"In you go." He pointed to the dark opening. I could see the red glowing veins of light leading down there.

Obediently, I lowered myself into the hole and landed on the ground with a small thud. General Carterra jumped in after me, but the guards did not follow. The hatch closed above us, blocking out the bright lights from the floors above.

Suddenly, the red glowing lights surged and lit up the room. It was probably the most alien thing I have ever seen. Five black spidery-looking chairs sat around in an arc, facing one giant, glowing mirror. The General moved forwards, running his right hand along the side of it, making it glow a bright white, before pictures and schematics began to appear, rushing before my eyes.

"Take a seat, Maddy. Do not worry for your life. If you had not obeyed my warning, then you would already be dead," he said slowly. Maybe he thought this was making the situation a bit better.

I took a seat in the middle chair facing the white disc, as it warped and faded in and out with pictures and voices that sounded very far away.

"Do you know what this is?" he asked, pointing to the glowing disc.

"No, sir," I said slowly, turning to face his cold gaze.

"It's a Tidesse," he said, mistily. "It has allowed the Gouteszi to remain as strong as we have for centuries. Its purpose is to retain all of our history, everything we have learnt and built. Each of the generals have one aboard their ships, and it helps to guide them on their journey away from the Motherland. The royals have one each, too. They live forever and rule forever, so the extra help of a Tidesse can be priceless. Very few have ever been made small enough to fit inside your pocket," he said, thoughtfully, as he looked deep into the glowing Tidesse. "I will admit, however, we have taken to letting the inhabitants of the planets we colonise do all the hard work for us," he said with a smile, standing up and running his hand along the Tidesse again, turning the pictures into darkness   once   more. "We used to be much like the humans, Maddy. Weak, stupid, squabbling amongst ourselves, until a higher power stepped in and we were transformed into what you see today: a magnificent race, powerful beyond belief. But with change, we lost the thing that one needs most for survival: versatility. Do you know what it means to be versatile, Maddy?" he asked, but did not turn to face me.

"To be able to adapt to change, sir," I said, quietly.

"Correct. Well done," he said, condescendingly. "We lost our creativity. Our minds no longer wanted to imagine or build or explore, but to take what we wanted, to rule over all. Look at us. Not one of us is born any more, but manufactured for the good of the colony. And yet, with each new class, our DNA is getting muddier. Heaven forbid how far away the Class Fours will be from our original form. Many centuries we have lived like this, perplexed by questions we cannot answer, lacking no other vision but control."

He explained all this very calmly before coming back to sit in front of me. "Humans are the closest we've been to what we once were so long ago. You're expendable - yes, but each of you are unique, with a different name and talent to the next. Earth is our best chance of making our race survivable again."

"And why are you telling me this?" I asked quietly, not breaking his stare.

His eyes flashed with excitement. "Because, Maddy, you're one of our best soldiers. Strong, rebellious… ha, you remind me of me in my youth," he smiled, leaning forwards. "We have reason to believe that if we have all that we know in one place, then so too do the humans. I am tasking you with the incredible job of locating it."

"But you have no proof that this knowledge exists?" I asked.

"When we first arrived here, the human government extended a hand of friendship towards us for both of our races to learn from each other, to share information. In our delegations, one amongst them caught my eye. He held with him a Tidesse, such as this one, but of a smaller size. He went by the name of Starr. There are no records of him anywhere within the Tidesse, and yet he carries something only royals have. Something about him leads me to believe that he may carry the information we seek. Regardless, a few mistakes were made before the information could be given to us, and war broke out, leaving us no choice but to carry on and conquer." He paused for a moment before continuing. "Do you like the Rebels, Maddy?"

"No, sir. I've captured and killed more than I can count," I said, calmly.

"But why?" he pressed on.

"Because I was ordered to, sir," I said robotically.

"No one has ordered you to kill them, but you continue to do it as a sign of strength," he said, with a frown. "There must be some reason you have such animosity towards them?"

"Only that this is my home now. I am not human, I am not anything but what I was created for… I am a soldier," I said, quietly. I wasn't sure if I was lying or not, but I knew if I was faced with killing a Raider or a Rebel, the Rebel would be down before they knew what had hit them.

"Good girl. You are different child, stronger than the rest... perhaps the lithuteum has made you a friend and not a soldier. That will be all," he concluded, with a smile.

It was strange that Carterra named the very metal inside my body as a friend. I did not think it was very alive: then again, the red veins glowing in the ship walls were proof that I was wrong about that. "When will I be doing this task, sir?" I asked, confused now.

"Oh, you won't have to wait too long. Just remember that when the time comes, don't get caught up with the excess of human emotions, the drama of feelings. We Gouteszi were quite glad when we got rid of ours. You have a purpose, and you make us proud Maddy. Get us the information we need and you will be rewarded," he said, still smiling, as he slowly stood up.

I wish that the Raider guards didn't have to walk me all the way back up to level two with the rest of the squads or else I would have run all the way out. My head buzzed with questions, and I could hardly believe that I had been invited all the way to the top – or bottom, at least. I didn't think anyone besides the general had been in there. My squad was forming its lines again as they collected their gear and put on their weapons.

"Maddy, hurry up," Kartiia called, softly, from the head of our squad, as she pointed to where she wanted me to stand.

My squad gave me looks of unbelievable surprise. I guess they all thought I would never have returned. I quickly fell in behind the last kid from the eastern squad receiving orders, his pack and weapons. When it was my turn, I barely noticed the searing pain of the scanner as I shoved my wrist in. I grabbed my pack: it was heavier than usual. This must mean we were going out on another mission. I secured my swords in their sheaths on my back, taking my fire-blaster eagerly from the woman's hands.

My mission orders blurred in front of my eyes, filling my head with new schematics and targets. I re-joined the north squad just as they were marching back up to the ground. It was a cool night. The rain from the day before had helped get rid of all the smoke, and the moon was already high in the sky, shining brightly across the courtyard. The trees seemed to have fully recovered now, glowing brighter, as if happy to be alive.

The Raiders had managed to make quick work of clearing out all the blackened remains of the buildings and houses that had stood before. Each squad went its separate ways, back to its quarters. I wasn't sure if all our orders were the same, but for the north squad, we were to follow the tracks made by the Rebels back to their base. This mission wasn't to destroy them but simply to sit and wait, counting their numbers, watching their movements and relaying the information back.

We reached the edge of the base and stopped, preparing to say goodbye to Kartiia, when she laughed a shrill laugh. "Oh no, I'm coming with you this time, children. You've lost a few and I'll just be here as an extra pair of eyes."

A couple of the other kids in the squad gave her a smile. Everyone felt pretty strongly about Kartiia, and I felt somewhat comforted by the fact that she was going to accompany us for this mission. We jogged out past the perimeter line we had run into the ground, and across the field to where the Rebels had taken their stand. In the bright moonlight, we easily found the huge tyre tracks from the Rebel trucks, dug deep into the mud. We all spread out and made a line, moving through the long grass, following the tracks north.

It was just after dawn when the tracks took an abrupt turn to the right, leading off towards a ridge cut high above a valley. The field turned into forest as we walked through a path the Rebels had hacked through. It seemed that they had put a lot of effort into getting their trucks through the bush. At every snap of a twig, or strange bird sound, we would freeze in our tracks, ducking down for cover. We might have looked a little stupid, but it was safest, especially since we didn't know how far off the Rebel camp actually was. I trailed behind Charlie, but he was being super annoying, bending over every few meters to hyper-examine the tracks, counting how many footsteps he could see and wondering aloud about how old the tracks could have been. The sun began to rise quicker now, and we continued to work our way along the ridge until we finally emerged from the forest and out onto rolling hills. The view was rather nice. There were huge dark mountains stretching high out of the ground, with dense forest on either side of a winding stream running down from the mountains. The tracks ran straight over the hill and could be seen engraving their way down towards a natural rocky break in the stream. Wade and Aiden led the way down the hill, with Charlie and me bringing up the rear of the squad. Kartiia seemed almost dazzled by the view, spinning round and round to try and take it all in.

In all my time with Kartiia, I'd never wondered how old she was. It was always hard to tell with the Raiders, but I guessed she couldn't be too old. Loren and Sam walked on either side of her, keeping her inside the safety of the group.

"She probably doesn't get out that much," Charlie whispered to me, as we watched Kartiia stop to pick up a wildflower.

I gave him a small smile. "I bet they all just fly everywhere. Then again, she's a Class Three. There's less control there," I said, quietly.

"Yeah, probably." He slowed for a little bit, making the space between himself and the rest of the squad larger.

I hung back with him, watching him carefully. His blue eyes watched me intently, but there was something else there. Curiosity.

"What did Carterra want to talk to you about?" he asked slowly, keeping his eyes on me.

I just shrugged. "Nothing much. Just telling me to keep in line, that's all."

"Oh. So – like a warning?" he asked, calming his voice.

"Yeah, something like that," I lied, with a smile. It was strange for him to show any curiosity at all.

We jogged back down the rest of the hill, retaking our place at the back of the squad.

"I think we'll stop here for a little while," Wade called to the squad. "Tracks seem to continue towards the base of the mountains. Loren and Sam, you guys are on watch. Everyone else, keep a lookout. We won't be here for long."

We all spread out. I made sure I got a little way from Charlie: he was making me a bit nervous. I sat down by the edge of the stream on a large rock and watched the water run calmly by. It was really pretty here. Tall trees covered the stream in shadows but where the sunlight did manage to touch the water, it sent sparkles glittering all around. The warm breeze rustled through the trees and little insects dipped up and down on the water. I wondered if, before the war, the humans took these places for granted or whether every day they would come down here and have picnics, or throw a ball around. Something, however, felt a bit strange; a little off. There were no birds. Not a sound came from the trees above.

Immediately, I got a sinking feeling in my stomach. I was always super paranoid when it got too quiet, but it normally didn't amount to anything. Somehow, I felt today would be different. I got to my feet, raising my gun a little higher, listening for anything.

"What are you do–" Sam began, but cut off as a spray of bullets came from the trees above.

Bullets ripped through his body and sent him face-first into the stream, blood gushing relentlessly from his back. We all jumped to action, taking cover wherever we could. I jumped up off my rock and over to the other side of the stream, blasting my gun up into the trees. The fireball tore its way through the trees, but collided with no Rebel. The bullets kept coming; this time, from the hill we had just run down.

"Stay down! Stay down!" Wade called from his cover behind a large rock on my side of the stream.

I ducked behind a thick tree and peered out, looking for the Rebels, when suddenly four black trucks came rolling down the hill.

"Wade! We have to go! We have to go now!" I called, as they tore their way towards us; Rebels with great machine guns bolted down to the trailers.

Wade looked out from behind his rock and saw the trucks, nodding in reply. "Get up! Move it! Go, go, go!" he shouted, leading the way back to the forest.

We followed suit, running hard for the dense forest, hearing the spray of bullets pelt against them. Without warning, a sudden sickening feeling came over me. It was as if all the energy in my body drained and my vision blurred as I fell forwards onto the soft grass.

Loren, who was just ahead of me, was lying on the ground as well, clutching her stomach in agony. With whatever strength I could muster, I got to my hands and knees and turned to look for the trucks behind me.

"Got one!" shouted a Rebel, as he jumped down from the back of one of the trucks. He made his way casually to Kartiia, whose body was lying lifeless and face-down on the ground. "A lady Raider!" he exclaimed with excitement, as he kicked her over.

My stomach churned with anger and pain. I wasn't hurt or anything. I hadn't been shot and even if I had, it was never enough to bring me to my knees. I tried to stand, but the world spun around me, forcing me to stay low.

"Look at them all," another Rebel said, quietly, nudging his friend by his side. "It's like they're shutting down, just like what the Major said would happen."

"Round 'em up!" shouted the first Rebel, with a smug grin on his face.

I reached for my fire-blaster, but before I could, one of the Rebels made it to me.

"Oh, no you don't!" he yelled, pulling the gun from my reach and examining it. "Sweet. Always wanted one of these." And with a quick swing, the end of my fire-blaster collided with my face, forcing me back to the ground. Angered now, I tried to get up again, but all there was was another swoosh of my fire-blaster and then darkness.

Chapter Six

I awoke quite abruptly, but felt too sick and tired to move. Wherever I was, it was cold and bright and I was lying on something extremely hard. I heard voices to the left of me. Concentrating as hard as I could, I focused in on what they were saying.

"I told you: when you kill their mother, you weaken them beyond repair. Shaw, explain it once more for these fools, will you?" a gruff-sounding voice said, wearily.

"They are made from living lithuteum; a biological weapon we humans understand very little," said the voice of what sounded like a very intelligent young man. "What we do know is this metal covers the bones, adds strength to muscles, and allows whoever obtains it to run faster, harder and longer. The Raiders tried for a long time to use adult humans for their experiments with the metal, but their bodies could not adapt. The children, however, with open hearts and minds, showing resilience beyond their years, were able to withstand the attack of the lithuteum on their body. They can see better, hear better and heal like you wouldn't believe. But, like children, the lithuteum must be nurtured and given clear boundaries, and so a bond must be formed between the Raider mother who carries the lithuteum in her body and the child it has taken over. When that mother is killed, the lithuteum will overrun the child's body and die with her."

"But how do they get the metal inside their bodies?" asked a young girl's wary voice.

"Perhaps our new friends here will be able to tell us that, once we give them a chance to regain control over themselves," Shaw answered heartily. There was an eagerness to his voice.

There were a few mutters and then quick footsteps came bursting into the room.

"Shaw! One of ours has started seizing!" came a young man's alarmed voice.

There were many more mutters, but Shaw – it must have been – ran from the room and out of the door.

"Major – why are we saving them again?" asked one voice from the crowd.

"Because they're useful and they used to be human. Let's give them the chance to prove themselves, shall we?" suggested the gruff voice.

"But if they tell the Raiders where we are–" started another voice, but was cut off by the major.

"They will not escape the Lifeline, there is no way. Don't you all have work to do?" he yelled, angrily, and with that, several pairs of footsteps shuffled away.

I couldn't help but feel there was someone watching me. Knowing that I wasn't going to be able to fight my way out of here, I narrowed my choices down to pretending to be asleep. It sounded like there were quite a few people in the room, some had laboured breathing and others moved with heavy footsteps, making a swishing noise as they went. With my curiosity getting the better of me, I dared to take a peek.

It took a moment for my eyes to adjust to the harsh bright lights burning above me. When I could finally see past the glare, I saw that I was in a white room, surrounded by tables cluttered with boxes and paper. I tried to turn my head slightly to the right. Out of the corner of my eye, I glimpsed several people standing at a table, looking down with great interest at a bright blue screen. They were dressed in white lab coats, their hair neat and tidy, all of them looking very prim and proper. These Rebels were obviously not the soldier kind… Maybe they were scientists, or doctors or something. I let my mind wander, remembering when we used to get our immunisation needles at school. I shuddered at the memory: I used to be so scared back then.

I desperately wanted to sit up, to demand to know where I was, and to see if my squad was here. My back was starting to ache on the cold, hard table. Patience was not one of my virtues. Knowing I'd probably regret it, I took in a deep breath and sat up, my head buzzing from where the Rebel had hit me with my fire-blaster. That was strange: normally it would heal pretty fast.

There were a few sudden gasps from the small huddle of lab coats, as they began to back away from me. A few escaped through a door to their right.

"One's waking up!" called one of the lab coats, panicking, down the hallway. I heard him take a big tumble, hitting the hard floor with a whack.

"For goodness' sake…" muttered a voice to my left.

I turned to look at the gruff voice I had heard before. Leaning against a silver steel desk was an older man, slim but still tough looking. He had a scar running back from his right brow to his dark brown hair; at least, what was left of it. He wasn't too tall and his face looked like it was set in stone as a constant frown. More footsteps came running frantically back towards the room.

My stomach started to lurch, and the room began to blur as it had by the stream. I hadn't felt so terrible in a long time, and I could feel the bump on my head beginning to pulse. I tried to swing my legs over the table, but before I knew it, countless men dressed in black ran into the room forcing me back down. I cried out in anger as I tried to get my body to fight back the way I wanted it to. I started by pulling one of the soldiers, who was holding my right arm, across the table. He landed on the floor with a loud smack, and just as I was reaching for one of the men on my other side, more soldiers came to hold me back down. I reached out again, wriggling under their grasp, when all of sudden I saw something that caught my eye in a terrible way. My hand was nearly as pale as a Raider's and my veins were black and spidery. In my confusion, the men managed to strap me down to the table.

"Give her a sedative," said a woman's voice to a small man in a lab coat, who nodded and left her side.

She seemed to have come out of nowhere, but perhaps she was the one who was watching me. She was tall, with long, blonde hair tied up and her black glasses positioned perfectly on her face. She was holding a notebook and pen, watching me curiously. The small man returned with a huge needle, and as much as I tried to struggle, he got me in the leg. The needle burned but gave me the sudden sensation of floating, as if I was lying on my back on a cloud under the bright light of the sun. But I was floating, or at least I was moving. The lights came and went as I passed under them.

"Get her over there, and strap her down tight," the woman's voice chimed again.

I was lifted off the table and onto another one, but wherever I was now, it was a lot darker and smaller. The voices, and sounds of the soldier's laboured breathing as they tied me down, seemed to bounce off the walls.

"I'm here, I'm here!" called the voice of Shaw, his footsteps booming as he ran into the room. His red, round face appeared by my side. "Maddy, I'm Dr Shaw. Don't you worry, we're taking very good care of you." This man looked down at me as if he knew me, as if he was worried. His brown eyes were red and appeared tired.

"All right, is she strapped in?" he asked one of the soldiers, quietly.

"Almost sir," he replied, breathlessly, "Done."

"Okay, let's begin," Dr Shaw said, quietly, as he and the other soldiers stepped away from me. "Don't worry, Maddy. It will be over shortly, then we can talk about everything that's going on," he said, loudly, but he wasn't really filling me with confidence.

All around me, I could see dark walls closing in. I tried to move my head, to see where everyone else had gone, but it was no use. I felt as if I was paralysed on the table. I heard a click as a door closed somewhere behind me and I waited anxiously in the darkness. Out of nowhere, bright red sparks jumped up through the walls, pulsing menacingly above me. I couldn't help but feel like I wasn't alone in here. Suddenly, six tentacle-like tubes sprang out from the walls, filled with vibrant colours, edging their way out of my line of sight behind me. With one swift movement, I heard the tentacles whoosh through the air before agonising pain filled my body, as each tentacle pierced into my spine like hot blades of iron. I screamed out in pain, wishing Kartiia was here to comfort me like she had when I was changed, but no one answered my cries. Like when I had been created, I could feel a hot, searing flood of liquid shoot through my body, covering my bones once more and stretching into my mind.

Lying there on the cold table, I could feel my body aching. I opened my eyes and tried to look around but I couldn't move all that well. I was still strapped down. I could hear the screams from a boy – he must have been in the machine – but I could also hear two people talking beside me.

It was Dr Shaw and the woman who had been ordering everyone around.

"She is incredible, Dr Shaw. And she was so strong even before the machine. You couldn't tell she was dying," said the woman with the black-rimmed glasses. "What will we do with them once they've gone through the machine?" she asked.

"Well, Eris, I have a feeling this one is special," said Dr Shaw. I could hear his footsteps getting louder as he walked towards me. "Maddy was the only one who woke up after being separated from the Raiders. Perhaps the bond wasn't strong enough for her, or she was too strong for the bond? Chances are if a child's body can adapt to one situation, they can definitely rework themselves to get out of it."

"You mean that her body was finding its own way out of the bond?" Eris asked, quietly. I couldn't tell if she was happy about that.

"Maybe," Shaw answered, slowly. "Everything is just theory with these kids. I'm so glad we finally have some. It's been quite difficult to learn anything by watching them and listening to the reports. I do hope they'll be happy here and will want to work with us…" He trailed off, dreamily, but got back on track, "Anyway, I think the major wants them all to go to the new dorms. I think that settling them back into as normal a human life as possible, the better they'll adjust. My team has used all of our resources to gather as much information about these kids that we can, so there'll be no need for them to go to the Infirmary."

"Do you think there'll be any effects from using the machine?" Eris asked, after scribbling something down on her clipboard.

"Again, this is a first for everyone. I suppose we will soon find out. But you know what's interesting..?" Shaw added, quietly. I flinched slightly in pain when his cold hand touched my arm. "Whatever alien chemicals are in that machine, they make their veins glow. It's really quite mesmerising. Interesting that it doesn't have the same effect on the lesser Raider classes."

"Quite," Eris answered, changing her tone. "Well, I'm here to keep an eye on this programme. We may be at the world's end, but I will have order. As you know, I was on the last convoy from Stronghold, and management would like to be kept fully aware and up to date with how these children go. The Raiders have definitely proved how useful they are, and we would not be investing so much time, energy and resources into failed science experiments."

"You expect them to fight... I see. I will do my best to inform you of everything."

"Oh, don't worry. I'll go where you go. I want to see it all first-hand," Eris said, brightly.

The boy's screaming stopped and I could hear the whirring of the machine come to a halt, as well. Dr Shaw left my side and I heard the footsteps of another person coming to a stop beside me. With another sharp sting, this time in my arm, I fell into a deep sleep, and for the first time in a long time, it was dreamless.

Chapter Seven

I was getting pretty sick and tired of waking up in different places. But this time, I awoke feeling very comfortable and warm. My body felt strange, like a giant weight I never knew was there had been lifted off my chest. I opened my eyes and found myself on the top bunk of a bunk bed. It was dark in the room, but I could see more bunks lined up on either side of the walls. The only light I could see was a faint glow from under a silvery roller door and from the new-found colours mixing in my veins. I stared at them, mesmerised in the darkness. The colours were vibrant blues and greens, reds and purples, mixing together. Every now and then, a flash of gold would emanate down my arm, fading as it reached my fingertips. I jumped down over the side of the bed, landing with a small thud on the concrete floor. On each side of the bunkbed were tall wooden cupboards. With curiosity, I opened mine and found a pair of black overalls, black heavy-duty boots, and a leather jacket. In the faint light, I saw a shimmer of red. Looking closer, I saw there was a thick, red band around the right overall pant leg and on the jacket. On the inside door of the cupboard was a mirror, and I caught a glimpse of myself. I was wearing long black pants, with a grey hoodie and khaki boots. My long hair was wavy, out of its usual braids, and my face didn't bear any mark of the life I'd lived, except for the glow in my veins.

I closed the cupboard door, uncomfortable from the stranger staring back at me and walked towards the other end of the dorm. As I did I passed other sleeping girls – my squad! Their veins glowed just as mine did, but they didn't wake. It seemed they had lost energy, some even whispering and calling out in their sleep. I tried to remember all their names, but with all the new replacements coming in when other kids died, it was hard to keep up. There was Loren, of course, her long blonde hair falling like a shimmering waterfall over the edge of the bed. There was Emily, a tall fifteen-year old with brown hair; Skylar, with short red hair and freckles; and Izzy, a brown haired, blue-eyed girl whose twin brother, Beau, was in our squad, as well. I'd never known her well, but her bunk was right next to mine.

At the very end of the dorm was a small bathroom and to my surprise, there was another bathroom at my end. After having searched the dorm, checking the cupboards to see that the other girls had suits like mine, my curiosity and boredom began to get the better of each other as I sat on my bed, staring at the roller door. What would I find out there? Was there a whole pack of Rebels just waiting for us, or was I in a house and I would find a kitchen or a living room?

Fed up, I jumped back down off my bunk and walked over to the roller door. Giving it a hard tug, it rolled back, revealing a large open space arcing around four columns in the centre. Taking a quick look around, I couldn't sense anyone else there, so off I went to explore.

Following white lights glowing underneath the grates in the floor, I strolled around the four silvery columns, stretching from the floor to the ceiling. Each column had a large door, and every now and then I could hear a swooshing sound, as something passed through them. I guessed they were lifts. There were no windows anywhere here, and there were big vents in the ceiling where the lifts disappeared, making me feel like they had to go up for air. We must be underground. On one of the walls, in front of the elevators, I saw a big white "37" stamped onto the silvery metal. I shuddered to think how far down that might have been.

There seemed to be another three rooms exactly like the one I had woken up in, but there was nobody else there: the cupboards were empty. Each roller door to the rooms had been painted a different colour on the outside. Mine was red, and the others were green, blue and violet.

It felt like forever, but finally the other girls started to wake up, although I wasn't sure that I was ready for the state they woke up in.

"Where am I?" shouted Emily, as she sat upright in her bed, looking frantically around.

"Don't freak out, but we're with the Rebels. I think we're underground or something," I said, quietly, as I stood on the ladder to her bunk.

Emily clutched her head, her brown hair falling around her face. "No, no no…" she trailed off, quietly. "They're going to be so mad. They'll never want us back after this," she said, softly.

Confused, I looked at her. "Are you crying?"

Emily sniffled a little before looking back up at me, big tears welling up in her eyes. "I don't know. I haven't really felt sad for a long time–"

She was cut off by Loren's scream from the bunk beside her. "My hands! My hands – they're different! There's colours!" she began hyperventilating a little now, "My head. What the hell happened?"

"Like I said," I began, loudly. "We're in a Rebel base."

I jumped down from Emily's bed and walked back to my own.

"Rebels?" Skylar said, quietly, fear in her voice. "Why are we still alive then?" she added as she, too, looked at her own colourful veins.

"We're soldiers: I guess they'll be wanting us to fight for them now," I suggested, as I slowly pulled back the sheets and made my bed. Mum used to hate it when I left it untidy. Her face flashed in my mind: it was like I could feel her warmth, her love.

"What are you doing?" said a small voice from below me. Izzy had walked over to watch me with a confused look in her blue eyes.

"What does it look like?" I said, annoyed.

"It looks like you're making your bed," she riposted, folding her arms.

"Well done," I smiled.

"But why?" she asked again.

"Because the sooner we get the Rebels to trust us, the sooner we can make a plan of getting out of here and back home. Or do you want to go against the Raiders?" I asked, as I jumped back down.

"Oh, okay," she said, happily, before walking back to her bed and making it.

Loren and Skylar began to make their beds, too. All I had wanted for a long time was to be able to talk to someone, but it was never these girls. I had wanted to talk to Charlie, Wade, or even Aiden: they had seemed more interesting to me.

Suddenly, a white screen rose up out of the floor in the centre of the room. We all jumped down to get a better look, confused by what it was. I moved closer, reaching out my hand to touch it, but it went straight through. All of a sudden, a tall figure emerged inside the screen; a man who I recognised as the major.

"Hello. My name is Major Scott Miller," he began, gruffly. "I'm sure you are all wondering where you are and why you're here…" His eyes weren't really looking at anyone, and his gaze didn't follow as I walked around the screen in interest.

"He's not really here, is he?" Skylar asked the rest of us, quietly, but the major continued.

"If you are the lucky ones who have made it to the base, congratulations. I am sure you are all aware now of your duties as the last-known survivors of the human race. You are at Saigo, a base built in secret by the United Nations. It is one of three bases in Australia, and there are several others across the earth which we keep in contact with as best we can. These bases make up the Lifeline, the last hope for the survival of our race. I'm sure many of you have travelled far and endured unimaginable sufferings, but know that you are safe here. Currently, the Raiders have gained control of most of the earth, some lands still remain free, but with limited resources it is difficult to regain any more. That is why I must ask a big thing of you: to help us, to join our fight and begin to retake our home, piece by piece. Others have not been so lucky and are still trapped inside the main cities, rounded up by the Raiders and forced to live in fear and squalor. It is our duty to do our best, to free them and to win this war for our earth. Officials from Saigo will be with you shortly and will help find a place for you in our community."

The screen faded away into the floor, leaving us standing there, the room a little darker now.

"They want our help?" Loren asked, loudly, with a smile, "We've been killing them for as long as I can remember."

"But you can remember before that, can't you?" Izzy asked, quietly. We all gave her a strange look. "I'm only saying that I feel different, and… and I miss my brother, and–"

"You miss your brother?" Loren asked, sarcastically. "We don't miss people. We don't feel anything. That's not what we're supposed to be."

"Loren's right," I began. "They want our help, but they expect us to have changed. We can't get caught up in all these feelings the humans have," I said, remembering what General Carterra had told me. "We are on the Raiders' side. We have to get back to them as soon as we can."

"Good. I hate the humans, anyway. As if we'd ever want to save them," Loren said, proudly.

The girls nodded in agreement. Izzy was a little bit slower to comply, but I knew she'd stick with us.

Outside the room, I heard the elevator whooshing its way down, but it stopped with a soft ding. The doors opened slowly, and several footsteps resounded as they filed out and onto our level. The tension built in the room with each footstep approaching our door. Like clockwork, we each ducked low and spread out along the beds in the dorm, waiting with bated breath.

All of a sudden, the round face of Dr Shaw appeared in the doorway. He raised his hands in the air with a small smile on his face. "I come in peace," he called into the dorm.

Two soldiers with guns entered right behind him, surveying the room.

"Come on, girls. I thought you might like to have something to eat? Maybe even see the boys?" he said, as though trying to tempt us.

I looked behind me at Loren, and whispered under my breath, "We're safer in numbers. We'll need the boys' help, too."

She nodded and with a devilish smile, bounded out from behind her hiding place in the shadows. The guards got a good scare but didn't raise their weapons.

"Well, I for one am starving," she declared happily, as she walked into the middle of the dorm.

Each of us followed suit, stepping out to follow her, with me trailing at the end of the line. I watched the soldiers and Shaw carefully, clenching my fists in readiness.

"Well, that's great. We'll take you up to level 25 for a spot of breakfast." He said this very happily, giving us each a smile as we passed.

I looked him up and down. He wasn't as tall or as big as I'd thought he was when I was being strapped to the table. I'd taken out much larger opponents with my bare hands before. Comforted by that fact, I gave him a small smile. There were another two soldiers waiting by the lifts, each holding guns. The metal doors opened and we each stepped inside. I could remember what the lift felt like whenever I used them before the war, but the sensation of zooming upwards in a metal box left me feeling a little nauseous.

As the lift came to a stop, the big metal doors opened to the cold world of the dining room on the 25th floor. There was no hallway to this floor; just one big room that curved around one half of the floor. As we stepped out of the lift, the familiar sounds of the boys' heartbeats filled my ears, and I was suddenly filled with the urge to run over and hug every one of them. The dining room had four long, metal tables, which shone under the bright lighting. It seemed even colder in here, but the air was a bit better than the lower level we'd come from.

Wade stood up when he saw us enter, and the four other boys followed his lead, watching us closely.

"Okay, ladies. You can go and join them now. There's plenty of food for everyone," Dr Shaw said, cheerfully, as he directed us over to the long, silver table the boys were still standing around. "We'll give you all about half an hour to eat, and then we'll take you to level 32." With that, Dr Shaw and the four guards left, the elevator swooshing away quietly.

I watched as they disappeared back into the lift. I saw that there was a small panel with two buttons on it that the soldiers pressed to call the lift. I walked quickly over to it and pressed them both, but nothing happened. A flash of red words sparked above the panel, reading 'LOCKED'.

'Well, no wonder they're leaving us here alone. There's actually no other way out except by the lifts,' I thought to myself.

I turned around to face the rest of the room from the lifts. I'd been so caught up in seeing the boys that I hadn't realised there was a large square hole in the wall. I walked forwards, feeling the eyes of my squad members burning into me, and poked my head through the hole. There was a large industrial-looking kitchen. It looked like everything in there was made of stainless steel: silvery steel was a recurring colour I kept finding here. Happy now that I had scoped out as much as I could from the dining room, I walked quietly over to the metal table and sat down across from Wade, who was still standing with everyone else, watching me.

"Are you kidding me?" I said, softly, as I looked at the stack of drinks full of thick, gross liquid in the centre of the table. "Raiders made us drink this mush, too," I said, getting angry now as I pulled one of the heavy glass cups towards myself.

"Wait – you're not actually going to drink that, are you?" Charlie asked, as he came to sit by my side. His eyes watched me anxiously as I brought the cup to my lips, taking a gulp of the purple liquid.

"What?" I said, after I swallowed it with some difficulty. "If they wanted us dead, we'd be dead. What's wrong with you all, anyway? Sit down," I said, looking around at them all.

Tentatively, they each took a seat and reached for their drinks.

"You know how you're defective, Maddy? Well, I think they've made us like you, too…" Charlie said, quietly.

"How do you mean?" I asked, trying more of my drink.

"Well, you know how you were asking Wade and me about video games and your brothers, the other day? Well, I know what you mean now… I mean, I remember it all," he said, quietly, looking into his glass. "I can remember my parents, and where I was when the war began. I even had an older sister…" He trailed off.

"Wait – you mean, with the Raiders, you guys never had dreams, never remembered anything about being human?" I asked, loudly now, looking around at them all.

They shook their heads and shrugged their shoulders.

"Oh, well, you guys were really annoying, actually. You were completely robotic. I just thought you didn't say anything because we weren't allowed to, not that you didn't know anything."

"It feels like I have lived two separate lives," Charlie said, quietly.

"Who cares? The Raiders are the ones we fight for, the ones who created us. That is the only thing you need to remember. These people are the enemy, the ones we've been destroying for the last four years. That's all that matters," I said, loudly, looking carefully at each of them.

"She's right," Loren piped up. "I hate the Rebels and I want to go home."

"But Kartiia's dead," Skylar said, quietly. "I don't know if I could go back without her there."

"How about we just see what it's like here before we decide whether we're going back?" Beau said, thoughtfully, looking at his twin sister, Izzy, who nodded in agreement.

"No," Wade's deep voice cut in. "We have a duty to the Raiders. We're going home." His word seemed pretty final, and everyone started to get to work on drinking their breakfasts.

Of the remaining boys, there was Charlie, Wade, Aiden, Beau and Mason. Their veins glowed colourfully under the bright lights, just as ours did, but I was beginning to see more changes that I hadn't noticed until now. Everyone looked uneasily around the table at each other, then at the doors, like they were nervous. I definitely wasn't afraid of dying or what was going to happen next, but my squad's once steady heartbeats were now pumping faster and more uncontrollably than ever. That wasn't the only thing: the way they spoke and had begun to express their feelings made me feel a little nervous about my plans to get us all out of here. Nowhere in my plan did I expect that my squad wouldn't want to go back to the Raiders.

After a tense half hour, the soldiers and Dr Shaw returned and led us back to the lift and down to level 32. The lift slowly came to a halt, and with a soft ding the doors opened and we were led out into a small hallway. On the wall was a white "32", stamped in big block numbers. The hallway, like the dorms on level 37, was a greyish zinc colour, the lights reflecting cold, silver shadows on the walls. A door stood ajar on the left side of the wall: it was the only door in the hallway. Bright light spilled in to the hall. I had the weird sensation that if I stepped through it, I would be burned. Aiden went first, followed by the twins, then the rest of us.

The room was large: it had white floors, white ceilings and mirrors all around. Huge lights burned brightly above our heads, bouncing off the mirrors. The mirrors, walls and ceilings all had black outlines of boxes dented into their surfaces.

"Welcome, children!" Eris's shrill voice rang around the large empty room.

We all made a line in front of her, where she stood by a doorway to another even smaller room.

"We haven't been properly introduced," she smiled, flashing her straight white teeth. "My name is Eris Black. I am here to watch over you all and see how you progress in your training. Now, I think I'll hand it over to the major." She turned to look at the small, dark room behind her, and from it emerged the figure of Major Miller.

"I'm sure you all saw my speech this morning when you woke up. We show that to all newcomers: that way they know who we are and what our purpose is. Your purpose, however, will be to fight. We have had many reports and have seen first-hand what you children are capable of. Now, from what I understand…" he looked to Shaw, and then back at us. "You must all be feeling a bit strange right now. I have no idea what it was like with the Raiders, and how well they treated you, but I will make myself clear now. Try anything – any attack or escape – and I will shoot you. If you hurt another member of this population, I will shoot you. And if you refuse to fight, I will shoot you." He looked sternly at us all, resting his hand on a holstered gun at his side.

I stifled a smile. I don't think they'd heard all the reports of us healing super-fast. Bullets weren't going to phase me.

"Now, today, we're going to be running a few little simulations, just to see what you can do," he said, with an unbelieving smile. "Simulation number one." He walked towards us with his smile getting bigger. "I want you to run to the end of the room and back," he said, pointing to the back wall about fifty-odd meters away.

I smirked a little and Wade gave me a 'piece-of-cake' kind of look.

"Off you go. We'll just be waiting in here," he said, as he walked back to the smaller room. I could see his faint shadow, sitting down, behind the glass. The guards closed the door to the hallway and followed Dr Shaw inside the room, also closing that door behind them. We were completely alone in this white little world.

"How hard can it be?" Loren said, smirking, as she began to jog towards the back wall.

A couple of the boys laughed and followed her. I hung back a little, watching as the squad charged off into the room, spreading out as they went. Others were a bit more timid than usual, but maybe it was the people watching us that was throwing them off their game. Shrugging my shoulders, I ran forwards, running past the twins, Skylar and Emily, when suddenly the room came alive. White boxes shot out from the walls, floors and ceiling, knocking Emily hard in her side, taking Mason down beside her. I could hear a few shouts of surprise and thuds as more boxes took out some of my squad members behind me. I ducked under a block coming down from the ceiling, then jumped high over the block receding back into the wall, passing Emily and Mason in a dazed heap on the floor. I was so close to reaching the wall when suddenly giant mirrors rose up out of the floors. In my attempt to dodge them, I got turned around, losing sight of the wall at the back of the room. This made me angry – when would there ever be mirrors in the field? I took a deep breath, dodging another couple of boxes before running straight through the mirror that I was certain was blocking my path to the wall, the glass shattering into pieces behind me. I ran forwards for the last few meters, touching the back wall before turning around to make it back.

It was a mess. Our squad was either lying on the floor, in the process of being knocked down, or in the twins' case, were too scared to move any closer. I screwed up my face in confusion, pushing my long hair off my face. Something was different and it was in that moment that I realised what had made us kids so successful under the Raiders command: without emotion, there is no fear. Fear holds us back from so much, and now that my squad members were back in touch with their human side, they realised they had something to lose… Their lives. I could feel myself feeling different, too. I was feeling guilt and pity. Watching my squad scramble was not something I could stomach. With a huff, I ran forwards to Loren and Mason, picking them up and swinging them one at a time over a block that kept coming straight for them. They dashed off to the back wall, clutching their sides. I could see another pile of mirrors creating a maze to my right and using a block that came shooting straight for me, I jumped high and landed on top of it, using it to see who was in the mirrors. It was Wade.

"Just smash your way through!" I called to him, and he gave me a nod when he saw me standing up high on the block. The block started to move rapidly back into the wall and I jumped down, running towards the twins.

I could hear that Loren, Mason and Wade, now having reached the back wall, were shouting directions to the rest of the squad. Beau and

Izzy began to shake their heads as I grabbed them by the arms and dragged them through the centre of the room.

"Just do it!" I shouted at them, as they began to pull away again. "Go!" I yelled, again, as I pushed them under a block that jutted out from the wall to our left.

It took a lot longer but we all managed to get back to the starting point, huffing and puffing, as we leant against the wall. The room seemed to power down, and the bits of broken glass from the mirrors sank down into the floor, like they were being absorbed by jelly. The door from the viewing room swung open, and we kids backed up and went back into a line before Dr Shaw, Major Miller and Eris.

"This facility is used to test agility, to train your minds to think fast, and make decisions on your feet," Major Miller began. "You all did quite well, considering you'd never been here before. All the surfaces in this room are fireproof and can absorb any object moving at high speeds, but only as big as an apple. The columns you see that jump out are connected to visual and sensory machines that can analyse high speed data and calculate their own attack against you. There are no tricks or ways around this facility: the only way you can conquer it is through hard work, and always expecting the unexpected. This has helped to train many of our soldiers, and it will do the same for you." The major walked down our line with his hands behind his back.

Dr Shaw cleared his throat before speaking in a very interested voice. "How did the Raiders train you, exactly?"

No one answered, but I could feel a few eyes on me.

"It was all in our heads. Besides, you learn fast when there's lots of people trying to kill you. And because we heal so fast, we had a few more chances to keep on fighting," I said, quietly.

"I see. In your heads? How?" he pressed on.

I took a deep breath. "Well, we would put our wrists into the scanner and our mission and orders would upload into our minds."

"Show me your wrist," he said, eagerly, holding out his hand.

I walked forwards, holding out my left wrist, and placed it into his warm hands. "There seems to be nothing on the surface," he said, examining it. "We haven't gone through all the scans yet, so I'll make sure I double-check your wrists. Thank you, Maddy. That is truly spectacular." He quietly let go of my hand.

"How do you know my name?" I asked, and stayed standing in front of him, my curiosity getting the better of me.

"Never mind that, child," Eris said, coldly, as she looked down at me.

"If you want us to fight for you, then we'll need some of our questions answered," I retorted, just as coldly.

But Dr Shaw just smiled down at me. "All in good time, Maddy. We just want you all to get settled in here. No one's fighting, just yet," he said, placing a hand on my shoulder.

I immediately jerked away from him, stepping back into line.

"Now, we can see what it's like when you all try to get somewhere by yourselves, and I'll thank Maddy for showing some leadership in trying to get the rest of you to finish this task, but how well will you do when you work together?" Major Miller smiled again.

The next few days carried on a lot like this. Steadily, we all got used to the training and to how we each had changed. Wade, it turns out, wasn't a natural born leader, and neither was I, but every time we had to do things in groups, it fell to me - maybe because I was more used to feeling the way I felt. It never felt like I'd lived two separate lives. I was beginning to like the routine, but I missed my home. Like Loren, I hated the Rebels and desperately wanted to get out. General Carterra's mission was in the back of my mind, never leaving me. I listened for anything that could give me clues as to where the Rebels kept their information, even when training. I noticed the golden sparks in my veins flash brighter and stay longer every time I listened. When I asked the girls, when we got back to the dorm, whether they could hear things through walls, they shook their heads. Even with having my squad to talk to, I still felt alone.

On the fifth day of training, we were doing excellently: the definition of teamwork. We were adapting a whole lot easier to the unknown, and the squad seemed to be growing in confidence. Every day we learnt more about the Rebels, and in turn we told them more about the Raiders. We made sure we didn't give anything too major away, but my main game was getting back to Carterra. I kept listening to that little room, hoping

they would let something slip about anything useful, when the gruff voice
of Major Miller rang in my ears.

"I think they're ready."

Chapter Eight

We sat at the silver tables, drinking our breakfasts quickly, with looks of distaste on our faces.

"Well, I don't think these are going to get better with time," Wade said, almost sadly, as he looked desperately into his cup.

"Honestly, I don't think we need to be eating this often, anyway," Charlie said smartly, with a smile.

From the end of the table, Beau cleared his throat, looking warily at us all. "I – er… I think it's not so bad here…" he said, slowly trailing off at my glare. "I just… I just…" he tried to begin again, looking anxiously into the bottom of his glass.

I felt Wade tense up from across the table, his grip tightening around his glass. "Get it out," he said, through gritted teeth.

I looked back at Beau, watching him carefully, feeling the anger rise up inside me. He looked nervously at Izzy, who gave him a small nudge of confidence.

"I only mean to say, that I like it here. It's safe and we're important to the humans–"

"Rebels!" Loren yelled loudly, slamming her drink on the table, the green slosh splashing onto the surface. "Say it, Beau – Rebels! They're nothing compared to the Raiders! I want to go home!"

"Maybe this is our home now!" Izzy shouted back, rising out of her chair. "I don't even think we could survive without Kartiia any more?"

"What's that supposed to mean?" Skylar said, quietly, flashing a concerned look my way.

"Well, that machine the humans used saved our lives… Maybe it's not a one-off thing," Charlie spoke smartly, pushing his blond hair out of his eyes. "I can see the colours in my veins getting fainter…"

"Who cares?!" Loren cut in again. "The Raiders will fix us, and they'll make sure we're all right. I just want to go home."

There was an awkward silence for a moment before I could feel the eyes boring into the side of my face. I took a breath.

"We're going back to the Raiders. The first chance we get, as soon as we're topside, we're leaving," I said softly,

"But Maddy–" Izzy started, hesitantly.

"If you want to stay, then that's fine. I'll meet you on the battlefield," I warned, looking her straight in the eyes.

There were a few shivers from the end of the table, but Loren smiled triumphantly, fixing her hair in the reflection of her glass.

After a few minutes, Loren broke the silence.

"Does anyone know why we're wearing these today?" she asked, grumpily, as she was deciding on whether her mission suit looked better zipped up or not.

I kept my gaze away from the rest of my squad, being careful not to catch their stare. Wade looked especially sullen.

Dr Shaw and the guards came a bit earlier today, and instead of hitting the button to the 32nd floor, Shaw pressed the one to the 12th. We all looked at each other, a little alarmed, but there was no stopping whatever was going to happen. We stepped out into the 12th floor. I looked down the long hall that seemed to stretch endlessly. As we were guided through, I took a look around. The walls were the same white colour as the training floor, but for some reason I felt even more boxed in. I could hear many heartbeats all around, the loud chatters of conversation and the humming and whirring of machines. Some humans in white uniforms passed us quickly in the hallway, averting their eyes. I could have sworn a few were even holding their breath. Other humans dared not enter the hallway but waited by the doors, clutching papers and folders to their chests. I tried hard to fight the urge to jump out and scare them, but I guess I was already getting a reaction I was satisfied with.

We passed several more doors on our walk down to the end of the hall. Two soldiers stood outside of the last door to the right. 'Mission Control' was stamped in black on the wall. They stood tall and watched us closely as we approached. I looked over to Charlie, who was walking slowly beside me. He gave me a small smile as the two soldiers directed us through the doorway.

Stepping through the doorway, we walked into a large room with dark walls covered in screens and radars. To the left was a large raised platform where many Rebels worked busily over blue screens on table tops, with maps and papers strewn across others. There were a few gasps from the humans as they noticed our presence. Dr Shaw led us to a stop in front of the raised platform, and we all turned our heads from side to side, trying to get a better look. I was pretty small, so I had to stand on my tiptoes to try and see past the Rebels' knees. Dr Shaw left us for a moment as he ducked into a small room on the far side of Mission Control.

"Shaw's a mad man if he thinks he's gonna get anywhere with those robots," one Rebel said to another, casting wary eyes towards us.

"I know. Honestly, they look just like children. How could they possibly have caused so much damage?" another rebel said to his friend, as they turned back to watch the radars on the walls.

My stomach began to fill with anger. I clenched my fists, biting my tongue.

Dr Shaw re-emerged from the room, followed by Eris, Major Miller and another man I did not recognise. Whoever he was, he was tall and pale, and walked with an unusual limp. He had a small amount of wispy, white hair on his head. He looked down at us all with brown, beady eyes, his mouth held in a somewhat half-smile.

"Children, this is Ronan Starr. He is the leader of the Lifeline Base Stronghold and has travelled a long way to be here with us today," Major Miller said, loudly, as he leant against the rail to talk to us.

"I just wanted to see you all once, and check in with my advisor, Miss Eris Black, on how well you were all progressing. I am very happy with what I have heard, and seeing you all stand before me fills me with a new hope for our future," Ronan Starr spoke very breathily but slowly, as he considered every word he said. He kept one hand inside his fading red coat, his dark eyes settling on each of us.

"Today, we're going to head up to the ground and you will all be meeting a few key members of Saigo. The Defence Force Unit, or DFU, that you'll be heading out with in future, is very anxious to meet you, as are some of our population. You will be on your best behaviour, and please do remember my warning," the major stated, almost threateningly.

"All righty, then," Shaw said, happily, stepping down from the platform. "If you would follow me now, children." He beckoned us towards him.

My anger didn't fade, but I was filled with the beginnings of hope. I looked up at Wade as he passed me. He nodded his head and spoke under his breath so that only we kids could hear: "Go time."

I took one look back at Starr as I followed Wade quietly to the door. He pulled his pale hand from his pocket and looked into a small round mirror. It reminded me of a small version of the Tidesse, like the one General Carterra had. My eyes widened but before I could get a better look, our squad was ushered back into the white world of Level 12. It was him. That was Starr: the one Carterra had warned me about. My mind began to jump into overdrive, knowing if we were going to get back to the Raiders, that Tidesse would have to be in our hands. The people in white uniforms stuck to the walls on our way back but I didn't care. We got to the lifts and filed in quietly, but I could feel the tension in the air. I knew my warning at breakfast was still ringing in everybody's ears. I only hoped that they would make the right decision. Shaw hit the button to Level 1. This level was full of sunlight, as vast glass ceilings ran along the length of the hallways above our heads. I looked up, glad to see the sun shining once more. It felt depressing being so far underground. The people up here were more civilian types than soldier, dressed in colourful clothes, smiles on their faces as they carried food or baskets of washing, going about their days. My eyes widened as I saw a few little kids run past, laughing and playing with a ball in the hall. I hadn't seen anyone younger than me for a long time and I doubted whether those kids actually knew there was a war going on.

We followed Shaw around the lifts and up the hallway opposite. It was a wide open area, with no rooms but plenty of little stalls, where people were trading things and making food. I saw the food stalls catch Wade's eye, slowing us down, but grudgingly he couldn't stop, and walked a little quicker to close the gap between himself and Shaw. We turned left down at the end of the hallway and through a small door, which turned out to be a staircase.

"The stairwell only goes down to Level 12," Shaw explained quickly, as he led the way up one flight of stairs.

We stepped through the door and found ourselves in a large warehouse. There were big trucks lined up in two rows with people working busily around them. Some were hauling big boxes onto the trucks, others were working on the engines. All we could see were pairs of legs sticking out.

"The main part of the base is comprised of eight buildings," Shaw began loudly, as we walked along the lines of trucks and out into the warmth of the sun. "They all circle around the Watchtower." He smiled as he pointed up to a large cement tower standing tall above the buildings which arced around it. The buildings had a few floors to them and were all the same colour of cold steel. I looked behind me, away from the Watchtower, and saw groups of young soldiers jogging, probably doing laps around the base; others were leading civilians from the centre of the base to what looked like large paddocks.

"We have horses back there, but we keep chickens, cows, pigs and sheep out on a farm about 2 kilometers away from the base," Shaw explained, as he followed my gaze. "Workers live out there on a weekly rotation and send in food, daily."

"Can we go out there?" Loren asked innocently, batting her eyes.

"Ah, no," Shaw said, with an equally sickly smile.

Suddenly I realised there was a faint blueish glow around the base. I peered up to look at it. It reminded me of the force field we brought down back at the Fishbowl. I wasn't surprised that they would have a force field; I just completely forgot about it. Also, surrounding the entire base was a thick concrete wall, tall and impenetrable looking, casting long shadows over some of the area. Suddenly, the whole force field above our heads shook and rippled, starting from the gates in the distance. I craned my neck and screwed up my eyes, trying to see what was happening. There seemed to be some sort of checkpoint; a shed or something beyond the gate. Four black trucks came rolling in to the base, speeding along the dirt road until their tyres met the road. The force field settled as the last truck had gone through.

"I'm betting we're going to have to bring that down if we're gonna get out of here," I said quietly to the squad, as they too watched the trucks push through the force field.

The trucks zoomed towards us, and my squad stood there in silence as we watched. I crossed my arms in front of myself, thoroughly unimpressed. As the trucks rolled around, several faces poked out from the windows, and there were even men riding in the trailers, standing and shouting in our direction.

"Raiders! Raiders! Here to get us!" they teased, as they drove past us, kicking up the dust off the road. "Help me, help me! They're so scary!" they called as they sped past.

The last truck slowed to a stop and Shaw jogged up to the driver's side. We all stood and watched intently, as did the Rebels in the trucks.

"Good scout?" Shaw said, loudly, as he leaned in through the open window.

"Not bad. The Raiders are crawling all over the place after we took those kids," the driver said wearily, but there was a lot of life to his voice. "Even tried to send a messenger out to us, but we made it pretty clear they're not getting them back."

"Hey, you!" shouted one of the Rebels from the trailer. He stood up, very tall and lean, but young. He whistled loudly as he pointed towards our squad. "Blondie?" he asked, again.

Loren looked from right to left, then realised he was talking to her, and gave him a smile.

"I'm surprised you're not dead yet," he said, sarcastically, "Either everyone would have tried to kill you by now 'cause you're that annoying, or you've tried to kill yourself 'cause you broke a nail!" He cowered, sarcastically, as he held his hand pretending to have broken a nail.

I could hear Loren's heartbeat rising, but before I could make a move to stop her, Wade stepped in front, blocking her path.

"Look at this jock!" the Rebel said loudly, pointing at Wade with a smile. "Keeping the girls in line? That's probably all you were good for." The other Rebels laughed along with their friend.

"Good one, Tag," said one of the Rebels, stupidly, in the back seat.

"Tag, is it?" I said loudly, walking to the edge of the trailer.

He looked down at me with eyes bright with excitement. "Oh, who invited the girl scout?"

"I'm sure I would be mad if understood that reference." I said loudly. "But," I continued, putting my hands on the side of the trailer, "The thing you'll learn about me is: I'm always mad." I smiled up at him and with one heavy push I tipped the truck up, lifting it onto two wheels.

Tag toppled backwards, falling with a thud onto the road. There were plenty of shouts around me; Shaw's being the loudest. "Maddy, put the truck down now!"

I obeyed with a smile and dropped it, the suspension heaving under the return of the weight. I walked back happily to stand with my squad, watching Tag with excitement as he got up angrily from the ground. He started to make his way towards me, raising his fists in the air, but several more Rebels came out and stood in between the two of us. I gave him a sarcastic smile.

"Honestly. You've been up here for all of two minutes and you've already picked a fight?" Shaw said, angrily (but somewhat impressed), as he came straight over to me. He brought me aside, separating me from my squad and kneeling down to look me in the eyes. "You don't have to fight us any more, Maddy. I really wish you would see that." He spoke almost sadly.

"Wait, your name's Maddy?" called the driver of the truck as he hopped out. He walked around the front of the black truck, and pushed past the rest of his Rebel friends, who had now been gathering in a circle around us.

He was tall and strong-looking, wavy brown hair and brown eyes. He looked at me with first confusion, then a sudden smile spread across his face.

"Maddy! Maddy, it's me. It's Jasper!" he shouted, as he ran towards me.

Shaw stood up, and in some strange reflex I stepped behind him, hiding from the young man rushing towards me.

"Jaz? Wait – is she the sister you lost in the beginning?" Shaw asked, full of wonder as he turned to look from Jasper to me.

Jasper was completely speechless, as he stood staring at me with his arms out. Feeling completely awkward with the emotion, I walked back to my squad and stood next to Wade.

"Who is he?" Loren asked, quietly.

"We need to get out of here," was all I could manage to say.

"Maybe today isn't the best day to be meeting new friends?" Shaw suggested, as he looked from our close-knit squad to the angry and annoyed faces of his soldiers.

"I don't have any problems with today. Please, Dr Shaw, we would really like to learn more about this place," I said loudly, flashing Jasper a stern look.

For some reason, there was no feelings but anger when I looked into my brother's eyes. The memories I had of Jasper were mis-matched and confusing. I felt completely detached from the emotions and memories of my brothers. I had a new family now, after all: one that was waiting, one that was counting on me.

"I think that's enough for the ground today," Dr Shaw said, slowly. "We'll explore the other levels," he added, nodding his head as he marched back towards the first warehouse we had emerged from.

Feeling deeply annoyed that we weren't going to be spending the day above ground, I trudged back into the cool shade and back down the stairs into Saigo.

We spent the next few hours walking down long, white hallways, seeing the human's school, where they all lived and what life was like for the civilians. There was an infirmary and a few floors devoted to growing plants underground and another few for training purposes. What I found most interesting was Level 41; an unnamed level but the one Dr Shaw told us he worked on. It was all white and seemed to contain only a few people in lab coats going from room to room.

A bustle of commotion sounded through the hallway coming from a room down on the left. Shaw shook his head.

"Gabe!" he called down the hallway.

Gabe came out from the room carrying a few boxes and crates with wires hanging out all over the place. He rested his chin on the highest box to stop it swaying backwards and forwards.

"Sorry, Shaw. Lee's got all the good stuff," he said with difficulty, trying to keep his chin still.

"This is Gabe, children. He is one of our techies. Just recently got back from capture at a Raider base," Shaw said, getting quieter towards the end.

"Oh, we know," Wade said shortly, looking at me.

Gabe lifted his eyes and saw us all standing there watching him. He noticed Wade and me, especially.

"Oh, sorry. I ah… um…" he trailed off as he stepped around us. "Back to… my room…" As soon as he walked past, I heard his footsteps quicken as he hurried off and disappeared up another hallway.

"Poor kid. Not sure what he saw at that Raider base…" Shaw said, slowly trailing off. "Well, anyway, I think you've seen all you need to. Why don't we go back for a spot of training–"

"Wait," Charlie cut in. "What about that machine? The one that replaces Kartiia's bond and is doing the weird light show with our veins…"

"Oh, that," Shaw said, looking at all of our eager faces. "That's on Level 42, and I'm afraid that I can't take you down there–"

"But you're a doctor, aren't you?" Charlie cut in again. "Couldn't you at least answer our questions about it all?"

Shaw processed this for a moment, then brought us all into a small white room with a desk in a corner and with a few rows of chairs in front of it.

We all took a seat and Shaw sat on the edge of the desk, facing us all with saddened eyes once more. The guards waited outside, closing the doors behind them. I was going to be sick. This was all very dramatic.

"What do you want to know?" Shaw said, quietly.

"Why the different colours in our veins?" Loren piped up, sounding almost upset. "I mean, can't we just choose one colour? Like pink?"

"I'm not sure. They seem to linger after the treatment. I believe that when they begin to fade, you'll need another treatment," he said, softly.

"Another?" Emily said, quietly, from her seat beside Skylar. The two of them looked positively terrified.

"Yes, well – this machine is not a permanent fix, you must understand," he answered slowly. "Nothing can replace the bond that was created when you were… ah, changed. May I ask, how have you all been after the bond was broken?" He watched us curiously, as none of us dared to speak.

Beau, however, broke the silence. "Different. It's like the lights have been switched on and I can remember things and feel things."

I glared at him from my seat at the back of the room. I knew he could feel my burning gaze and he dared not to look my way.

"Really?" Shaw said, eagerly now. "And whose side are you on, if you don't mind me asking?"

"Well…" Beau murmured, quietly.

"We're human again," Izzy said, from his side. "And I don't think we meant that much to the Raiders. I mean, we were useful, sure, but not cared for. I don't think we ever had a choice, anyway. We were all taken from our families and were turned into little soldiers… I like it here."

"Does anyone else agree with what Izzy has just said?" Shaw looked from face to face, resting his eyes uneasily on me. "Maddy?" he asked.

The rest of my squad turned to look at me. I put on a smile and spoke confidently. "I completely agree. There's nothing I want more than to fight the Raiders."

Loren sneaked a smile at me, seeing straight through my lie.

Shaw, however, gave me a big smile. "Good… Good." He trailed off, stood up and walked back to the door. "The guards will take you back up to your dorms. I think you've all earned an afternoon off. The lifts to your floor have been unlocked and you are now free to roam between levels 15 and 37. I expect your best behaviour, as always."

The squad got up and began to file out but Shaw stopped me. "Maddy, could I have a word? It'll only take a minute," he said, quietly.

"Okay, we'll be on 25," Wade said.

"She'll catch up with you all a bit later," Shaw said to the rest of my squad as he closed the door behind them.

"Please, sit down." Shaw moved back to his desk. I did as he asked, feeling completely out of place now in the empty room. Why was it always me who had to be talked to alone?

"Maddy, I did not know that Jasper and Max were your brothers," Shaw said quietly as he came to sit in the chair beside me.

"Neither did I," I said, keeping my face still. "I don't really remember them that well."

"Don't lie," Shaw cut me off. "I mean, you let on that you know nothing, Maddy, but I can see you feel differently to your friends."

"Well the Raiders said we were all unique… Different qualities and all that," I said, getting annoyed now.

"Yes…" Shaw looked at me with concern in his eyes. "Max and Jasper have been at Saigo from the beginning. They're two of our best Defence Unit soldiers and really mean a lot to everyone here. I just really don't want to see them get hurt, so if you could find it within yourself to let down that angry guard you've got going on," he said, waving his hand at me. "Then maybe you would be a lot happier here. Maybe you could even fit in and go back to your family."

"My family, Dr Shaw, is my squad. I don't want to fit in and I'm not angry," I said defiantly, folding my arms in front of me.

Shaw sighed, and looked down at his hands. "Maddy, you are already on thin ice."

"What's that supposed to mean?" I said, angrily.

"It means that everyone knows who you are. Over the years, we've watched you and your 'squad' attack our convoys, and bring down our bases. You would hand over and kill countless people, young and old; you showed no mercy, no sign of humanity or compassion for your own race. You, along with the Raider Generals, have been one of our most-wanted targets. Major Miller is taking a great risk in letting you stay here. If Ronan Starr had not intervened, then you would be wasting away on the ground where we'd found you." He said all this quite threateningly. "You have the chance to make a difference, to choose the right thing and help your people. Please, don't force our hand. Don't make us have to end you."

"Whatever you say," I stated loudly, trying hard not to crack a smile and concentrating hard at staring at the white wall in front of me. I felt almost happy. This was a sign of how good I was, how much the Raiders had needed me. I was the one setting in the fear; I was the one doing my job right.

"You can go back to your friends now, Maddy. I'll leave it there for today," Shaw said quietly, as he got back up and moved over to his desk.

I jumped up and made a move to the door but Shaw spoke one last thing before I could leave.

"Your friends listen to you a lot. You have a big influence on them, which is quite amazing considering you're the youngest and definitely the smallest. Good or bad, you are a leader. Maybe you should try listening to them for a change."

With a huff, I pulled open the door and marched my way back to the lifts, pushing the up button. The doors clanked open and I stepped inside, pushing the next button to the 25th floor.

"Wait – hold up!" a voice called out and a hand stuck out into the lift, reopening the doors. Gabe stepped in and pushed the button for Level 8.

He turned to look at me and then, with fear, turned back to the doors, which had just closed. He sighed and stepped back, his back against the cold wall, keeping his eyes on me.

"So, are you on our side now?" he asked quietly, as the lift went slowly upwards.

"Haven't decided yet, Gabe. I see we didn't manage to catch you," I said, with a smile. He shuddered when I said his name.

"Yeah, we were pretty lucky. Honestly didn't think I was going to get out of that Raider camp alive. Good thing you guys were like robots..." He slowed down, pausing for a moment. When he realised I wasn't about to kill him he went on. "Are you really as dangerous as everyone says you are? I mean, you attacked this base a few years back when we were trying to get the force field up, and you took out the Stadium and the cities..." he trailed off, as I gave him an uninterested look.

"If you keep talking, you might find out. Besides, you've seen me kill before..." I said, shortly. I looked at Gabe: he was young too, and maybe he would accidentally answer some of my questions. "So what does a techie do exactly?" I asked him, as the lift rolled up past level 31.

"Invent stuff like weapons and gadgets. We fix a hell of a lot of stuff, too. This place doesn't run on its own. We also try to decipher what all the alien weapons do. We've got a whole heap of them just waiting to be tested," he said, quickly.

"What about information?" I asked, slowly. "We were just given a tour of Saigo, but there's no library or that many books," I said, giving him a small smile.

"Oh, well, there's heaps of stuff at the schools on levels 5 and 6. But Mission Control keeps electronic records of everything," he said, eagerly answering my question.

"And you're into gadgets and things like that. I noticed Ronan Starr has something he keeps in his pocket–" I began.

"Oh, that mirror?" Gabe cut in. "He takes it with him everywhere. Never seen him without it. I think it's from his old politician days when he had to look good all the time, 'cause cameras would follow him everywhere. Funny man, that one. Seems like he's been around forever."

The door of the lift opened and I found my squad waiting, spread out across the dining room. It looked like they had already had a yelling match.

"Thanks, Gabe," I said, as sweetly as I could, as I stepped out of the lift.

He smiled back and gave an awkward wave to the rest of the squad as the lift doors closed again.

"What was that all about?" Skylar asked, quietly, standing on the left side of the room with Emily, Beau and Izzy.

"Nothing to worry about," I said calmly, as I walked into the centre of the room, looking from side to side. "Something wrong?" I asked.

"Only that they're traitors," Mason said, through gritted teeth.

"You heard what Shaw said: we can't leave, even if we wanted to. We'll die without that machine," Beau said, defensively.

"You've made your decision then?" I asked, turning to the four of them.

"Why can't you all feel the way we do? Don't you want to be good, to be on the right side?" Izzy asked, frustrated.

"I call that a difference in opinion," Loren said, judgementally, folding her arms in front of her.

The four of them looked at me, waiting for my answer. "You know I'm not squad leader right?" I shouted, looking at Wade.

He shrugged his large shoulders. "I was all right when I was being told what to do. I don't have the ideas you have…" He trailed off.

I sighed loudly and looked back at the four of them. "I told you this morning: make whatever decision you like, but when it comes down to Raiders or Rebels, I know where my loyalties lie. If you're on the wrong side, then I'll cut you down just like I would any other enemy. If you guys hadn't noticed, you've only been mentally aware for a week: me, the whole time. I don't feel the way you do because feelings get you into trouble and will get you killed. I learnt that a long time ago. So do what you want." I walked back to the lift and pushed the down button.

"Anyone who would like to get out of here can come with me," I said, as I turned back to them all.

"But if you leave, you could die," Emily said, quietly.

"What's the point of living if you're not doing it right?" I said, as the doors rolled open.

Wade, Loren, Charlie and Mason marched over to me, stepping into the lift. Aiden hung back, looking from side to side, but eventually walked over to join the others.

"Sorry," he said, quietly, as the lift doors closed.

"So how are we going to get out of here?" Loren asked, turning to me.

"Don't know yet," I said, truthfully. "But if we want to get out of the base alive, we're going to have to plan it really well. There's another thing…" I paused, weighing up whether I should tell them all about my secret mission from General Carterra. "There's something we need to get, to bring back for the Raiders. I don't know how he has one, but Ronan Starr has something the Raiders need."

"How do you know?" Charlie asked, quietly.

"Just do. Now we're going to have to scout this place out, just like we did before, but this time we're already on the inside. We have the disadvantage of not being able to sit for all hours of the day, but make mental notes of everything you see and hear. Now that we've been left to roam a little more freely, there'll be more trust – something we will need to maintain – so best behaviour from everyone. This isn't going to happen overnight, but we will make it out. Who knows? If they trust us enough to send us on missions, we won't even need to make a break from Saigo."

"Okay. Sounds good," Wade said, encouragingly. "But what about the others?"

"Act like nothing's wrong; like nothing's changed. Don't tell them anything, and we'll speak to each other about this stuff well away from them," I instructed.

"I can't wait to go home," Loren said, longingly.

"If we play this right, you won't have to wait long," Charlie riposted, with a smile.

Chapter Nine

We woke early to the bright light of the screen rising out of the floor in the centre of the dorm. Major Miller didn't appear there today, but there was a giant map of Saigo with directions back up to the first floor. There were flashing lights leading from our floor all the way up and then back to the hangar we had been in the day before. In the top right-hand corner of the map was a message:

'Together, Defence Unit One and the Northern Raider Squad will join for training and drills with the intent to combine as a Defence Taskforce for Saigo. This taskforce will lead Saigo to a new age of security, closing the gap between the Raider and human defence forces and bringing the humans victory. You will be the lifeline to the Lifeline Bases.

You will all report to Hangar One at 0600hrs and remain until a cohesive taskforce is attained.

I expect to hear only good things,

Signed

Ronan Starr.'

With a huff, I turned back to my cupboard and pulled out my mission get-up, quickly getting dressed. It was already 0546, according to the clock on the wall. I tied my long hair into braids and ran into the bathroom to brush my teeth. It took us only a few minutes before all we girls were standing waiting for the lifts – although Loren took a little more time.

We stood in two separate groups: Loren and me on one side and Izzy, Skylar and Emily on the other. I saw Izzy throw me a couple of uncertain looks, but she didn't say what was on her mind.

"How long is this going to take, do you think?" Emily asked, as she re-tightened her pony tail.

"Who knows? I just hope it'll be interesting," Skylar said quietly, as she watched the numbers count slowly away as the lift approached us.

"Oh no, the Defence Unit One people… Are they all the boys we met yesterday?" Loren asked me, as the lift doors opened before us with a clank.

"I think so," I said, casually. "But who cares? At least I showed them we're not weak."

"Good point. But there are a lot more of them than us," Loren said, as she watched Izzy carefully push the button to level 1. "We'll just stick together – right, Madds?" she asked quietly, looking from me to the others.

"Yeah, if you want. I think you should just keep away from that Tag guy," I said quietly back.

We made it back to Level 1, Loren and I hanging back as we followed the other three girls down the darkened hallway and up the stairs into Hangar One. The morning air was fresh and cool on my face, and it was nice to breathe it in. If I had the chance, I would have laid on a small patch of grass in the base and waited while the sun rose, warming up my skin… But there was no time for that, as the tall dark figures of the DFU were slowly marching around. A few dim lights gradually turned on around us and their tired faces came more into view. The door from the stairs opened and closed several times as the boys straggled through. Wade looked tired, his short hair standing up. Charlie's hair was even worse: it was all up on one side. Like yesterday, we all split off into two separate groups, eyeing each other closely, but watching the humans even more carefully.

"Argh, why so early?" Wade asked, quietly, stamping his foot in annoyance.

"Well, I can see we're all here," declared a bright voice, as Dr Shaw stepped out of the shadows ahead of us.

We all faced him. His eyes were twinkling brightly in the dim light.

"Today, Defence Force Unit One is going to take you through some drills. You are going to work together, and you are going to try your hardest." He gave a little nod towards us when he said that. "Dr Black and I will be supervising but the training will be led by Wally," he said, pointing to a tall dark man standing with his arms folded across his chest. "And, as you all may have guessed, we would like you to be out on missions soon, working the perimeter and bringing our people home. So,

I'll hand it over to Wally." Shaw smiled brightly and took a step back to join Eris in the darkness, although I could still see her white lab coat glowing in the light.

Wally stepped forwards, his dark brow furrowed with a sense of determination, but he spoke calmly and clearly, and I could tell by the way the Rebels changed position that what he said mattered. They stood up straighter, gave him their fullest attention, trying their hardest not to look as tired as they were.

"So today we'll be on the ground, going through a few drills and getting to know one another and see where we each fit into this new team. I think I'd like to alternate between the training levels and the ground, just so we can learn to work together in pressing situations. What I want from you all, today, is to listen and learn and do the best you can. We don't have to be friends and we don't have to be enemies, but we can still make the most of this unique opportunity. We'll start with running the perimeter of the base... That'll get us warmed up. Now remember – we're a team, so we move together. We don't leave a man behind. We're as strong as our weakest member." Wally said this to everyone. He did well to seem quite unbiased about the situation.

I looked over and could see my two brothers standing there with their mates. They were watching me carefully, but I gave them a fierce look and turned away. I could remember only bad things about them. For some reason, seeing them was making my insides squirm; something I wasn't going to be able to put up with for long.

Before we knew it, we were running laps around the entire base. When I state 'laps', I should probably be saying a marathon. I never realised how big Saigo was, but it didn't really phase me. My body moved steadily, jogging along in the cold morning air as the sun slowly pinked the sky. Wally stopped us so many times, yelling loudly and angrily.

"Get in line!" he ordered, as Mason began to run ahead of the jogging pack we had formed. "We move together, we stay together!" he shouted as we continued to jog.

I was beginning to get frustrated. It felt like I was walking on the spot and I felt almost sick listening to the panting and heavy breathing of the humans around me. With the time I had to spare, I began to look along the lines at all the people. I recognised the faces of my two brothers, Jasper and Max. They seemed to be keeping a painfully watchful eye on me, and I averted my eyes every time they looked my way. I was glad to find a few girls on the team, although you can't really tell in the bulky mission uniforms. They seemed to be keeping up pretty well with us all.

Of course there was Tag, jogging with an amused look on his face, winking to his friends, who grinned wide toothy smiles back, like there some inside joke. I presumed the joke was us.

After about an hour, Wally led the way back to the hangar, and we all jogged in step behind him.

"Well done. It took less time than I expected for you to get it into your heads to move together, but I think you get the point," he said, speaking loudly to the group.

The sun was truly beginning to rise now and the warmth was working its way around the hangar, seeping in through the windows and creeping slowly towards us from the hangar door. He gave us a few minutes to recover. Basically, we kids stood around waiting patiently whilst the humans got water and sat down, wiping the sweat from their brows.

The day turned into a mixture of learning first aid (which was weird: normally we Raider kids healed too fast to do anything about it), teamwork exercises and finding our place in the group (I was down on the bottom rank because I'm the youngest and 'reckless and angry' – according to Wally) and learning what goes in the trucks on missions and how to load it up and take it out. Whatever we did, Wally turned it into a lesson and would give us feedback every single time. It was truly the most boring day I'd ever experienced. With the Raiders I would be building houses, at least, or running the perimeter with my fire-blaster in my hand. Here, it was bubble-wrapped and safe inside our force field.

We spent the next three weeks like this, going back and forth between the training levels and the ground. Wally would start the day making us run in formation around the base for an hour or two or three, and then we'd either break off into groups or we'd be given a mission, like getting everyone to the other white wall in the training room, making sure our buddies wouldn't be burnt alive by flames shooting upwards from the white floor, or ensuring the white blocks wouldn't come crashing down on us all. Tag was a rude awakening for our squad: whether we were all on the same side or not, Tag and his five friends made sure we looked like we screwed up. On one occasion, when no one but his friends were looking, he pushed Skylar into Mason, shoving him in front of a white block that crushed him into the wall opposite.

My brothers and I steered clear of each other. Sometimes, I would catch them talking together but whenever they saw that I was close by, they stopped. I wasn't sure if they were going to work up the courage to talk to me, I sure had a few things to say if they did. On the other hand, I wished they would just go away and leave me to get back to my life: the more un-human, the better.

To my delight, the days did get more interesting. I would find myself racing as fast as I could, trying to beat our time to load up a truck. I even liked saving those Rebels when the white room turned into a full-on battlefield when we played 'Capture the Flag'. The white everything turned into a dark night, or a blue sky, as we trudged along through long grass or rock floors towards an enemy ahead. This was what I lived for. I found myself getting a pat on the back by the Rebels as I would lead the way towards the flag, making sure to respect Wally's wishes to get everyone on our side home alive, as well. I was beginning to understand what Wally meant by teamwork, and was playing the part very well. But in the front of my mind remained my mission: to get the Tidesse from Starr and get the hell out of Saigo.

In our free time, the five of us, who had our hearts set on getting back to the Raiders, worked tirelessly over our collection of information. We would meet at a different place every day and piled all of our information about Saigo into an empty book Charlie had found in his cupboard. We added the things we saw and things we didn't understand, and fixed the things we had worked out, and what we knew to be true. This book became tattered in no time; the pages became heavy with drawings and little notes, but through the amount of times we had each read it, it was all etched into our minds. We picked up that the next envoy coming in from Stronghold was on November 2nd and knew for a fact (thanks to my awesome listening skills) that Starr would be on it. I overheard Eris and Shaw discussing how they were going to report to Starr how far our little Defence Taskforce was coming.

"Yes, he will be pleased," Eris said, happily, as she peered out behind her clipboard and looked at us all in the training room.

"They're finally working as a team. Even the younger ones have a place to belong," said Dr Shaw, even more excitedly. He never sat down any more, but stood intently watching our combat training. "It is a shame though, that the children still lack emotional qualities," he said, thoughtfully.

"A shame?" Eris responded. "I think it's the exact opposite. Soldiers, born and bred to fight, and we didn't have to lift a finger. And think of it, all the other children out there. The chances of us winning this war climb higher and higher with each one we take."

And when we weren't adding to our book, we went and visited Gabe, who became less frightened of us with every meeting.

"So, you want me to make another mirror, like the one Ronan Starr has?" he asked, hesitantly, as he looked from Charlie's sketch to my face.

"Yes, please," I said, politely.

He blushed a little, but went on. "But why?"

"Well… ah…" I began, but luckily Charlie rescued me.

"We just want to be more like you guys. We want to make Starr proud of us and the work we're doing. We want to give it to him, as a… Oh, what do you call it..?" Charlie said, slowly.

"A present?" Gabe queried, looking at us with confusion. "Wait – you don't know what that is?"

We played dumb and shook our heads.

"Well, generally, when someone's already got something, they don't need a second one…" he trailed off, with a smile.

"You said it yourself: that mirror is really important to him. If he breaks it or loses it, who knows what could happen?" Loren interjected.

"Yeah, that's right. The Raiders always said 'Why prepare for what you can't see? Why not take the chance to see everything at once?'" Mason said. It was odd to hear him say something smart, and to be put on the spot, too. I was impressed.

"Oh, well, all right. I guess we all have to learn from each other," Gabe said slowly, scratching his head as he looked back down at

Charlie's sketch. "Now, I've never held this thing or seen it up close, so it won't be exactly perfect."

"Close enough will be perfect. Oh, and if we could keep it as a surprise for everyone, that would be awesome. Thanks, Gabe" I said, with a smile.

He blushed again and cast his eyes back down at the sketch, setting to work on a blue screen on his desk. We all stood and watched him quietly. It was barely a minute before he spoke again.

"Are you guys going to watch me do this?" he asked, looking up at us all. "I mean, I just can't concentrate when I've got an audience," he tried to explain.

"All good. We'll just go then," Wade said, just as awkwardly. We all left Gabe to it.

We waited patiently for one more week, counting down the days in our minds until November 2nd. When it finally came, we stashed our book under a loose grate in the boys' dorm (when none of the others were there, of course). We took it in turns carrying the beautiful replica of Starr's Tidesse, waiting for the chance when we could make a swap.

It was early morning and Wally had us out running in formation around the base. Our speed had increased and the human's endurance had definitely improved. When we made it back to the hangar, Eris and Shaw were accompanied by a large group of guards surrounding a few well-dressed men and women. Among them was Starr. We slowed to a stop in front of them, standing still with our eyes forwards, just as we kids had done with the Raiders.

Ronan Starr stepped out from the huddle of people, his red coat glinting in the sunlight. He addressed us, opening his arms wide, his smile small. "Congratulations. I see you have created a well-oiled machine here," he nodded at Wally. "I have heard many great things about you all, and believe you are ready for the world beyond Saigo." He looked longingly out, past the force field. "I—" but he was cut off.

Loud explosions cracked over our heads as Hornets buzzed angrily above us, sending the force field shivering and quaking. The people in front of us screamed and made to dash back to the stairs into Saigo.

Wally shouted to us all, as he ran forwards towards Starr. "Get everybody inside, then gear up and move to the perimeter!"

I looked at Charlie and he nodded as we both dashed towards Starr, as well. Another explosion cracked over our heads, making the ground shake when the ripple from the force field hit the ground. It knocked us all forwards, bringing Starr to the ground. Charlie raced forwards to behind Starr, and I reached for Starr's hand to help him up, distracting him.

"Please, sir, you must get inside," I instructed him.

He nodded, shaking his head as he looked back towards the stairs where the other men and women were taking refuge. Charlie stood up and helped Starr up by the elbows, allowing me to guide him back to the stairs. Once he was inside, we closed the door and ran back to the trucks to get our gear.

"It's done," Charlie said, flashing me a small smile when no one was looking. The others didn't have to ask: they'd heard Charlie say it under his breath and were now giving each other looks of relief.

"Keep it safe," I said, as quietly as possible to Charlie, as we each geared up, me putting on my swords.

"All right – move to your positions at the gate. Protect it at all costs!" Wally shouted as he led the way towards the huge break in the wall.

Wally reached for his walkie-talkie as he went, shouting questions to the watchtower. "Are there any ground forces moving in?" he called through.

"Unclear, sir. They've dropped too many bombs around the base. There's too much smoke to get a good look!" called the other voice, panicking.

We made it there in no time. As practised, the ten of us kids waited by the force field before a large hole ripped through it. We then moved out and took a knee, waiting for any ground attack through the smoke. The field closed behind us and we were all alone outside of Saigo.

"Do we go now?" Loren whispered, looking to me.

"No. Now is not the time," I said under my breath, as I watched the smoke rise slowly. The buzzing seemed to reside and there was an eerie calm that set over the base.

"I agree: we're too close to the base. They'll shoot us before we get the chance. We have to make a run for it on a mission or something," Charlie said, quietly.

"What are you all whispering about?" Aiden asked angrily, lowering his weapon to look at us all.

"Shut up. Eyes out," Wade said quietly, raising his gun before him.

It felt like forever, but only a minute had passed. The smoke rose higher and higher into the blue sky, when suddenly out of the haze, tall, white figures glided towards us. I hesitated for a moment before pulling out my swords.

"We can't kill them," Loren said, anxiously.

"Play the part," Wade said, through gritted teeth.

I lunged forwards, cutting down the first Raider in my way. I felt a sinking feeling in my stomach… I was betraying them. Black blood spilled out over the short green grass, as the Raider writhed in pain. I plunged my sword into its chest, feeling the life drain away. It had been a long time since I'd killed anything, and it took me a few extra seconds to peel my eyes away from the dead Raider and get back to reality.

Like we had done when defending the Raider base perimeter, we cut down everything in our path, except this time black blood pooled at our feet and the Raiders actually did a pretty good job of fighting back – then again they'd only sent some Class Threes through. I dived through the legs of one Raider, letting Wade (who was behind me) kill him, whilst I ducked and weaved around the next Raider, cutting him down in a single blow. We fought on and on, every now and then I'd come across a terribly large Raider, holding its gun at my face, when suddenly I'd be saved by a bullet that came flying from nowhere – the humans were acting as snipers behind us. It took about an hour before the Raiders began to retreat, realising that we weren't going to let them through.

We were pretty battered, but we'd done well considering we were a divided group and that we hadn't fought for a long time. Wally told us to stand guard outside the force field and wait for further instructions, when out of the smoke I could hear heartbeats approaching.

"Wait, there are more coming!" I shouted to my squad, as I peered through the smoke that was beginning to fade, but not fast enough.

"That's enough!! Wade… Maddy? Charlie?" called the voice of someone we all used to know… Callum.

We turned to look through the smoke, and saw the small figures of Raider-human kids coming into view, their weapons at the ready.

"We're here to bring you back. Nahla is here, too. She'll take care of you all!" he called, as the Raider squad leader stepped out of the smoke, too. She was very tall, and like Kartiia she watched us with very careful eyes, but there was some kindness.

"Oh please Maddy… Can't we just go?" Loren pleaded, as she looked from me to the group of twenty Raider-human kids before us.

"We can't fight them all, Madds," Wade said, loudly.

"We don't have to fight them all: we just have to stop one," I said cruelly, as I grabbed my fire blaster off my shoulder and shot a blast at Nahla, sending her backwards with a shout. Her back arched and she choked and spluttered as hot burning black blood poured from her mouth.

All at once, the other children began to fall where they stood, the bond breaking them away from the Raiders and towards their humanity. I watched with wonder, but Loren didn't seem to take it so well.

"Why would you do that?" she shouted, as quietly as she could. Her blonde hair was all ruffled after the fight, and her cheeks flushed bright red in anger. "We were so close. We could have just gone, or better yet, turned around and stormed the base."

"We need the Rebels' trust, Loren. I don't care what you think, but this is the way it's going down, so either stay here on our side or make a little squad of your own," I threatened.

Her eyes darted to and from the boys, but their eyes didn't meet hers.

"They're gonna be all wrapped up with their new presents we've just delivered them. We have the Tidesse, and even if Starr notices it's missing he's not going to think it was us. Don't you see? Now we're the squad that's gonna go out there. No suspicion: just good old keep your friends close and your enemies closer," I said in a hushed voice, explaining myself to them.

They seemed all right with my answer and kept their mouths shut as we dragged the kids through the force field and into the waiting arms of the rest of the Defence Force Unit. I could see Dr Shaw had emerged from the stairs, looking eagerly at the twenty new little toys he was going to get to play with.

The squad rallied around us kids as we all met up back at the trucks. There were plenty of pats on the backs and cheers of delight. Even Tag said we'd been brave, even if it was in the most condescending way.

I looked around at all their happy faces, and knew for sure, how happy *I* was going to feel when I got to stab them in the back.

Chapter Ten

Another few days came and went. We spent most of our time walking around the long sweeping corridors of the floors we were allowed to visit. There was no more talk about the Tidesse or any plans of escape: instead we waited, keeping our book and the Tidesse hidden under the grate. I had seen General Carterra use the Tidesse on his ship but it wouldn't work when I tried to use it on my own, something I was severely disappointed about. We did not go to the ground after the attack; we didn't see Shaw or Eris or even the Defence Taskforce. The boys dorm was as far down as we could go and I tried desperately to hear anything, but it was too far. We watched the lifts, waiting to see if any came or went from Level 42 where the machine was, and when it did, we'd call the lift just to see who it was, making up a lame excuse to get out on any level.

"Shame you couldn't give Starr your present," Gabe said, almost sadly, as he joined us one morning for breakfast.

I tried to match his sadness. "Yeah," I muttered quietly, but it didn't feel too convincing. Gabe bought it, anyway.

"Well, after they rushed him back to Stronghold, I don't think he'll be back too fast. He's just too important to the Lifeline," Gabe said, thoughtfully as he looked at the drinks that were on the table before us. "Wait – you guys aren't going to drink those, are you?" he asked, turning his nose up at them.

Wade looked at him in an almost thankful way. "At least someone here can understand how terrible this stuff is," he said, loudly.

"Yeah, well – on Level 6 we have all this fresh food, and there's bread they bake every morning. The way the smell just fills the air…" he trailed off, dreamily, but was brought back to reality when he looked down at the drink I pushed towards him.

"Go on. Live a little on the wild side," I said, with a small smile.

He gulped anxiously and brought the drink slowly to his mouth but was saved when silver screens rose up along the walls, reading:

'All Defence Taskforce members, please report to Hangar One in fifteen minutes. Mission awaits.'

"Oh, sweet," Gabe said, looking at the writing on the walls. "I wish I could go on missions. Oh, actually last time it didn't go so well…" he said, trailing off once more.

I gave Loren an *'I told you so'* smile. We raced back down to the dorms and got ready in our mission get-ups. We all met back up in Hangar One and Wade gave me a little nod to let me know he had the Tidesse.

"All right, this is it. We've had a few days off, but we're gonna be going out further than we've been before," Wally began loudly to us all. "Scanners have picked up a large mass that has come out of nowhere and begun to grow exponentially over the last two days. We believe this is another pit, one that's been uprooted and moved to a new place so as to keep its prisoners alive. These places are the worst and I know some of you have lost friends and family to them, so I need everyone to keep a clear head and stay focused. We're gonna drive out there and scope it out. We'll make a plan of action when we see the place." He finished there and turned back to the five black trucks parked in the shade of the hangar.

"All right – load the trucks, gear up and we'll get this show on the road," he ordered, loudly, and we all moved to action like clockwork.

Wade and I jumped into the back seat of one of the trucks – I was squished in the middle. On my other side was Davy, a nice young guy with short, black hair and a few freckles on his nose. Wally was driving our truck and I felt happy that I was going to be close to the action. With a roar from the engines, we all rolled out, one after the other, arcing our way along the road before straightening up, heading for the gate. We stopped as we waited for a man in a little shed who seemed to be doing a lot of work as he ran around the place. The force field lurched and warped, the small man gave a yell and Wally edged towards it. The truck seemed to be covered in a blue net for a moment, like we were being swallowed up, when suddenly we popped out on the other side of the force field. We drove on fast down the dirt road, past the farms and crops that had black holes burnt into the ground from the attack the Raiders had made. I looked out, feeling the warm air whip into the truck from the open windows. I could almost remember a happy memory, something that I used to like – driving with dad with the windows rolled down and the music turned up.

We headed north for a long time along the bumpy earth. We dipped and bobbed up and down in our seats as we worked our way around lakes and forests. There seemed to be a bit of a track carved into the ground: perhaps the rebels had used this route before. Every now and then, we'd stop and get out to stretch our legs, but we spent hours sitting in silence as we headed towards this unknown mass.

"So, what was it really like with the Raiders?" Davy asked me, curiously, from my side.

"How do you mean?" I replied. He had broken the four-hour silence. I had a feeling he'd been working up the courage to ask for a while.

"Well, where did you sleep?"

"In a bed."

"Really? And were you guarded or anything?" he pressed on.

"No. We had our dorms and we weren't allowed to leave them until Kartiia came in the morning," I said, calmly, keeping my eyes out the front.

"Oh, the Raider – was she like your mother, then?"

"Not really. I mean she was responsible for us, but the aliens… They don't even have parents," I explained to him.

"Oh, I didn't know that. What did they make you do?"

"Fight. Run the perimeter; go on missions and build houses – you name it. We did whatever they told us to do," Wade answered for me.

"Those jagged black things that stick out of the ground in the bases…" Wally cut in. "What are they?"

"They're the top end of a ship," I answered, quietly.

"A ship? You mean there's a whole spaceship under the ground?" he asked, in disbelief.

"Well, what about you guys?" Wade asked, eagerly, now. "How did you get to Saigo?"

"Well, I came here with my whole family and have been fighting ever since," Davy said, happily.

"Yeah, you're one of the lucky ones," Carter chimed in from the front passenger seat. "I lost my girlfriend and my parents to the pit, but I managed to get my two younger sisters to Saigo."

"I got my little brother here but that's all. My house got crushed when I went to take him out for ice cream. Never got to say goodbye…" Wally trailed off, slowly, a hint of weakness in his voice I'd never heard before.

"How did you become what you are?" Davy said, cautiously.

"Well, I don't remember, but Maddy does," Wade responded, quietly.

I gave him a look, but answered, anyway. "They opened up our back and poured this liquid living metal in. It covers all our bones and can only survive when there is a bond created by the Raider mother who carries it."

"Woah…" Carter exclaimed, under his breath. "Did it hurt?"

I rolled my eyes. "No, it felt like I was lying on clouds," I retorted, sarcastically.

No one really spoke much after that, and we drove on until the ground began to get too bumpy and hilly to continue. The sky was beginning to get darker as heavy rain clouds started to close in around us. Wally led the way to a clearing inside a small forest, parking the truck under the shade of the trees. The others followed suit and we all jumped out to gather around Wally, awaiting further instructions.

"Cover the trucks. We'll head out on foot. We've got a few k's left before we reach the mountain range where the mass is," he ordered.

A few people went over and grabbed out a couple of tarp-like covers that were tucked into the third truck. Between them, they spread them out and cast them over all five of the trucks, fastening them to the ground with huge pegs. It looked absolutely ridiculous but when I turned back again, the trucks were gone. Instead, the clearing looked like more forest, like there were about forty more fully-grown trees that sprouted up and stood swaying in the breeze with the others.

"Holograms?" Charlie guessed, quietly. "Gabe would know," he said, even more quietly.

I agreed with him. Gabe would know what these wonderful things were, but now was not the time to get sentimental.

We trekked on, splitting off into four groups to attack each angle of the mass. We stuck close together in our groups, keeping the formation Wally had ensured was drilled into our minds. We reached the top of a hill and judging from a few gasps from those ahead of me, I knew I was in for an interesting sight.

From up on the hill, we could see what looked like an entire Raider camp. To our left we could see a larger, winding river, making its way down from the mountains that towered before us. Many large tents stretched along the river: a bright, blue light shining brighter in the dimming sun, sat above each one. The tents stretched from the bottom of our own hill to the hill of the other side of the wide river. They covered the land around the rocky ridge and the grassland across from where another group would have the perfect lookout. It was on that grassland that we could see Hornets, all lined up in a row, ready for action. I could see the beautiful trees, glowing ominously, spread out amongst the camp. I could feel them calling to me like an old memory.

A kind of anger began to rumble from somewhere in the depths of my stomach. I looked out at the pit from on top of the hill: the clouds were growing ever darker as they threatened to give way to masses of water to crash upon us all. Large, dagger-like stakes thirty feet high jutted out of the ground in the valley below, enclosing a large area full of little people aimlessly wandering around. The ground was blackened as if the earth had been scorched beneath their feet. No trees or grass could be seen inside the pit, and small groups of humans sat closely together, huddled against the cold wind that was beginning to pick up.

"Horrible. Just horrible…" Carter muttered wearily, from my side.

We waited and watched on the hill all night, writing down everything we saw and how often Raiders would walk in and around the camp. They didn't seem to be allowed to move freely: it was more as though they were an army of eight thousand confined to their quarters until they were told to move out. Regular guards patrolled the rows of tents and several Hornets constantly buzzed low over our heads.

By mid-morning, three days later, Wally radioed to the groups to make their way back to the trucks. We didn't bother setting up camp: it looked like Wally was already working on a plan, anyway. I could feel the excitement beginning to grow. The Tidesse in my pocket was so close to being back where it belonged.

"So, what did we all learn?" Wally asked as we sat down around the trucks. We raised the tarps: that way we could stay hidden underneath them and have our own little camp.

Wally had his own notepad and pencil, ready to write down everything we had all learned. We all spoke freely about what we had seen and heard. There seemed to be some pretty important Raiders there - not that anyone knew who they were – but there were a few tents, bigger than all the rest, with constant activity and a pair of guards at the entrance at all times. Everyone was getting approximately fourteen minutes of perimeter checking before the pair of Raiders went back to the tent to give their report and wait for the next round. It was the same all over the camp – it made me feel a little embarrassed that they would stick to their routine.

"They have so many Hornets," Izzy said, quietly, as she held out the piece of paper she had scribbled notes onto. "They're keeping them all on that grassland across the river, but they are only using two for patrols for twelve minutes every half hour."

"All right, that seems manageable enough," Wally said, with a smile. "What about you guys?" he asked, turning to Tag's team.

"We saw a few tents that were guarded more heavily than the ones we think the leaders are in, but no one goes in or out, except for one pair of Raiders at 0900 and 2100 hours. We think they're just checking on weapons or something…" he said, sheepishly, roughing up his hair.

"Well, the weapons and this army's leaders are surrounded by hundreds and hundreds of tents filled with Raiders. If we can get in there and blow them up, that would be good. Especially if we manage to take out the authority, then the others won't know quite what to do. That river…" Wally began thinking it over in his mind. "It runs all the way through the camp, doesn't it?"

"Yeah," was murmured around the group and Wally nodded with a smile on his face.

"Ok, so this plan is going down at night… Tonight." Wally looked around at us all. With no objections, he continued. "So we're splitting up into several teams. We've got enough Catch Cable to go around most of the camp on this side of the river. The first team will go slowly and *quietly* around, laying down the cable as far as you can. The second team will go in whilst the cable is being laid and set a few Warpers around the place. The third team will take the smaller amount of Catch Cable to the Hornets and cordon it all off. The fourth team will put just one Warper in the centre. Those Hornets will go off all by themselves." He gave a smile before continuing.

"We know the times the patrols come out for both the Hornets and Raiders, and we know that the only activity is taking place in the leader's tents and the guards stand watch outside their weaponry tents. The fifth, sixth and seventh teams will be going for a little swim," Wally announced, with a smile.

"Brilliant," Carter laughed.

"These teams will set four Blitzers around the place. Try and get as close to the weapons tents as you can. Each team will jump out of the river, one by one, depending on which target they have. How does that sound?" Wally asked, almost hesitantly. It was quite a risky plan, but it sounded like a lot of fun… I wish I'd be able to stick around for it.

"What about everyone who's left over?" Jasper asked Wally.

"They'll bring the trucks around and find a way across the river, then bust out our people from the pit when the camp is getting destroyed," he said, with a smile. "All good? Jaz, can you lead that team to the pit?"

No one answered but Jasper nodded his head. He looked like dad, the responsibility weighed heavily on him. I could see it in his eyes. Everyone began to divvy up who went on each team and that the left-over people were going to break the humans out of the pit. I was with Davy and we were Team Six – the Blitzers (we got one each). Davy explained that the Blitzers are a bit like firecrackers; at least, that's what they look like when they go off. There was the main piece, the centre: a big black rectangle that was pretty heavy. It had six long wires attached to it, spreading out to six other smaller parts. When the centre goes off, it sends a huge shockwave first which sets off the other six, and then it opens up and obliterates everything within a thirty-meter perimeter. The smaller ones jump out further when they go off, adding another twenty meters. It sounded pretty cool.

"Are we actually going to go through with this?" Mason asked, quietly, as he admired the Blitzer I was carefully stuffing into my pack.

"They're all on timers and we know where they're getting put. We'll warn them with time to spare," I said, in a low voice.

"But what do we get when we bring this back to Carterra? Why are–" he began again, but Loren cut him off.

"Don't you start, Mason. Maddy is going to run in and give the Tidesse over to Carterra, then we're gonna take him straight to Saigo. It's nearly over. We're almost home."

I looked up at their faces. Charlie didn't meet my eyes but kept looking at everyone else. Mason looked very confused, all of a sudden, and it was making me just a little nervous. Wade met my eyes however, but I knew he was beginning to think this was wrong. At least Loren was on my side, but she wasn't the one I wanted.

"Hey, Maddy?" Jasper's voice met my ears from behind me and I slowly turned around to face him. This would be the first time we'd talked properly. Max stood beside him, warily.

"Be careful, okay? Maybe… Maybe when we all get back to Saigo, we could talk?" he suggested, quietly.

"We understand that lots has changed but we're family, and always will be," Max added, with a small smile.

"Did Mum and Dad ever find you?" I asked, slyly. I already knew the answer.

Max shuddered a little. "No… They didn't."

"Do you think they're proud?" I asked quietly, as I put my swords onto my back, in their holsters.

"I don't know what to think," Jasper said, quietly. "But I hope they'd be happy we were still alive and together again."

"Right. Well, when you two humans die, let them know I said hi. And we're not family," I added, with a small smile, walking around them and back to meet up with my squad, who all gave them sour looks.

We packed up quickly, running round the camp, shoving all our kit back into the trucks. All geared up and ready to go, with our plan ready, the weapons distributed and the packs waterproofed, we took off back up the hill towards the Raider camp. Jasper and his team stayed behind, driving the trucks back out of the clearing and around the edge of the forest towards the river. We ran hard for a while together, until we began to split off, running in our separate directions for the plan. We all began to slow down considerably when we edged our way along the top of the hill. We were so close to the Raiders. The rest of us who were left continued up to another hill: this one was quite bare and rocky, and in the darkness it was hard to see, but eventually we made it to the top of the river. We all waited anxiously for the time we had set to jump into the river. We had planned for all the bombs to go off at exactly 2000hrs. The time now: 1925. A few golden Hornets buzzed along threateningly in the cool night air, but the six of us at the top of the river hid up in the trees just inside the tree line.

The time came to go, but now that it was here, my tummy was being filled with butterflies. Was I getting scared? In our teams, we all jumped out of the trees, taking one big look around in the darkness before jumping into the river. Davy and I held onto each other as we dived in, making sure we would both get out at the same time. No one had mentioned how incredibly deep and cold this river was, but I couldn't agree more that this had been a good idea. The water rushed into my clothes, chilling me to my bones. You know what? I don't think the Living Lithuteum likes the cold…

Davy stayed close by my side as we drifted along in the cold water, being slowly pushed along by the current. My breathing started to get a bit faster, but I was managing okay. The sooner we were out of this water, the better. We drifted along with the current and about thirty seconds later, two figures were scrambling up the river bank, dashing into the cover of darkness beside a tent. Charlie and Max swam over to the right side of the river beside us, as Davy and I kept to the left, and about forty-five seconds later, it was our turn to get out. My limbs were numb, which didn't help, as we climbed up the river bank, putting our packs back on our backs. Lying on our stomachs in the mud of the river bank, we peered out over the side at the tents, listening for the sound of any approaching soldiers. Davy was just about to jump up when I heard a Raider walk by. I grabbed him by his pack, forcing him back down again, waiting for him to pass. He mouthed the words 'thank you' to me as we waited the extra minute. With no more Raiders in view, and all the sounds coming from within the tents, we dashed beside the first tent in front of us. It was a small tent, full of sleeping Raider soldiers, positioned on the bottom of the hill. We stayed here for a minute assessing the situation before us.

The large tent that we suspected contained leaders had six guards; one on each side of the tent and two covering the entrance. These tents must have been made out of some special material because no matter how hard I tried, I could not hear anything inside it. Two rows across from the leader's tent was one of the large weaponry tents, which was just as heavily guarded as the leaders'. Davy and I dashed across the small spaces between the tents towards our target. Hiding in the shadows once again, we decided where would be the best place to put the Blitzers. Davy quietly unzipped his pack and pulled out his Blitzer.

"Okay, I'll put mine here. You go round to the other side and set yours," Davy mouthed to me.

I gave him a small nod, glad now that I was going to be left alone. I dashed back behind the tent and all of the way around to the other side of the leader's tent. Just as I was edging closer to the second weaponry tent, a tall, white Raider emerged from the tent to my left, walking wearily straight past us towards a tent down at the other end, of the bottom of the hill. Must have been the loos. I froze in place for another minute before venturing closer to the weaponry tent. I held my breath the entire way, dashing across the small walkway in between the tents in the dim light. I was now right up against the side of our target. I took off my pack, lifted up the bottom of the tent and shoved it under the tent, then wriggled in myself. There were no guards on the inside, thankfully, and it had a large open space in the middle where I could place my Blitzer. The tent was full of what looked like bombs and barrels full of something. There were shelves with golden balls of light shining brightly, just like the energy that powered the Hornets. If I was right, then this would be one massive explosion. I waited for a moment, thinking about whether I should set the Blitzer or not, but made up my mind that if I was changing teams tonight, I'd come back and turn them off. That thought brought me back to the fact that we were on a time limit. I set the Blitzer carefully in the centre of the tent, spreading out its six other parts around it, especially near the barrels and the golden Hornet globes.

Listening hard for any footsteps around me, I took a deep breath and crawled quickly out from under the tent and ran across the walkway without looking. I looked down at my watch: fifteen minutes to go. Perfect. I knew that Davy would already be back in the river by now, making his way down to the rally point by the pit. Feeling the Tidesse in my pocket giving me an awful weight in my stomach, I stood up, turning back to the Leader's tent, when I heard a commotion come from its door. Getting closer towards the golden light, now beaming out onto the dusty ground, I saw a tall Raider step out from the door. General Carterra.

"Where is he?" Carterra whispered angrily out into the darkness. I could see just behind him: there was a man on his knees, his head dropping slightly.

I backed up into the darkness, listening hard to who Carterra was speaking to. I kept my head down, knowing my veins and eyes were glowing golden.

Off in the distance, I heard a reply. "We have the Rebel, sir, and we're bringing him now."

For some reason, I felt a wave of anxiety once more, but I pushed it away. Out of the darkness two Raiders emerged, dragging Davy by the arms. Carterra stepped back out of the way, as they entered the tent. He looked back out around the tents and gave a blood-curdling smile.

"You too, Maddy. Inside," he said, quietly.

My heart leapt with a mixture of happiness and fear, but I obeyed, standing up out of the darkness, taking a few steps towards him.

"That's my girl," he said, almost proudly as he opened his arms wide.

Knowing I was crazy, I took one look back into the darkness before I followed him into the tent.

Chapter Eleven

The lights were bright in my eyes, or perhaps that was the shock after having been hit in the face a good few times. I could feel warm blood trickling down from my head, but I managed to keep my balance. I looked around the tent: there was a large wooden desk sitting in the centre. Carterra leaned against it with an interested look on his face.

"So, Maddy…" he began, his voice quiet. "We sent in an entire raiding party and you killed them all. You defended the humans and killed your own people."

"I was just playing the part, sir," I said, through gritted teeth, looking up into his cold, dark eyes. "We were too close to the Rebel base and wouldn't have been able to make a break for it without getting caught up again." I spoke breathlessly, trying to explain myself.

"And the other children – why did you kill Nahla? Why would you have handed them over?" he asked, straightening up now.

I looked to my left and could see Davy lying still on the floor, small breaths escaping every now and then. "Because then we could get out. The information I have is far more important than losing twenty kids."

His cold smile returned as he came to kneel before me. He was still so much taller than me.

"So, you have it? Starr's Tidesse?" he asked, with curiosity, his cold eyes searching my face.

I nodded. "Yes, sir. But you need to mobilise your army. A lot of destruction is about to be caused." I looked down at my watch. "You have about ten minutes left."

He looked taken aback. "Our force is too large to be taken…" he said, doubtfully, still watching me intently.

"You're wrong. They're going to destroy the camp, then take the pit," I said, quietly, still holding his stare.

He stood back up slowly, and looked down at the second man on his knees. "Did you have anything to do with this, Walker?" he asked, menacingly. "I know you've been in contact with your precious Lifeline…"

"Go to hell," said the man, gruffly, without lifting his eyes. He looked middle-aged, with short brown hair; he was stocky but looked strong for a human.

Carterra smiled, then held out his hand to me. "The Tidesse, Maddy. Give it to me."

I took my eyes off the man and looked back at Carterra. Now I wasn't so sure. I reached into my pocket and obeyed, putting the glowing Tidesse into his pale, outstretched hand. I heard his heart begin to pump louder as he took the Tidesse in his hand, examining it.

"They will be pleased," he whispered with a grin, looking around at the other Raiders in the room. "Thank you, Maddy. Your mission is complete. I am proud," he said, slowly, but didn't look at me. "Go and wake the guard. Tell them we've been infiltrated and need to evacuate," he ordered the other Raiders, who moved quickly out of the tent, leaving us three alone with Carterra.

"What would you have me do?" I asked Carterra, awaiting my orders.

He laughed loudly, pocketing the Tidesse. "Oh no Maddy – you can't possibly think I have use of a dying child," he sneered, as he walked behind his desk and began to rifle through it. "Look at you! The humans have made you weak. I mean, honestly – you children never cease to amaze me." He stopped and looked me in the eyes once more. "You're expendable. Nothing but a shell. And now… Now that I have all the information I need to build force fields and weapons of our own, we'll be unstoppable… Just what the sovereigns desire."

Carterra moved back to me, almost gliding across the room. "I know you don't feel anything, but Maddy – I want you to know: you were the best of our vilest creations. There is no place in this world for crossbreeds like you. Your reward will be freedom from that," he said, resting a hand on my shoulder. I stared at him, understanding every word but not daring myself to believe it.

Suddenly, his hand moved to my neck, beginning to choke me with his strength. I fought back now, feeling the anger and betrayal well up from somewhere deep inside me. I swung myself up and kicked off his face with all my might. He let go of me with a shout, and I dropped to the floor. I scrambled to my feet, grabbing my swords as I tried to catch my breath. I lunged forwards, swinging my swords with all my fury. One collided with his leg; the other he managed to halt by catching my arm. He pushed my arm back and I dodged the sword coming for my neck, slicing deep into my shoulder.

"Come on, Maddy. You can do better than that," he teased, pushing me back.

I forgot about the searing pain in my shoulder and took a run at him once more. He ducked and I jumped up onto his desk, turning around quick enough to dodge his fist. I kicked him hard in the face, bringing one of my swords down into his chest, which he managed to mostly dodge, but I got in a good slice. He howled out in pain, before grabbing me by the legs and throwing me across the room. I hit the floor with a thud and tried to get back up, but he kicked me in the stomach, pushing me further towards the door. I could have sworn I heard one of my ribs crack, or all of them, but I dropped my swords as he went for another deafening kick to my face. The room around me started to spin. I couldn't see for a moment, as the right side of my face began to pulse and burn with pain.

"Oh, I'm going to enjoy this, Maddy," Carterra said, as he leant down to pick up one of my swords.

I didn't realise it, but the man who had been kneeling had sprung to life, grabbing one of my swords and plunging it into Carterra's back.

He yelled out in pain once more, stumbling back to his desk.

"Come on – get up. Get the thing you just gave him," Walker's gruff voice rang loudly in my ears.

I shook my head and got to my feet, wobbling around on the spot. I looked at Carterra, his body heaving with pain as black blood poured from his chest. Walker went to grab Davy and began to drag him to the door. I ran over to Carterra and grabbed the Tidesse back out of his pocket.

"They'll never accept you… Not after this. You're worth nothing, Maddy…" he uttered, on and on.

I put the Tidesse back into my pocket and looked in his cold eyes. "I would have done anything you told me to… I promise. I'll be the

Raiders' living nightmare. Congratulations – looks like you created something after all," I said, angrily, but I smiled at the end. His eyes widened when he heard my promise. I felt almost happy that I'd manage to make him feel scared, just once.

"Come on, kid. We've got barely a minute left!" Walker called from the door.

I left Carterra's side and scooped up my swords, putting one on my back and keeping the other in my right hand.

"I'll take him," I said to Walker, as we shifted Davy's almost lifeless body from his shoulder to my own. "We're going out and to the right. Run straight for the river," I ordered.

"Right," Walker said, quietly, staring at me with a confused look. "Have we met before, kid?" he asked.

I shrugged. "Most humans who've met me are dead. So I'd say no." I gave him a small smile and wiped the blood out of my eyes with the back of my hand.

I led the way back out into the cold night. It felt like so much time had passed, and yet the commotion in the tent hadn't been heard by a soul. There was, however, a lot more commotion as the Raiders began to wake up all around.

We ran as fast as possible, dodging the confused Raiders. I cut down the ones who had noticed us as best as I could, with Davy on my shoulder.

"There!" shouted a guard, just as we'd made it to the edge of the camp facing the river.

"Rebels!" another shouted.

This was it: no matter what happened now, we just had to run for it and hope for the best. Walker ran straight out into the open and slid down the muddy bank, waiting with open arms for me to pass Davy to him. I lowered Davy towards him and tried to follow, but was caught by a spray of bullets from behind me. I screamed out in pain as one hit me in my right calf and in my lower-left back. I fell into the river, feeling the cold water rush into my wounds, numbing my body even more than before. I dived under the water, trying to escape the next shower of bullets from the surge of soldiers searching the river. Under the water, I felt everything shake. I came back up for air and rolled onto my back, watching as bursts of light filled the air, stretching high up into the sky as our Blitzers went off. Up and off in the distance, I could see the Catch Cable ignite, sending a blue force field-like dome stretching high up over the flames the Warpers had created, enclosing the camp in its own little world. I watched as the frightened Raiders ran out towards the edge of the camp, seeing with confused, horror-stricken faces that there was no way out, the dome now boxing them in. The flames rose high up to the roof of the dome, which then suddenly turned a violent silvery red colour. The Raiders were now at the dome walls, hundreds of them banging on the wall, trying to dig their way out, but it was too late. The top of the dome bubbled and warped before crashing down, pushing the flames across the entire camp. The same thing happened to the Hornets, and the Raiders who were left stood lifeless on the edge of the river bank, watching it all burn to the ground.

I gave a small smile, proud of the destruction we had caused, but couldn't help but feel absolutely stupid for thinking Carterra thought anything more of me than just a shell. I drifted with the current as I watched the camp explode, but the flow pushed me into Walker and Davy, the three of us riding the cold water all the way down past the camp. With extreme effort, I pushed the two of them towards the left side of the river, shoving them up the muddy river bank. We sat there for a moment, breathing deeply and shaking furiously. My body ached all over and I threw up a bloody mess. My body was trying to heal itself: I threw up the bullet that had gone into my back.

I stood up slowly and put my swords back into their holsters on my back, dragging Davy to his feet, wiping blood from my mouth. He was kind of awake now, but he shook forcefully in my arms.

"Where to now?" Walker asked, breathlessly.

I pointed up towards the towering dagger-like wall that was surrounding the pit.

"Half our taskforce blew up the camp. The other half is going to try and bust out the humans from the pit," I said, breathlessly.

I dragged Davy along quickly, Walker by my side, keeping an eye out for any Raiders.

"So who are you, exactly?" he asked quietly, as we trudged along, still soaking wet.

"Doesn't matter. I'll get you back to your people, then you can go back to Saigo."

"You're from Saigo?" he asked, excitedly. "I've only ever heard about that place…"

"So, what? The Raiders caught you and put you in the pit? They've kept you alive from the very beginning?" I asked. We were walking around the dark edges of the pit now, getting nearer and nearer to the gate.

"Yeah," he said, sadly. "You have no idea what it's like in there. I really thought we'd be all killed. At least, that would've been the nicer thing to do…" he trailed off when the sounds of revving engines filled our ears.

The big black trucks rolled up to the gate of the pit. One went crashing straight into a few Raiders who were standing guard, holding their weapons at the ready. Their pale bodies were squished right into the pit wall.

It filled me with happiness seeing them die. This was a weird night. I propped Davy up against the wall, and pulled my swords off my shoulders. I didn't feel too good, but I was still in good enough shape to fight.

"I'm gonna help them get in there. You stay with Davy, and stay out of sight," I ordered Walker, as I began to run back to where the five trucks were being used as barricades against the raining fire of Raiders' bullets.

"Wait!" Walker called. "I don't have any weapons." He showed me his empty hands.

I sighed and reluctantly shoved one of my swords into his hands, feeling a part of me disappear as I handed it over. He looked like this wasn't what he meant, but it was better than nothing.

I ran along the pit's jagged black wall, edging closer to the gate. There were five Raiders, all standing in front of the gate, skirmishing with the humans at the trucks. I jumped over the dead bodies of the three Raiders that just got crushed by a truck and leapt out, stabbing the first Raider in the head. His body dropped to the ground with a heavy thud. I ran forwards, taking out the next and the next, stabbing them hard in the backs, and then kicking them to the ground with all my might. I managed to take out the other two before they turned their guns to me. Even injured, I was still fast.

There were suddenly loud screams of terror coming from the pit behind me. I turned back to look but only caught a glimpse of white, gliding past the gate.

The others joined me as they ran up from the battered trucks.

"Thanks, Maddy," Jasper said, quietly, as he joined me. He looked different to me somehow. Or perhaps I was looking at him differently.

The screams got louder, and some people even began to shout at us to hurry. I turned back to the gate, peering into the darkness, when suddenly a white Raider burst out in front of me, reaching forwards with a bloody hand. I managed to escape his grasp as a few of the taskforce hopped back in their trucks, turning them around to face away from the gate. Others attached chains to the back of each truck and to the gate. The Raider backed away with a smile; back towards the screaming people. With one hard, coordinated pull, the gates came clean off, crashing to the ground in the darkness. I stepped out and peered in through the hole that had been busted open, looking in at the pit. There were dim lights sitting high up on the walls on the inside. I looked around at the many still bodies of the humans, standing there, watching us. They were all huddled into a group in the centre, fast moving glimpses of white flashing around them. Suddenly, another scream burst out from the right side of the group and I saw, to my horror, a young girl being dragged away from the group, a blood curdling scream escaping from her. I ran towards the girl, holding my one sword tightly in my hand. I felt a little uncomfortable without the other.

"Hey!" I called angrily, as I ran over.

The Raiders head snapped back to my direction, still holding the girl up by the throat, blood now pouring from her chest. He dropped her with a heavy thud on the black earth and sneered.

"Welcome to the pit, little one," he said, menacingly.

"Yeah, right!" I yelled, as I dived for him, burying my sword deep into his stomach. His spine snapped with a crack and his knees buckled as he fell to the ground.

Another Raider came bursting out of the darkness then. I went back for my sword, trying my hardest to pull it from his chest, but the Raider got to me first. He took one giant swing, and I managed to move fast enough to put up my hands to block him, but even then he sent me soaring, hitting the pit wall.

There were gunshots then as the rest of the taskforce came in, trying to kill the rest of the Raiders in the pit who were making grabs for the humans in the centre. I shook my head dizzily as I tried to stand but for the third time tonight, the Raider came up to me and kicked me hard in my chest. If my ribs were broken before, then they were shattered now. I could even feel shards poking into my lungs, making every breath feel like fire. As he went back for one more kick, a gunshot echoed around the walls, and the Raider fell to the ground before me, black blood spilling onto the ground. For some reason, the heavens began to open: like now was the right time for that. I got up slowly, feeling my head spinning, blood dripping from my mouth. I stumbled forwards to the girl who lay silent on the floor. She looked a few years older than me, and I couldn't help but feel a little jealous that she was gone… It was over.

"It's all right!" Jasper called, loudly, to the many people standing there. "We're from Saigo! It's time to get out of here! This way!" he called, as he began to lead the way back out of the pit.

Some were hesitant at first, and then all at once, the sound of hundreds of footsteps and quick beating heartbeats filled my ears. Some people laughed as they ran through the rain, raising their hands in happiness. Others continued to cling to each other, horror struck and shaken, being led wherever they were supposed to go, averting their eyes from the dead that were all around.

"Maddy?" called Wade's voice, as he jogged to my side. He had a big cut across his brow but other than that, he looked all right.

"Are you all right?" he asked, worry beginning to fill his voice.

"I handed it over, but…" I trailed off as I watched the happy faces of the humans file out of the pit, forgetting the girl and her tragic fate. "Wade… We've been lost for so long…" Tears began to fill my eyes. "We did this. We were proud of this…" I said, quietly, looking at a scene I would have once called a victory.

"Hey Madds, it's okay. We're all alive, we're going back to Saigo and we're gonna fight for the humans. I think this is where we're supposed to be. Doesn't this feel right?" He said this kindly, grabbing me by the arm. I spluttered blood everywhere as he pulled me to my feet.

"Please – stop… Can't we just sit for a moment?" I asked, breathlessly.

"Let's go, guys!" Carter called to us from his place in the trailer on the back of one of the trucks.

Wade looked from me to Carter, before lifting me up into his arms. "We're just kids, Maddy. We don't know what we're doing," he said, quietly, as he carried me away, following the last few humans out of the pit.

"I don't want to feel, Wade… I can't stop it, I don't want it… We're terrible, horrible people, and we deserve all the hurt in the world," I whispered.

"Come on… Let's go home." Wade hugged me a little closer to him, walking out the gate.

Walker had dragged Davy to one of the trucks and helped put him in the trailer with a few other injured people from the pit.

He saw Wade carrying me out and ran over, a concerned look on his face.

"Damn it, are you okay?" he asked, worriedly.

"All good. She'll heal soon," Wade said, breathlessly.

"Well, honestly, I thought I was gonna die back there. Thanks for interrupting, kid," he said, as he handed me back my sword. "I'm really glad I didn't have to use that… Guns are more my style," he added, with a weary smile that made his brown eyes light up.

The rain poured down hard on us as we trudged back down by the river, keeping a wary eye out for Raiders. My lungs had managed to heal enough so that I could breathe without coughing up blood. The golden fires still burned high into the sky as the camp continued to be razed to the ground. All of us kids in the squad spread out around the two-hundred odd humans we'd rescued from the pit, weapons out ready for the chance of another fight.

Walker re-joined some humans in the middle of the group talking loudly and laughing with delight at the fact they were free. He seemed to be pretty important to a lot of them, as they spoke highly of his bravery and how he would always stand up to the Raiders. Turns out he was the ringleader for a few breakouts and even led an attack killing twelve Raiders, but managed to get four people out of the pit.

The sun began to rise slowly as we were nearly half-way back to Saigo. It had rained on and off all night, but now the sky was turning a clear pinkish-red colour.

My wounds were starting to heal but I didn't feel any better. Jasper got everyone to stop for half an hour: that way the humans could have a break. I was filled with relief that I'd get to sit down.

The whole of my squad – Aiden, Beau, Izzy, Emily and Skylar included – sat together under a tree. I lay flat on my back, feeling the warmth of the sun reaching my bones.

"You guys did really well," Wally said, happily, as he walked by to check on us. "Honestly, the whole thing went better than I'd expected," he said with a laugh. "Oh, and Maddy, you've got something on your face." He pointed to me with a smile before walking away again.

"There's just blood all over you, that's all," Charlie said, kindly.

"Great," I muttered, looking back up at the sky.

"Did it really go all to plan, though?" Aiden questioned, as he looked at the five of us who'd wanted to leave.

"No," Loren huffed, giving me a dirty look.

"I've already told you. Carterra tried to kill me. He said we were shells and that we're expendable. I think I got his message pretty loud and clear… We're never going back and why would we want to?" I was getting angry again, but I looked up at the sunlight peeking through the leaves of the tree above and that seemed to help.

"Well… I would like to stay here now, too," Charlie said quietly.

"At least you've all come to your senses," Izzy said, triumphantly. "But Maddy, what was the plan anyway? Were you just gonna go in there and ask for everything back, the way it was?"

"I told you, I saw Raiders pull Davy in there," I said, slowly. I had told only Wade and Charlie what had really happened: the only problem now was Walker saying what he heard and saw.

"Oh, well – that's a big leap, isn't it? Going from hating the Rebels to saving one," Izzy said, slowly, but I gave her an annoyed look and she averted her eyes, stopping her line of questioning. She gave Beau a bright smile.

I was happy when I could finally see the blue arcing force field covering Saigo. It glinted in the sunlight like a beacon in the distance. More big trucks came out to meet us as we trudged along the sodden ground towards Saigo. They picked up a lot of the weariest and weakest of the humans and drove them back, helping them first before those who could hold on just a little longer.

There was suddenly a loud, happy shout from the front of the group; most of the noise made by Walker.

"Jasper!" he called happily, in a concerned kind of fatherly way as he ran towards him.

Jasper turned around to look, when his face cracked an alarmingly happy smile. "Dad!" he called back, as they ran forwards and hugged each other.

Max was up at the back of the pack with us, and he gave me a worried look before running forwards to join Jasper and Walker. The humans laughed and cried happily around them, saying things like, "Oh, they've been reunited, how wonderful!" and "I wonder if some of our families are at Saigo, too."

The air was filled with excitement and the pack began to move a little faster towards the blueish dome.

Me, however, I stopped dead in my tracks. It took only a moment before the three of them looked back at me. I had a sudden sinking feeling.

"Maddy? You all right?" Charlie asked, looking at me strangely.

All of a sudden, Walker came running back. I didn't know what to do: do I stay put, do I make a run for it? But before I could decide, he was there, standing in front of me, his eyes filled with tears, his heart pumping loudly from his chest.

"I knew it," he said breathlessly, before running forwards and bringing me into his arms.

Everything in my body told me to push him off and I tried, but he held me too tightly. I felt like I had known Walker, but couldn't be sure. The way his eyes had lightened with life every time he smiled… The way he spoke, the way he moved. I tried to fight it, but memories began to flood back into my mind and I became a little breathless with the force. All of a sudden, feelings washed over me, stronger than I'd ever felt before. I was happy and sad; angry at myself, confused… All these things were just words to me before, but now… Now they were real. They meant something; they were worth something. And there he was, holding me in his arms like he used to… My dad.

"Dad?" I whispered slowly, feeling tears well up in my eyes.

"I didn't even recognise you… Look at you! So strong, you're all grown up." He held me in his arms, tears running down his smiling face.

Suddenly, a sick feeling coursed through my body, overtaking everything else. I dropped to my knees and as my vision began to blur, I could make out that the veins in my hands had begun to turn a sickly black colour again. I looked up and saw the rest of my squad falling, too; some even writhing in the dirt in agony.

"Maddy?" Dad called loudly, panic in his voice as I, too, fell. "What's happening?" he yelled to the rest of the taskforce, as they ran over to us. I could feel the black rise into my throat, making me cough and splutter as I began to choke.

Before I blacked out, I could see concerned, blurry faces, lifting me and my squad into the trailers of the trucks and driving us to the gates of Saigo. My mind rushed with worry and fear; I didn't want to die. I had only just felt the real feelings of living. For the first time in a long time I wanted something… I wanted to be human.

Chapter Twelve

I awoke back in my bunk bed in the dark dorm of Level 37. I could hear the other girls breathe deeply as they slept soundly in their beds. I felt so comfortable in bed, but I couldn't help but feel nervous, having not remembered anything after the bright light of the sun on my skin as I was driven back to Saigo in the truck.

I sat up quickly when I remembered where I was… Saigo. I smiled happily, looking around at everything I had taken for granted the first time I had awoken in here. I looked down at my hands and could see my veins had returned to the same beautiful array of colours mixing and flowing through my body. Must have gone through that machine again… The others had been right: we couldn't have survived away from Saigo.

I climbed slowly down from my bunk and sat on the one below. I opened my cupboard and saw my reflection. I didn't look tired, my eyes seemed a little brighter than usual, but maybe that was the chemicals. My long hair was out and fell over my shoulders onto my black t-shirt. Then, with a sinking feeling, I remembered the Tidesse. I looked up at the mission suit hanging on its hook and pulled it down, searching the pockets, but it was nowhere to be found.

'They have it. They know…" I thought, nervously, as I put the suit away and closed my cupboard.

I put on my jacket and my boots and made my way out to the lifts. "LOCKED" was in bold letters, flashing above the button. This made my stomach churn. I turned back around and looked at our red roller door. Feeling bored and annoyed that I couldn't still be sleeping soundly, as my squad was, I walked back around the lifts, facing the green roller door, when I stopped. More hearts were beating slowly in the green-coloured dorm. I walked forwards slowly, curious now, when I remembered: the other squad kids we'd handed over when Saigo was attacked. I opened the door slowly, but not very quietly: it creaked the entire way. I sneaked inside and took a look at who was here. I didn't know any of them, but I was almost excited for the chance for new friends. There were ten of them all spread out across the bunks in the room.

Getting bored again, I walked back out to the lifts and walked around and around until everyone else began to stir.

"Maddy?" called Loren sleepily from the roller door.

"Yes?" I answered back.

"Oh, I thought you were gone," she said, happily. "That was really weird, us all dropping like flies like that," she added, putting her hair up in a bun and joining me on a walk around the lifts.

"Yeah, I'll say. It felt horrible, but at least I didn't wake up before going into the machine again. That was terrible," I said, with a smile.

"Wait – you woke up once?" she asked, perplexed. "Man, it must suck to be you sometimes," she laughed.

I gave her a smile back. "Lifts are locked cause of the newbies. I think we're gonna have to wait for guards to come and get us or something."

"Well, I can't believe I'm going to say this but I'm starving, and I'm really glad that we're back," she said, a little annoyed, but happy all the same.

It took another half an hour until we heard the lift make its way towards us, stopping with a soft ping. The newbies hadn't yet emerged from their dorm, but I could hear them all shuffling around, huffing and acting all angry. Some of them were even making plans to bust out, like we had. Four guards stepped out of the lift and went straight to the green dorm room and escorted them back. In the red dorm, we watched from the door as they filed into the lifts, giving us unimpressed and even scared looks. After they had left, the lifts to our floor became unlocked and we rode up to Level 25 for breakfast... I think. It was hard to tell without windows in this place.

We were greeted happily by the boys sitting at our table, waiting for us. I gave them a smile as I sat down, pulling a reddish-green-looking drink towards me.

"Do you have the Tidesse by any chance?" Charlie asked me, under his breath.

I shook my head. "Hope they think it's just a mirror."

For the first time in a long time, we actually enjoyed each other's company, each taking turns describing what part we played in the destruction of the Raider camp. The newbies looked on with disgusted looks on their faces. It was interesting to see how much more lively we were than them. I knew I had changed: I could feel things, understand someone else's fear and excitement as they told me their story. My mind kept wandering back to my dad and my brothers, wondering if I could ever make things right again.

The white screens arose on the walls, the message today reading:

To celebrate our victory and welcome new friends, there will be a feast tomorrow night on Level 1. This is an open invitation to all of Saigo. Please arrive by 1800 hours.

We hope to see you there!

There were murmurs of excitement from our table, but the other kids didn't look too thrilled about it. We hung around to talk for a lot longer than usual, before Dr Shaw emerged from one of the lifts.

"Good morning, children," he said, happily, looking around at us all. "I was wondering, Maddy – could I borrow you for a little bit?" he asked.

I shrugged my shoulders and swung my legs back from over my chair, walking over to him.

"Good… Good," he muttered, as he led me back to the lifts.

We stepped inside in silence, as he pushed the button to Level 12.

"Mission Control, Dr Shaw?" I asked, confused.

"Yes, yes… Ronan Starr would like to have a word. He was quite impressed by your effort on both the attack on Saigo and on your last mission," he said, with a smile.

"Oh, all right." I said slowly, feeling that anxiety well up inside me once more.

"Don't be nervous. He's a very good man. Very important to the Lifeline," Shaw assured me, with a smile.

It took a moment before Dr Shaw spoke again. "Your father would really like to see you, Maddy," he said, quietly.

I didn't answer, but kept watching the numbers tick away as we rose higher and higher.

"He is quite upset, you know. You really scared him…" he trailed off. "You know what? Even before the invasion, I was always cooped up in a hospital and I will always regret the time I never spent with my family," he said, with a look in his eyes that made me think he was reliving some old memories.

"Really… Before the invasion, I was just a kid, I remember that now. I can feel all of it," I said, slowly, before looking back up at him.

"Good, Maddy. You are very different to the other children; something I'm sure you've realised by now. For some reason you couldn't let go," he said, with a smile, "But you don't have to be so angry all the time. It's not a bad thing to show that you feel."

I nodded, thinking his advice over in my head before saying, "I didn't want to be here, to tell you the truth. But now… I mean, I know that we're not human and you keep us on separate floors from them, but – well, we are… Human, I mean. This place means something to me now, because I can understand its worth… It's – ah… It's hard to explain…" I trailed off.

"I get it, Maddy. A lot of people thought I was crazy for bringing you kids here, but now look. All it takes is a leap of faith. You don't know what people are capable of when they're not afraid, but it's worth even more when they do the right thing despite their fear." He smiled and straightened bodily as the doors opened up on the white world of Level 12.

'I'm afraid now,' was all I could think as I walked beside Shaw back to Mission Control.

We stepped in to the dark room – after the guards let us through – and Shaw led me over to a small room on the right-hand side of Mission Control. He opened the door and gave me a small smile. I stepped through the door, I could hear my heart beating faster… It never used to do that. Sitting at a white table in a white chair was Ronan Starr, smiling his usual small smile, his dark eyes piercing my own.

"Maddy… Maddy. So good to see you, my dear. Come, take a seat." He gestured to the chair across the table from him, as he spoke kindly.

I heard the door behind me close with a click and I shuddered on the inside. Obediently, I took the seat across from him. It was as if Starr and I were both trapped in a windowless white box.

He didn't speak for a long time, keeping one hand in his red coat, the other tapping the table.

"So, Maddy… Are you beginning to like it here?" he asked, slowly.

"Yes, sir."

"And your friends do, too? I mean, I suppose now that you like it here, they do, as well?" he suggested, his eyes twinkling.

"I like it, sir, but I cannot speak for my friends."

"Yes, yes, of course. Well, I'm going to make this quite simple," he said, with a smile, as he took out his other hand from his pocket, placing the Tidesse on the table.

I looked from his face to the Tidesse and back again, concentrating hard on keeping my heart steady.

"What is that?" I asked, curiously, leaning forwards to take a better look, pretending my best to act dumb.

"Ha!" he laughed. "You're good. A quick thinker, I like that about you, Maddy," he said, happily, as he too leaned forwards. "This, as you already know, is a Tidesse. Now stop lying and tell the truth."

I sat back in my chair, thinking about my options. One: if I don't come out of this room alive, everyone will know it was Starr who killed me. Two: I'm a pretty good fighter, and I'm sure I stand a way better chance than him. Three: I'm pretty sure it's just him and me in here with no one else listening or watching, and he's already admitted to having a Tidesse, so he's incriminating himself, anyway.

I gave him a small smile, leaning back into my chair. "Everyone keeps saying how important you are to the Lifeline."

"I am… A leader of sorts," he said, speaking calmly once more. "I attained this a long time ago and carry it with me. It holds all the information of this world," he said, gesturing to the Tidesse.

"And others? But you're not human, are you? I know for a fact that only royals and generals of the Gouteszi hold Tidesses."

"Human, of sorts, but try telling anyone that and they'll think you're crazy. No one would ever turn against me, you understand," he said, almost threateningly now.

I didn't answer but tried my best not to break his stare.

"I will not explain myself to one as young and – different as you," he said quietly, choosing his words carefully. I already knew he was referring to the fact I was a 'crossbreed' or whatever. "I will say this: I have been watching you from afar and know for a fact that those children will follow you, that they listen to you. I know you met with Carterra and had your little heart broken when he wouldn't take you back, so don't think I don't see through your little act. I'll have you know that my family is on its way, and no matter whose side you or I are on, we will all be in trouble."

"You're talking about the royals, aren't you?" I asked, slowly.

He nodded. "When they come – which they will – they will seek to overrun this entire world. For now, yes, we're all safe in our bases, running out when they get too close, but the real war is coming."

"So? Why are you telling me this?" I asked, curiously.

"Because you took this from me. You and your little friends have been planning under our noses and I need you to understand. Your kind seems to be a vital resource for the human cause, and I need someone I can count on, to be my eyes and my ears. Someone who will can fight and win against the Raiders. As you can see, I don't get out much. So tell me, what do I need to do to keep your kind in the game?" he asked, quietly.

I was taken aback. "So, wait – you and I – we're on the same side?"

"Yes."

"Because what, you screwed up and mum and dad kicked you out of the planet-dominating family business?"

"That's enough!" he shouted, rising a little out of his seat. "Know your place," he said, quietening down a little.

We sat in silence for a few seconds before I answered his question.

"It was nice working with humans on the mission, but they slowed us down. If this is going to work, we'll need squads of our own. You're going to loosen the rein and let us have some normality. We get to go to all floors–"

"No," he cut me off.

"All floors, except 42," I said, changing my request.

"No. How about floors 1 to 41 except the schools, the kitchens, Mission Control and the Population Living Quarters."

"Fine," I said, slowly. "We get to eat something other than that mush you give us."

"Dr Shaw insists that that mush contains everything you need for your day," Starr explained, calmly.

"Fine. At least throw in a biscuit or Weetabix or something."

"I will suggest it to Shaw. Anything else?"

"Of course, we'll need to go and get the other kids from the Raider camp. We're not your soldiers. I'll follow Major Miller, and we're doing nothing any more for the Raiders," I said, slowing down.

"That I can understand," he answered.

"And when your family comes, where will you be? Which side will you be on?" I asked, watching him carefully.

"I suppose you'll just have to wait and see. But for now, the humans are safe. I will need to see progress and your best behaviour," he warned.

"That I can understand."

"Good. Ha, look at us. Two non-humans deciding humanity's fate," he said, with a smile, as he pulled the Tidesse off the table and back into his pocket. "I will see you at the feast, Maddy."

And with that, he got up and walked out of the room. I sat there for a moment, almost dreamily, as I thought about what was just said. Starr was a Raider: he wasn't just any Raider either. He was a royal; a sovereign. Why had his family kicked him out? Why did he care so much about Earth and the humans? How did he not look like a Raider? Were there more of those machines I had seen in the Armoury back with Carterra? And if he was a Raider, who else was?

I felt nervous about the times ahead, the war ahead, but I wasn't afraid. These nerves were going to prepare me, to make me stronger. But at least, hopefully, I could make our lives a little easier, and I knew for a fact that squads of kids like me were what worked best for the Raiders, so now it was going to work for the humans. I felt terrified that it fell to me to lead the kids but I remembered what Shaw had said... It's worth more to do the right thing despite your fear.

I got up from my chair and walked back out of Mission Control, where Shaw saw me and came bustling back over.

"Maddy – your father is up on Level 4. Starr just told me you kids are now allowed up there. I can take you to go and see him if you like?" he suggested, but I shook my head.

"I don't–"

"Don't worry, Maddy. You don't have to know what to say or do. You just have to go and try." He patted me on the shoulder and led me back to the lifts.

"No – Dr Shaw, really. I mean, I can fight and kill things, you name it, but this is something I'd rather give a little more time to prepare for. I mean, I was on the same team as my brothers for the last month and they meant nothing to me… They won't understand," I whispered quickly as the doors opened.

"Fine, fine. But I expect you to give it a try tomorrow night at the feast," he said, raising his eyebrows.

"Yes, sir," I said, a little relieved. I stepped inside and pushed the button back down to Level 37. Shaw didn't follow.

"I'll see you tomorrow night, too. There's still a lot of training to be done with the new kids. Thank you for giving them to us." He waved goodbye as the doors of the lift closed, and I drifted back down to the girls' dorm.

Chapter Thirteen

I stepped off the lift to the sound of a squeal coming from our dorm. I bolted out and through the red roller door to find an unexpected sight. Loren was beaming with happiness as she held a yellow dress up to her body, spinning in circles around the dorm.

"What is going on?" I asked, slowly, as the other girls went to check their own cupboards.

"They must've come when we were having breakfast," Skylar said happily, holding up a blue dress.

I walked over to my own cupboard and took a deep breath. I opened the door slowly, as if I was waiting for something to jump out at me. As soon as I saw the dress, I closed the door immediately.

"What, don't you like yours?" Izzy said as she waltzed over, opening my cupboard door.

"Oh, that's beautiful, Maddy," she said, as she took it out.

It was a white dress with big red and pink roses imprinted on the bottom half. It puffed out a bit and had three-quarter sleeves.

"It is pretty…" I said slowly, feeling my face begin to blush. "But, I can't wear that… It's not practical." I snatched it back out of Izzy's hands and threw it over the bed. "Honestly, where will I put my dagger, or my swords?"

"They're not meant to be practical, Madds," Izzy giggled, as she sat down beside it. "We're going to look beautiful; we're going to have fun. This is the part of living we've all forgotten about. We can't let everyone else have all the fun, can we?" she asked, looking up at me with her big blue eyes.

"No," I guessed.

She smiled back. "Now ladies, how will we do our hair?" she asked, as she jumped up from the bed and waltzed back down the other end.

No one asked about my talk with Starr, which I liked. All the girls seemed rather obsessed with the feast tomorrow night. They spent the rest of the afternoon trialling hairstyles and table manners. It was strange to see how the other girls were so interested in all this stuff. I was only ten when the war started, and I had two brothers. The odds of me knowing these things were stacked against me.

We spent the next day roaming around the new levels we could explore in twos and threes. I stuck with Wade and Charlie, of course, and we decided we'd go to Level 41 to see Gabe. With all the preparations for the feast going on up on the higher levels, we couldn't even bother with waiting in the lifts to get to 1, even if it was just to feel the sunlight on our faces. Gabe was especially excited today, bustling around his tiny room, with bits and bobs and gadgets scattered all across the place. He would keep muttering to himself, furrowing his brows, and then shout and run to the other side of the room to start work on a completely different project.

For Charlie, this little place was like heaven. His bright blue eyes were alight with excitement as he kneeled down to explore a glass box that seemed to be filled with a little ecosystem.

"Oh yeah, genetic mutation was crossed off my list years ago…" Gabe said over his shoulder, as he tried to twist open a jar full of nuts and bolts.

He seemed to be struggling, and looked over at Wade who was standing like an elephant in the small room, his arms folded across his chest. Gabe gave him one look up and down, then shrugged and handed Wade the jar. He smiled and popped the lid off with ease. I could have sworn I saw Gabe gulp: Wade did look kind of menacing.

"Hey, did you guys get dresses – oh, I mean, like normal clothes yesterday?" I asked, watching a metallic ball roll around through a maze, as I sat at a table.

"Yeah, Charlie's dress is pink," Wade said, teasingly.

"Hey no! I don't have a dress!" he called back, cracking an annoyed smile. "I got this blue shirt and a pair of black pants…" he trailed off.

I looked over at Wade and asked seriously, "Did they find a tent for you to wear?"

It was his turn to get a little embarrassed as Charlie laughed at him.

"Nah, just this white long-sleeved shirt," he said, rubbing the back of his head. "Do they really expect us to wear normal clothes? I mean, I've never really been out of my mission suit," he said, uncomfortably.

"You guys will be fine," Gabe said, consolingly, as he turned back to face us. "Everyone is really looking forward to seeing the people who saved them, especially when they thought you had all died when we brought you back in," he said, with a smile.

"Oh, right," I said quietly. Now something was expected of me, I was starting to feel nervous again. I heard footsteps come running down the hallway, and I snapped my head up, catching the glimpse of my golden eyes in the reflection of the metal table.

"What is it?" Wade asked, as Charlie straightened up, too.

Loren burst through the door, a look of utter annoyance on her face. "Maddy, we have to go. Come on," she announced loudly as she ran towards me, pulling me from the chair.

"What? Wait, nothing's wrong, is it?" I asked, confused now.

"Everything will be if you don't come with me right now," she said, as she began to pull me back out of the door. "We've only got two hours left to get ready for tonight... I can't believe I let you go wandering around this long," she huffed.

"Girls..." I heard Gabe mutter to Charlie and Wade, as we left the room.

Loren marched me all the way back to our dorms, where I could hear the others laughing loudly. The newbies weren't here. Probably training on Level 32 with Shaw, Miller and Eris.

"Come on, I'll do your hair," Loren said, happily, as she led me to the other girls.

I sat on the bottom bunk uncomfortably, getting my hair tugged this way and that. I got dressed in the bathroom quickly. It was strange to see so much of my legs bare, as the dress only went to the top of my knees. I tried not to look in the mirror, but accidentally caught a glimpse. Loren had braided the top half of my hair really loosely, and let everything else fall. Tearing my eyes away from the stranger in the mirror, I put my boots and jacket back on.

"No, no, no..." Izzy said, watching me carefully as I left the bathroom. She was wearing a black dress with pink flowers all over it.

"What..? This looks fine," I said, shoving my hands in the pockets.

"You're ruining that beautiful dress, Maddy. Come on, please – just humour me," she coaxed.

"Fine, but the boots stay. I'm not going to fight in anything but my boots," I said defiantly, taking off the jacket.

At about quarter to six, we all lined up – the newbies too – at the lifts. We all looked very different with our hair brushed and styled in different ways. I hadn't seen so many different colours being worn at once, but I was glad I didn't stick out too badly. Some of the new girls were still wearing their boots, and a couple even their jackets.

The lift slowly rose from the lower levels, where the boys' dorms were.

"Ooh, here come some boys… Game faces, ladies," said Loren, excitedly.

Everyone had a little giggle as the lift slowly came to a stop. The great metal doors opened and there to meet us were all the boys from the new squad. The newbies looked relieved and squished inside with them.

"We'll catch the next one, then," Skylar said to them, with a smile, as the doors closed once more.

We waited a few more minutes, but finally a lift on the other side came to collect us. We filed in and waited with nervous tension in the air as we rose slowly to Level 1.

We must have been the last few to arrive for when we stepped out of the lift, people were already sitting at one long wooden table. There were bright golden lights floating in mid-air above the tables that were laden with hot food and salads with vibrant colours. The smell was incredible: fresh bread, baked vegetables with butter all over, different smells of cooking meats and the unmistakeable scent of lavender came from beautiful flower arrangements spread out on the table. That was just the food. The people looked so happy, wearing even more colours with bright earrings, talking in a lively way amongst those they sat with.

Feeling immediately uncomfortable, I listened hard to hear for Wade's or Charlie's voice and found them whispering, a bit further down on the right.

"Maddy – your eyes… They're glowing again," Izzy whispered, looking at the nervous faces of the humans as they watched us carefully.

"This way," I said, quietly, and the five of us walked quickly around the floor.

The table seemed to stretch around the whole floor, with some breaks in between every now and then so people could get from side to side. I breathed a deep sigh of relief when I saw them all sitting in the middle of one particularly short part of the table, empty chairs on either side.

"Maddy!" Wade called loudly, raising his hand to call us over. "Maddy?" he said again, as he took a double take.

I could feel my face blushing and looked down to avoid his eyes as I made my way over to the table. I sat beside Charlie, across from Wade, with Izzy coming to sit beside me. We all shared awkward smiles as we looked each other up and down. It was so strange to see us all out of black.

"You look really nice, Madds," Charlie whispered in my ear, as he poured me a glass of water from a blue jug.

The chairs around us slowly filled as wary people began to sit down.

"They look so normal," I heard one woman whisper to her friend by her side. "You couldn't tell that they're robots who've killed so many people…" She trailed off.

"I know… Do you think they're safe?" the other woman asked.

"Perhaps if you got to know them, then you would know they're the ones who are keeping you safe," Walker strolled past the ladies, leaning in as he spoke to them.

They blushed but looked a little taken aback being caught out, sending almost apologetic looks our way. Walker, Jasper and Max came up to us and sat down across the table from me, next to Wade, who gave me an uncomfortable look.

"How are we all doing tonight?" Dad asked, loudly, with a lively smile. He looked a lot better, well rested and clean. His brown hair had been cut a little shorter, and I could see the resemblance between him and his sons. "Maddy," he nodded to me.

I stared back at him, unsure of what to say or do, considering the last time we'd met I'd basically died in his arms, but Izzy rescued me… I think.

"So, what was your first name, Mr Walker?" she asked, making him peel his eyes away from me.

"Tom," he said, with a smile. "You kids can call me whatever you like… Major Walker, Walker, Tom… Dad…" He looked back at me again.

I heard Charlie take in a deep breath. "Can I leave?" he asked sarcastically, but Izzy spoke again.

"You're a major?"

"Yes. Before the invasion, I was a major in the Australasian army. We were at the front lines of World War Three, and I can tell you fighting aliens is a whole lot easier than your fellow man," he said, wearily.

"So, how did you manage to survive in the pit?" she said, almost painfully. It was a pretty big question to start the night, but Dad shook it off and answered her, still as happily as before.

"By sticking together. The Raiders don't understand how strong we can be, how compassionate and brave humanity is," he said, with a smile, passing the water to Jasper.

"And you've been there the whole time?" Izzy continued.

"At the beginning, I was brought to Alewar. The Raiders thought I was dead – just about, too – so they'd left me on the side of the road." He laughed, before continuing. "Anyway, I got picked up by a small unit of Alewar as they were looking for survivors. I was a major there for a couple of years, but people began to get scared… They used to let the Raiders just bomb them day and night and no one would be brave enough to go to the ground and push them back. There were a few other little problems I had there. They were losing their humanity… So, I led a team out on a mission and long story short, we managed to widen our force-field perimeter by another 200 meters. The people came out and began fighting back, but my crew and I got caught up and dragged into the pit." He shrugged, trying to casually shake off what seemed to be a horrendous experience.

"Hey guys!" called Gabe, as he jogged up to sit by Wade.

He took one look down at who was sitting with us and whispered quietly, "Ooh, awkward…" He raised his eyebrows at me, obviously sensing the tension.

Luckily, the white screens rose up all around the walls, breaking through the loud chattering of the floor. Starr was sitting behind a table, next to Dr Shaw and Major Miller, looking cheery and happy in the golden glow of the floating lights. He stood slowly, and all around everyone began to rise from their seats, as well.

Following suit, we kids all rose, looking around curiously, but keeping an eye on Starr's happy face.

"Dear friends," he began, delightedly. "Look how far we've come. Each one of you standing here represents the life we hold so dear. I first would like to welcome those who have joined us from the pit. I know how difficult your journey must have been, but rest now knowing you are home. Second, I would like to congratulate our new friends, the children rescued from the torment of the Raiders, now joining in our fight for freedom." I could feel eyes look our way, and necks craning around to get a better look.

"You, too, are home." He smiled warmly, his eyes piercing mine even through the screen. He cleared his throat and began to speak once more, reciting something that the people all around us began to join with him. He raised his glass, and others followed suit once more. "We are Saigo, a Lifeline for the human race. We bring hope and light and stand together in our fight. We will not be overcome by the weight of our task, nor will we be afraid. We stand together as one, as humans, we prevail."

And with that, everyone raised their glasses and took a drink, toasting the speech.

"Enjoy!" Starr said, happily, as he sat back down, the screens fading to black and lowering from the walls once more.

I looked at Wade, whose eyes seemed to bulge at the food before him. Chicken, lamb, roast potatoes and soups, fresh bread and butter… it went on and on. He looked around as if waiting for someone else to begin, but Walker smiled at him, slapping him on the back as he threw a bread roll onto Wade's plate. Wade gave him a look of the greatest admiration before sinking his teeth in.

"Look at him," Charlie said, quietly. "This is gonna be a blood bath."

I laughed with him as we both reached forward for whatever took our fancy. I loaded up my plate with a bit of everything. I talked to Charlie and Wade, keeping my eyes away from my family. It was super awkward but I couldn't help but feel sad. Here I was, sitting across from the people I had once known so well, the ones I loved above all, and yet I couldn't work up the courage to look them in the eyes.

"So, you kids must have had a wild ride?" Dad asked, bringing our attention back to him.

"How do you mean?" Loren asked, from beside Izzy.

"Well, you got pulled out of your lives and made to fight for the other side. It just seems pretty unfair that you get whispered about behind your backs. Some people have been hidden safely inside their bases for a while now: they've forgotten what it's like up there."

"It's only weird now that we're back and we've started to remember again," Izzy answered, quietly.

"Hey, Maddy – I forgot to thank you for saving my life back there in the camp," Dad said, happily.

"Don't mention it… I was just doing my job," I replied, quietly.

"What job was that? Saving the humans from the pit, or trying to re-join the Raiders?" he asked, curiosity in his eyes. "You've been out cold for three days and I've had some time to think about your behaviour."

"I knew it," Izzy whispered from my side. "I knew you were planning something… I knew it," she said again, looking at me with wide eyes, then back at Beau.

"I've already told you, Carterra wanted nothing to do with us any more. I just wanted to be sure…" I said to her, through gritted teeth.

"And now Maddy? Is Saigo the last resort? You'll leave when something better turns up?" Dad asked, pushing now.

"Something did, actually." I said, looking him straight in the face. "You turned up."

He looked at me with happiness in his eyes, but I continued.

"I didn't want you anywhere near me. I was contemplating throwing you to the moon, but it was– It was like someone shoved my heart back into my chest. But, of course, we all went down before I could do anything about it."

"But that's what it was like when I first woke up in Saigo, after Kartiia died," Izzy said, quietly. "You mean, you haven't felt anything all the way up to three days ago?" she asked, sadness rising in her eyes.

I shrugged. "What can I say? I'm a good liar."

"Man, you really are defective," Charlie said from my side.

"But we're here now; we understand now. I know whose side I'm on, and I can't wait for the next chance I get to stick it to the Raiders."

"I agree," Wade said, proudly, through a mouthful of chicken. "I'm with you Madds. Let's burn them to the ground."

"Your enthusiasm is noted, but there's no way Major Miller is gonna let you kids run around on the ground by yourselves," Dad said, shaking his head.

"Wanna bet?" I said, with a smile.

"Honestly," Jasper said, annoyed, throwing his knife and fork down a little too hard. "Maddy, if mum was here, if she could see you now…" he trailed off, shaking his head. "You're just a kid, you should be in school. No – wait, you should've died… I'm sorry we left you behind, but I wish that you would have died, Maddy, instead of becoming this… this monster. This is no way for a kid to live."

Dad shot Jasper an angry look, but Wade was the first to talk.

"Dude, I don't think you can talk… How old are you, anyway? Besides, if we were dead then I'm sure your dad wouldn't be sitting here now, and we wouldn't have blown up a Raider camp," Wade said, defiantly, turning to look at Jasper.

Max looked worriedly at Jasper, putting a hand on his arm. "All Jaz is saying is that we're at war, and things are different now and we get that, but you need to get yourselves in check. Be realistic–"

"We are being realistic," Charlie cut in. "For four years we kids have been taking down every human base the Raiders pointed at. We're faster, stronger, we've been trained… Statistically, we're your best chance."

Dad sat back in his chair looking at us all with an amused smile. "All right, all right… That's enough," he said, breaking apart the glaring stares across the table.

"Besides," Jasper began again. "How could this war get worse? I mean, we're doing pretty well. We'll have the Raiders destroyed in no time."

Dad shook his head. "Don't be so sure. I heard many things from the Raiders… They really liked to lord it over us in the pit that there were more coming. Word is, there's a higher power. The Raiders that are here now are just preparing the planet for them."

"What?" Max said, quietly.

"Carterra even called them something… What did he say, Maddy?"

"He called them the sovereigns," I said, calmly, remembering Carterra's face of happiness as he spoke of them. "I've only ever heard small stuff over the years… Talk of a higher power above the Raiders, the ones who were like they were before," I said, quietly.

"What do you mean 'like they were before'?" Charlie said slowly, thinking it over in his mind. "Class One? Originals?"

"Carterra told me himself that the Raiders lost their ability to create. They manufacture themselves now. There's nothing inside them that is new or different and it's been that way for centuries. Maybe the sovereigns are the beginning of everything about the Raiders?" I guessed.

"Who knows?" Dad said, quietly. "But if there are more coming, then we humans with our guns and hiding places won't be enough to fight back. I just don't agree that you kids should get free rein."

"Don't worry about me, dad," I said, quietly. "I've managed to survive without you this long…" I smiled. "I know where I'll be when they do come. I'll be on the front line, ready to show them what their last creation is capable of. And I'll do my best to die there, Jasper… You can have your wish," I said, angrily.

The night moved slowly from there. No one really spoke much, except for Loren who, it seemed, couldn't help herself but fill the empty air. I gladly listened to Charlie and Gabe, who spoke for ages about science projects and inventions they could think up. It would have been quite amusing if it weren't for my father's stare boring into the side of my face. I knew he wanted to say more to me, as did I, but here was definitely not the time nor place. Besides, I knew that I loved them and all; it was just that I had no idea how to express that. Having the emotional level of a ten-year old doesn't really help.

After a dessert full of pancakes and fresh cream and berries, the loud chatter from the floor began to ebb as people turned in for the night. Dad, Jasper and Max were among them. Dad politely said goodnight to us all and told me he expected to see me again, now that we were allowed on more of the levels.

After they had gone, I could feel the eyes of my squad on me.

"I can't believe you just spoke to your dad like that?" Gabe said, with a smile, "My dad would've slapped me into next week."

"That's highly impossible," Charlie said to him, seriously.

"But Maddy, honestly. I really think you should go and see them again. You can't leave it like that. They probably think you're a crazy killer or you're suicidal…" Izzy said, caringly… I think.

I just nodded, but the rest of the squad moved in closer, and we joined our own little huddle across the table.

"So, what did Starr want yesterday?" Wade said, quietly.

"Yeah, you didn't think you'd get out of telling us, did you?" Loren said, happily, with an eager smile.

"He didn't want much…" I began, slowly. "Look, as soon as I got there, he took out the Tidesse and put it on the table. He knows what it is and he knows we took it, but he didn't really care. He just said that we were really important."

Mason rolled his eyes from his place beside Loren. "How many times will we have to hear that, do you think?" he said, grumpily.

"Well, he wants us to stay, and so do I. So I asked if he'd make life a bit easier for us," I began quietly. "I want you to know that I'm in this only if you guys are… Yeah, I still have family and I think they mean a lot to me: it's just that you guys mean more now. If you don't want to stay, then we'll leave. But if we do stay, then know that we're fighting. That we're not going to stop fighting until we save the humans and get our world back."

There was silence for a moment before Charlie broke it. "Sounds good to me. Civilian life would be boring, anyway," he said.

Wade nodded his head. "I'll follow you, Madds."

Everyone else began to agree. Beau even thanked me for including all of our squad, even if we hadn't been as united as we once were.

"I think it's about time we started to work like a squad again, except this time as friends," Beau said, with a small smile, looking at us all.

"Well," Gabe said, cheerfully, watching from the sidelines. "I'll be your techie!" he said, proudly.

"Thanks, Gabe." I laughed as he raised his hand high in the air, a sheepish grin spread across his face.

"And every squad needs its leader," Izzy said, boldly, from my side.

Again, all eyes fell to me, and I could feel my face redden once more. "No way. I'm the youngest, and I'm not that smart. I make decisions based on feeling. Not to mention how short I am. Plus, that's Wade's job…" I began throwing a hissy fit.

"Whoa, whoa…" Wade said, throwing his hands up with a smile. "The jobs yours, Maddy. Even if you're defective… You're the reason we're all here, anyway."

"I agree," Loren said, smiling.

"Me, too," said Aiden and Skylar together.

"You helped Beau and me when we were getting beaten up in that training room, and that was before you could even feel anything… Who knows, Maddy, maybe you'll be the one who cares the most?" Izzy said, proudly.

"Well," I began, stunned, before cracking a smile. "Fine. But you guys are so gonna regret this."

Chapter Fourteen

The next few days brought challenges of its own. Starr had announced that we kids would be getting a hangar of our own, and we were to get sorted and prepared before setting out to rescue the rest of the kids from the Raider camp we used to call home. Dr Shaw would come and check on us regularly, and a pair of guards always stayed with us: I don't really know why.

"Well, well. Moving to the big leagues!" Tag shouted, as he and some of his friends walked into our hangar.

"I can't say I won't miss you, Tag!" I shouted over my shoulder, as I lifted a black crate full of Warpers, Blitzers and a few other things I was going to have to ask Gabe about.

"Wow, you got brave fast, kid," he teased, as they walked to the side of the truck. "So, are you feeling better now that Daddy's a major?" he asked, condescendingly.

"Nah," I smiled at him. "But just you wait. We kids – we're gonna give you a run for your money. And then some."

One of Tag's friends whistled from his side, looking at me with disbelief and anger on his face.

"So, how about you guys get lost, before I throw this truck at you?" I said, with a smile, resting my hand on the side of the truck, pushing it slowly off its wheels.

"Tag, let's go…" his friend said from his side, as they all began to slowly back away from us.

"You watch your back, kid," Tag warned as he backed out of the hangar and disappeared into the bright day.

I turned back to look at my squad, who had frozen in their places and watched me. "Come on, guys. These trucks aren't gonna pack themselves," I said, with a smile.

"Cool," I heard Beau whisper under his breath to Aiden as they lifted another black crate onto the other truck.

"Someone's on our side now," Aiden answered back, happily.

"But how will we bring them all back without them dying on us?" Beau asked at the dinner table, after we'd spent the whole day setting up our hangar and new squad trucks.

"Or killing us?" Emily asked, cautiously, as she wound spaghetti around her fork.

"I've been thinking about this, too, and I'm not sure," Charlie answered. "There's too many of them to put into the trucks, even if we knocked them out. We'll have to find a way to get their Raider mothers to do what we say."

"Or we can make them chase us," I said, quietly. I took a large gulp of orangey-yellow liquid. Shaw made a compromise that we had to eat both the mush he gave us and small amounts of the good stuff.

"Chase us?" Izzy said, interested now. "But how?"

"Well, I'm sure we're number one most-wanted on the Raiders' list. I bet they're keeping an eye out for our next move. It'll be easy. All we have to do is knock on the front door and then run for it," I said, with a smile.

"Wait, that's not your plan, is it?" Loren asked, a little nervously.

"No, but that's the quick version," I said, with a smile.

The newbies sat at the dining table on the other side of the room, watching us carefully, whispering amongst themselves. They were beginning to get used to the way things ran here, but still, neither side had spoken yet. They all wore the same black mission suits as us, except they had a green band around their right leg and arm, whereas ours was red.

Wade caught my eye and nodded over to them. "What are they saying?" he said, in a whisper.

I listened hard and easily focused in on their voices.

"They're just like us. Just another squad. Why can't we go with them?" one girl said, in a hushed voice.

"Because we don't belong here. The humans are only letting them up to the ground because they want to get rid of them…"

"That's stupid."

"Yeah, why waste all that time and energy on them?"

"Why waste it on any of us, you mean? They had a whole feast just to welcome us all and all that training, we must be important…"

"What did the Raiders ever do for us, really? I mean, think about it."

I looked back at my squad and told them what I heard. "They're just going through the motions, just like we did," I said, quietly.

"Yeah, except they didn't have you leading the rebellion to get back to the Raiders," Izzy said, quietly. "We really should get to know them. Maybe they could help?"

"But can we trust them?" Skylar chimed in, slowly.

"Only one way to find out," I said, flashing them a smile before turning around, swinging my legs over the chair. "Hey, how are we all doing today?" I asked, as I walked over. "I just wanted to say that we're on the same side…"

"What?" one of the boys asked, confused, looking me up and down.

"We mean a lot to the humans. Way more than we did to the Raiders. They're gonna need us, and we're gonna need them if we want to continue to live as well…" I said, smiling.

"And what? You want our help on this little mission you're going on?" the same boy asked.

I could already tell this guy was going to be a thorn in my side. He sat higher than his other friends at the table, probably because his head was full of hot air. His short, black hair shone under the bright lighting and his brown beady eyes watched me intently, as if begging me to pick a fight.

"If you mean rescuing our friends, then yeah. But don't get me wrong: I don't need your help. You guys are going to stay behind and protect Saigo from what we're bringing to them," I said loudly to the rest of them.

He laughed and stood up, walking over to me. He was about a foot taller than me, but I wasn't afraid.

"The name's Jack," he said, proudly, putting his hand forward to me to shake it.

"Maddy," I said, just as proud, shaking his hand with a tight grip.

"Well, aren't you just the cutest, ordering us all around…" he said, condescendingly, bobbing down to look me properly in the eyes.

"Thanks," I said back, a little dopey, "Now what was I saying– oh, right…" With a smile, I grabbed Jack by the front of his collar, slamming him hard onto the cold floor with a smack.

"Don't forget what we are," I said, condescendingly, as he struggled under my grip. "We were made to fight for the Raiders, but when they see you they won't care whose side you're on. You'll be dead before you know it," I added, as if I was teaching a lesson. "Plan is to retake the other two squads like us and bring them here. We're going to need back-up, so if you guys are done freaking out, we've got work to do."

I stood back up, releasing Jack from my grip. Two rather large guys came over and pulled him quickly up from the floor, as Jack massaged the side of his face.

"What do you need us to do?" asked a blonde-haired girl.

"Stop thinking about escape and get ready to fight. We're going to bring a whole lot of mayhem to Saigo if we're gonna save the other kids. The humans will need you to stand beyond the force field and to cut down as many Raiders as you can. The weakest point in the force field is at the gate, and that's where we'll need you," I ordered as I stood my ground.

"Life will get easier if you help. We're strong, we're brave, and so let's show the Raiders what they're missing out on. What they took for granted. Wasn't it your squad who let the humans into the Raider camp?" I asked, walking a few steps towards them.

Some of them dropped their eyes, their faces reddening.

"We still killed a lot of humans," Jack said, proudly.

"But you let them through. How did Carterra treat you after that?" I asked quietly; hopefully kindly.

"He… He…" the girl began again, but stopped.

"He broke our legs," said a boy who was still sitting down. He had dark hair with hazelnut eyes. "I mean, I know we heal fast and all, but they held us down and snapped them in two. We couldn't even fight back, couldn't stop it from happening. I know that we were being controlled…" he said, sadly.

"Okay," I said, quietly. "Who's your squad leader?" I looked at all their faces.

Just like with me, their eyes turned to the boy who had just spoken. He raised his hand slowly, as Jack gave a huff.

"My name's Rory," he said slowly.

"All right, then. I'll let you know when we're heading out. For now, train hard. And don't be strangers," I said, with a smile.

Rory nodded back at me with a smile. Jack and his two friends huffed back to the lifts, obviously having had enough of everyone.

I took my seat again back at the table. "We're gonna have to watch out for those three," I said, quietly. "But other than that, I think it went pretty well." I took a bring drink of that mush again, and got tucked in to my dinner.

"Cool," Beau whispered under his breath to Aiden for the second time today. They exchanged big smiles, before tucking into their own dinners.

I was beginning to find it hard to sleep. Memories floated around my head, regrets stayed with me and feelings surged through my veins just like the chemicals from the Raider machine. I'd never second guessed myself before, now it seemed like that was the only thing I was good at. We had been waiting for a whole week now for Major Miller to give the okay to go for the mission. My dad was a major again and I had a feeling he was holding up the process. I walked along the dimly lit 41st floor. Most of the lights had been turned off now that all the techies had gone to the higher levels, to their own living quarters. I walked around the entire level for a few hours, thinking, concentrating, and preparing myself for what things might come my way on this next mission. I mean, sure – we kids have fought alongside each other for the last four years, but that was when we weren't afraid; when we didn't stop to think about the consequences.

I had begun to walk in only the spaces, missing the lines in the grey floor – I think this was a game once – when out of the silence came a whisper.

I stopped in the middle of the hallway, looking up and turning back to look behind myself, but no one was there. I stood still a moment longer, listening for any sound of someone near, but there was nothing. No heartbeats, no sound of breathing, just silence. I turned back to step carefully into the next space, when I heard the whisper again, but this time it didn't fade. I kept going.

I walked slowly towards the sound, which had me heading straight for a wall at the end of the hallway. The whispering got louder and louder, turning into small voices – men, I think. Something about the way they spoke made me feel they all had colds: their voices crackled, and faded in and out. I reached the end of the hallway and came to a stop in front of a doorway. The sound was coming from inside here: it had to be. I took a deep breath and turned the handle. The room was dark, except for one small light in the ceiling that flickered on and off. I turned to my right to see the place where I had believed the sound was coming from, but there was nothing. The sound remained, but the wall was bare. I stepped back out the door, and double-checked nothing was on the wall outside the room, and then ducked my head back in to see the wall, bare as well. Frustrated now, I moved forwards, resting the side of my head against the wall.

"Great, now I can really add crazy to my list of problems," I muttered angrily to myself.

I ran my hands slowly around the wall, hoping for something to prove me wrong. I was just about to lose hope when I felt the rough edge of the wall sticking out above my head. I curled my fingers around it and ripped it away, taking off a whole grey-coloured panel. Carefully, I put the panel aside, the voices sounding like they were egging me on. Inside the wall, there were many cables all bunched together, running straight up. I reached out – hoping electrocution was something I could heal from – and touched them. Nothing happened. The voices began to fade once more and feeling desperate, I moved closer, pulling the cables apart from each other. Suddenly, I felt a big zap, as I reached out for a red cable at the back of the wall. A small burst of blue light came from me to the cable and then disappeared as quickly as it had come. In that moment, the small voices became booming bellows in my ears. It was as if I was standing right in the room with a very angry invisible man.

Intrigued now, I reached out once more, and felt the surge again, blue light shooting around my veins and then up through the cable. It was as if I was the cable, as if I had been stretched and wound around all these little parts, connecting to the next bit and the next bit, all the way up to the top floors of Saigo. There was a small buzzing in my ears, but the voice of the yelling man was one that I recognised.

"We have wasted enough resources on these children. It is one thing to let them up to the ground with a taskforce, but by themselves? Huh, it's preposterous!" Major Miller yelled angrily into my ears.

"I gave you a direct order, Miller, and I expect it to be followed. These children–" Starr began sternly, but Miller cut him off.

"Orders are orders. Here we go again!" Miller yelled furiously. "My men have trained hard, the human race has lost so much and you want me to put my faith in these monsters!"

Starr began again. "These children are the hope for our future. They are one thing being controlled by the Raiders, and well – you've seen what they can do when they have their own minds, their own free will."

"Might I say…" the cool, shrill voice of Eris Black chimed in. "Major Miller, the other Lifelines are retaking their land, they are fighting well and truly above and beyond what Saigo is doing. Perhaps, you have let your pride stand in the way of progress. These children will perform far better than any human soldier you have… because war is what they were created for."

"Pride?" Miller said, angrily. "I put my people first, and this is not happening, whether you think they're better or not. Those children will not leave Saigo again unless accompanied by a taskforce trained to deal with them."

"Major Walker," Starr said, loudly, his voice crackling a little. "I know you are there, too."

It took a moment, but then my father's voice sounded in my ears. "Yes, Starr."

"You will temporarily relieve Major Miller and let the children up to the ground. This is an order and I am trusting you to enforce it."

There was another moment's silence, but my father answered coolly. "I believe the care of Saigo has been entrusted to Major Miller. By all means, you can come back on the next envoy, but for tonight, tomorrow and however many days it takes, I will not remove Major Miller from his duties. And I do believe we have attained the only machine that can keep these children alive, so let's hope we don't break it before you get here. Surely, that would be disastrous. Thank you, sir. Goodnight."

There was a jarring sound, like someone had hung up a phone, before everything went silent once more. I took my hand away from the cable, watching the glow fade once more, feeling even more confused than before.

"Fantastic," I muttered, as I put the panel back on the wall, banging it into place.

I left the room and paced up and down the hallway, thinking of my next move. If Major Miller wasn't going to let us do our job, then we were going have to make it happen ourselves. The next envoy wouldn't be back for another two weeks, and who knew when the sovereigns would get here..? Maybe we'd have the smallest window right here and now to prove our worth, and it was beginning to close. Okay, so what's first? I began to think, forming a new plan in my mind. Getting up to Level 1 would be easy enough: the real problem would be the force field. Maybe we could figure out how to open it, or threaten the man who controls it to let us through? We could still get the eastern squad kids to be our back-up when we bring the Raiders back with the kids. Major Miller was probably going to tell us not to go on the mission tomorrow morning, so I was sure we'd be monitored a little closer if we tried for an escape. Now was the time to go… I looked down at my watch: 0105hrs.

"Do-able," I muttered under my breath, as I stuck my hands in the pockets of my jacket.

I ran back to the lift and pushed the up button.

"Get the squad, tell the newbies, get out…" I repeated in my mind over and over. When I finally reached the boys' dorm, I ran out, heading straight for the red roller door. I pulled it open loudly. I could see a few shadows jump in their beds, one fairly large one sat straight up.

"Wade," I whispered, as I ran towards his large body in the bottom bunk.

"Maddy?" he asked, dazed and sleepily.

"No time to explain. Get everyone up and ready to head out on our mission. Stay quiet, and tell Rory we're going now, but only Rory. In five minutes, we'll all meet up on the girls' dorm," I said, grabbing his arm and squeezing it tightly to let him know he wasn't dreaming.

"Okay, okay," he answered back, but he laid back down and rolled over.

I rolled my eyes, and ran around to the other side of the bed. "I mean now, Wade!" I shouted as loud as I could in a whisper, dragging his trunk-like arms over the side of the bed, threatening to drop him on his head.

"Okay, okay – I'm up," he said, pulling his arms away and getting out of bed. "Goodness sake, Maddy, we're not all as energetic as you." I saw a flash of white teeth in the darkness as he gave me a quick smile, before dashing off to wake the other boys.

"Five minutes," I said, sternly, before running back out of the door and to the lift.

The girls behaved worse than Wade did.

"But Maddy, it's one o'clock in the morning," Loren whined as she ran her hands through her messy hair.

"Get up," I said, sternly again, as I ran over to get into my mission get-up.

Five minutes later and we girls were waiting in front of the lifts for the boys. They came finally, thirty seconds late, but at least they were here. The lift doors opened and the boys began to clamber out, wearily.

"Hold up, go back in," I said, annoyed, throwing my hands in the air. "Can't get to the ground from here."

The lifts doors closed with a clank and I pushed the button to Level 1. I could feeling the eyes of my squad burning into the back of my head, and I turned around with my arms raised, giving them a small smile.

"Last time you woke me up in the middle of the night, it didn't end so well. Hope this time's different, Madds," Wade said, with a smile, folding his arms across his chest.

Chapter Fifteen

I explained everything as quickly as I could, although I skimmed over the part about me hearing voices in the walls (which I was quite sure were connected to Saigo's communication tower, I don't know…). With quick thinking, I said that I was up on Level 4 to see my family and had overheard the entire yelling match. Izzy was very proud of me, which gave me a small guilty feeling in my stomach for the lie. They mulled over the information, but didn't have much time to get it straight, as the doors opened up to the quiet, peaceful world of Level 1. It had returned to its usual way after the celebration feast, and the bright clear light from the moon shone through the glass ceilings, making long white rectangles on the floor. We edged along the hallway slowly, and up the stairs out into Hangar One. Running down the back of the hangar, we went through another two doors and found ourselves in our own hangar.

In the middle, a light had been left on and it shone down over the two black squad trucks. Suddenly, I heard a small chink of tools. Charlie, who was by my side, froze in his place, his eyes fixed on the trucks. We edged closer, as quiet as we could, but stopped when someone's two legs could be seen sticking out from underneath one of the trucks.

Wade stepped in front of me, flexing his shoulders and neck as he moved closer to the pair of legs. With one swift movement, he grabbed hold of the person by the ankles and yanked him out from underneath the truck. He gave a soft shriek, but almost began to scream when he saw Wade's face.

"Gabe, shut up," Wade said quietly, putting his hand over his mouth.

"I knew it, I knew you were out to get me… So big and – and tall. The way you can open jars… Oh, no. You're not going to rip my head off like a lid, are you? No – please, please…" Gabe carried on and on.

Charlie ran over and pushed Wade away, stretching out his hand to Gabe.

"You're so dramatic," he said, with exasperation. "What are you doing here, anyway?"

Gabe turned to look behind Charlie and Wade and saw the rest of us standing there in the darkness. He gave a slight jump, but then smiled back, devilishly.

"Just making some adjustments to your ride… What are you doing here?" he asked, now curious.

"We have to go. Maddy said this is our only chance to go on the mission and that Major Miller is gonna stop us," Mason said, quietly.

"Oh, okay," Gabe said quietly, looking at me. "Well, I can get you through the force field," he said, shrugging his shoulders.

"Sweet," Loren whispered from somewhere behind me.

"Yeah, I'll just need to borrow someone to come with me to the checkpoint. Oh and look…" Gabe said, proudly, as he turned to the side of the truck and pulled white paper off it. A red line streaked its way through the black across the side of the truck.

"See? It's just like your arm bands and everything. Now, you guys look the part." He took a small bow before running around to the other side, and pulling the paper off. "Made the stickers myself, too. Oh, and the engine's fine, just kick that stuff out of the way…" he trailed off, pointing to his tools spread out underneath and beside the truck.

I turned back to my squad. "Load the trucks, gear up and wait. Listen out for anything. If something happens, use your walkies," I instructed, as I put my swords onto my back, and put my own walkie on the inside upper pocket of my jacket. "I'll go with Gabe." They set to work, as I turned around and led Gabe back to the door of our hangar.

We walked down the small lane in between the two hangars and made it out into the open, the bright moonlight shining on the ground. I edged my way along the front of the hangar, hearing Gabe's heart beating close behind, but nothing else around me. I stopped at the corner of the hangar and looked out across the clearing to the next smaller shed in between the hangar and the wall. There was a lot of ground to cover, and the moon was so bright with no clouds in the sky to help us out.

"I can't hear anyone around…" I whispered as I listened once more. "Closest people are in the watchtower, and there's another in the checkpoint." I turned around and looked up at the dark shadowy tower.

"Don't worry, I know for a fact that Big Kev is on watchtower duty tonight, and that guy is a heavy sleeper," Gabe said, with a small smile.

"What does that mean?" I asked.

"Only that I may have wanted to take the trucks out for a little spin and so… I added a little drop of something to his drink," he rushed through the last part, but I had heard every word.

"Awesome," I said with a smile, and stood up straight. "Wait – how were you going to take the trucks out if there's patrols around?"

Gabe shrugged. "Oh, right. Didn't think about that..." he said, looking down at the gravel on the ground.

"Maybe you should confide in me the next time you want to do something sneaky. I'm a pro," I said, with a smile, as I grabbed him by the arm and pulled him out onto the road.

We dashed over to the shed, which took us a couple of minutes. Then, when Gabe had caught his breath, we ran for the wall which stood tall and terrifying in the gloom of the night. The wall was even bigger than I had thought, now that I was standing right next to it. We edged around and made it to the huge iron gates. Gabe ran back to the edge of the wall, where there was a small black box fixed to it.

"I got this…" he whispered, happily grabbing a torch and balancing it in his mouth so he could see what he was doing.

It took a few moments but Gabe paused, spitting the torch onto the ground so he could speak. "Maddy, I've nearly done it. Get ready to run to the checkpoint, otherwise Steve will alert the entire base." He touched the last two wires together and with a huge creak, the iron gates began to roll apart.

"Oh, and don't kill anyone!" he shouted in a whisper after me as I ran through the gates.

"Wade, get those trucks moving, keep it slow, and head lights off," I whispered through my walkie as I ran to the side of the checkpoint.

"Got it," he whispered back.

I ducked down low underneath the windowsill of the small checkpoint – it was like a small, one-storey house that had just one room, with windows on all sides. I crawled along the ground, aiming for the door at the back, listening hard for where Steve might be.

"What the–" I heard a man's voice say from right above me.

He gave me a fright, and I jumped to the wall, tucking my legs under, hoping he didn't see me. Steve was sticking his huge head outside the window, watching the gate open, with his own mouth hanging open. I took my chance, remembering Gabe's warning to not kill anyone. I grabbed Steve's head and pulled his body out of the window. He gave a short yelp, and hit the ground on his back with a thud. I put my arm around his neck, and the other holding back his fighting arms. It took nearly ten seconds, but his body began to relax, his arms flopping down by his sides. I let go of him and sat him up against the wall of the checkpoint, listening for a heartbeat. Knowing he was still alive, I jumped up and crawled in through the open window.

"Maddy!" Gabe whispered from outside the window. "What did you do? I told you not to kill him. Oh, I'm so sorry, Steve... How am I going to tell your wife..." he trailed on and on, before I ducked my head back out of the window.

"He's not dead. His heart's still beating. Now, get in here... The trucks are coming," I whispered, as I grabbed him by the arms and pulled him through the window.

The one room was pretty big. To the left side, there was one long table stretching out, covered in controls and flashing lights. There was even a screen hanging from the ceiling showing a computer-generated diagram of the force field and Saigo. Another screen was showing heaps of numbers and levels that would keep changing by rising and falling together. On the other side of the room was a bed and what looked like a small kitchen. There were also stacks of books and manuals sitting in all different ways on a large bookshelf, as if they'd been used so many times that they each got shoved back in without any real order.

"Cool," Gabe said, slapping his hands together. "I interned here once, but I lacked – patience," Gabe said, sarcastically, as he ran his hands over the many controls.

I could hear the trucks rolling up now, the eager heartbeats of my squad coming closer and closer.

"Okay, so what's first?" Gabe said, taking a step back, before his eyes lit up with enthusiasm and he got to work running backwards and forwards around the checkpoint.

The same static sound began to fill my ears, and I stepped closer to the controls to see where it was coming from. I walked up to the screen with the numbers and levels, and somehow knew that one switch, in a locked case, in particular controlled them. I reached out my hand, feeling the electricity well up inside me, but Gabe noticed and swatted my hand away.

"Good try, but that's the switch for the power core," he said, with a smile. "We never touch that one, or else it cuts the power to the field." He pointed back to the screen with the levels and numbers. "Besides, the watchtower and mission control all have to flip their switches as well and we don't want them to know we're in here, do we?"

I didn't answer, but felt a little more confused.

"Gabe, do you know anything about Living Lithu–" I began to ask, but was cut off by the sound of the trucks rolling up beside the checkpoint.

Gabe gave me a concerned look, but I shook my head. "Well, thanks, Gabe. We've got our walkies so I'll tell you when we're on our way back. Rory from the east squad knows we're leaving tonight, so just tell him when we'll be here, so his squad can help fight off anyone else who decides to follow us," I said, with a smile, walking back to the window.

"Wait – your walkies won't get that good a range. Here," he said, quietly, shoving a smaller, black walkie into my hand. "My own design," he shrugged. "I've got another one in my workshop, and it'll save us from being overheard."

"Thanks," I said, happily, as I tucked it into my jacket pocket. I wanted so badly to ask him what he knew about the metal that was in my body… Wanted to know if I was going crazy or if I was going to need to add cyborg to my list of problems. But I knew now wasn't the time, so I just asked, "We ready?"

Gabe nodded. "Good luck."

I smiled once more before ducking out of the window – nearly landing on Steve – and jogging round to join my squad in their trucks. I jumped into the passenger seat of the first truck, sitting beside Wade as he drove slowly towards the edge of the force field.

"Good thing Gabe is just as annoying as you, Madds, otherwise we'd be waiting all night for Charlie to figure out the force field," Loren said happily, but annoyingly, from the back seat.

Gabe stuck his head out from the window. "Good to go," he whispered, and Wade drove into the blue net-like force field.

It felt like we all held our breath, hoping we would get through, that no alarms would go off, but just like before, the truck was covered in a blue net for a moment, like we were being swallowed up, before we suddenly popped out on the other side of the force field. I turned round to check the other truck made it through before taking another breath.

"Well, that was kind of easy," Skylar said, from the back seat, a triumphant smile spread across her face.

I rolled my eyes again, and turned back in my seat, putting on my seat belt.

"Woah, Madds! A seat belt… Seriously?" Wade asked, with a smile.

"Yeah. You're driving mate: better safe than most definitely sorry," I smiled back at him.

Wade laughed and kicked the truck into another gear, streaking past the countryside, the cool breeze coming in through the open windows, the blue-net force field of Saigo disappearing in my rear-view mirror.

Chapter Sixteen

It was mid-morning when we made it to the edge of the valley Kartiia had died in. The little stream still flowed happily along, the trees swaying in the light breeze, sunlight glistening on the surface of the water. We parked the trucks under the trees and spread out along the water's edge, looking ahead to the way towards the Raider camp.

"Raiders are faster than us, Maddy. Are we really going to be able to run away from them," Skylar asked, with concern, her red hair shining in the bright light.

"Remember what used to happen…" I began, kindly. "They'd send us kids out first to our quadrants to protect the perimeter from any ground attack, then the Raiders would get into their Hornets and attack from above."

"Oh yeah… But do you think they'll have changed their ways?" Charlie asked quietly, bobbing down to run his hands through the water. "I mean, Carterra is dead now, isn't he? Someone else must be in charge."

"That's true, so I think we'll try to scope the place out for a few days. See if there is anything we could use to our advantage. Anyway, I was thinking that we'd go and take the two Raider mothers left. That way, we can try to just get the kids out of the camp first. I know that the kids are a priority, but if we can destroy the camp, too, that'd be awesome," I smiled.

"That is, if the kids come quietly," Aiden murmured, thinking things over in his head.

"Yeah… we've got a lot banking on the Raider mothers doing what we say, and us being able to run away fast enough," Loren said, beginning to sound a little sceptical.

"The Raider mothers aren't soldiers, Loren. They don't know how to fight. Their job is to take orders and make sure their kids follow them," I said, quietly. "Don't you remember bringing Kartiia here? She was completely unaware that there could be any danger… She didn't understand."

"Okay. So, say the mothers do what we say and they bring the kids out of the camp quietly… Do we really have to make a ruckus and set the rest of the camp on our tails?" Mason asked, now.

"Yes," I answered, flatly.

"Yes?" Mason asked again, a little confused.

"This is our job – remember. We are fighting back, destroying as many of the Raiders as we can," I said, quietly, explaining it to him calmly.

"Yeah, I know that, but why not one mission at a time?" he said, becoming agitated, pulling at the grass.

"Because we may not get a good shot like this one. Think about it: we take the kids, who are their protection, from the ground. All the other Raiders go to the Hornets but they'll be fighting nothing. They'll expect the kids to be protecting the perimeter, and we can all just waltz in. If we get seen, we can just pretend we're on our way to our quadrant," Wade said, cheerily.

"Okay. So we'll put a few Blitzers around the camp and then run for it?" Emily stated, happily.

"No. The Raiders have ships under the ground. That's what we'll need to destroy if we want to do this right," I answered, firmly.

"Okay. Well, there's three ships, aren't there?" Izzy said, unsure, sitting next to Beau on a huge rock in the middle of the stream.

Charlie nodded. "HQ, the armoury and one of the supply buildings," he answered, beginning to draw a little diagram in the dirt.

"I think we'll leave the supply building. It might come in handy. Besides, not many Raiders go into that one, so it'll be easy to clear it," I said, thinking out loud. "HQ and the armoury we definitely need to destroy. We'll put Warpers around the surface of the camp because they'll do a better job. The Blitzers we can set up inside the ships. HQ will probably need one Blitzer every few floors…" I said, trailing off as I walked slowly back and forth across the rocks in the stream.

Wade watched me carefully as I walked around, throwing rocks into the stream. "Maddy?" he asked, quietly.

I turned to look at him.

"Do you think this would really work?" he asked, in a low voice, looking back down at the stream. "I mean, it's a long way to bring forty kids and two Raiders back to Saigo and that is if we don't have anyone following us…" he trailed off.

I looked around at the uncertain faces of my squad and gave them a smile. "Are you guys using those feelings again?" I asked, putting my hands on my hips. "I'm nervous, but I'm not afraid because I have all you guys to fight alongside with. Stop overthinking, and take a deep breath. The more you think about it, the worse it'll feel. We have the upper hand, we have the coolest weapons and if things don't go to plan then I'll come and get you myself and we'll all go home." I took a few steps closer to them all. "The reason why the humans need us is because we're different. They use their feelings way too much and for us, with the Raiders, we were unstoppable – all because we couldn't feel. I know things have changed, but we're still like that; we move the same as we did, fought the same way, now you're just a little more aware, but we are the only ones who are gonna be brave enough to fight. You just have to believe it," I said, encouragingly.

"All right," Wade said, standing up, throwing one last rock into the stream. "Let's do this."

Hesitantly, but eventually, everyone else rose from their places, fixing their weapons over their shoulders, zipping up their jackets, preparing for a fight.

We hid the trucks underneath their special tarps, taking only the Blitzers and Warpers with us, dispersing them into each pack. We deliberated taking the Catch Cable along, too, but the camp was too big to do it properly, so it stayed. We ran across the stream and up the hill to the edge of the ridge, cut high above the valley below. Before we knew it, we found ourselves trekking through the thick forest once more, our path darkened by the thick canopy of trees overhead. We walked for a few hours before we finally made it back out to the long grass clearing. The Raider camp was only just visible in the distance, and I felt myself shudder at the thought that I once called this place home. I led the way back into the trees, and walked quickly, and as quietly as possible, towards the camp, my squad following close behind. As we got closer, I could tell the land around the camp had been cleared, and there were more houses and buildings being added that had to be rebuilt after the humans attacked. New additions to the camp included four lookout towers standing high amidst the buildings, Raiders standing up there keeping their eyes on the ground below, and the sky. My heart began to sink as I realised there weren't any good vantage points to settle into to get a good chance of scoping the camp out.

"Well – damn," Aiden muttered, when he saw the towers. "That's gonna make this a bit more interesting."

"I guess we're going to have to split up," Beau suggested.

"Don't know how we'll get to the forest on the other side of camp without being seen. But maybe we will be able to see a bit more, the closer we get," I said, turning back to lead the way forward. "Listen really hard now, guys: they might be in here getting wood…" I warned in a whisper.

We stepped carefully through the forest, stopping for every small sound and ducking in behind the trees and scrub when we did hear something. I pulled my swords out, just to be prepared. We went on for another fifteen minutes when we could see the base more clearly. The three ships with their dagger-like tails pointing up in the air remained. There didn't seem to be much change to the layout of the camp: I could still see HQ and the courtyard where the kids' dorms were. The Armoury was still sitting like a box on the ground, the black daggers surrounding it on all sides. Newly built buildings and small houses arced around HQ as the centre of the camp, small lanes winding in amongst them. The trees had grown larger and doubled in amount, spreading through the entire camp like a patchwork of glowing nightlights. They were still my favourite trees, but now we had the same glowing characteristics as them, making me wonder if they had something to do with the machine which was keeping us alive.

"Okay, so it's still mostly the same. Just bigger," Charlie whispered.

I nodded with a smile. Suddenly, the sound of several trudging footsteps reached my ears from deeper inside the forest. "In the trees. Hide," I whispered quickly to my squad, as I grabbed Skylar by her pack and pushed her up a tall tree to my right.

I shoved my swords back in their holsters on my back and followed Mason up a fairly large tree just ahead of me. We scaled the branches, getting higher into the dense cover of leaves. Catching my breath, I lay on my stomach, watching the forest floor from thirty feet above.

The footsteps became louder, and it sounded like there were quite a few of whoever they were. A minute later and about ten kids, carrying heavy-looking stacks of wood, walked out from the trees. I could feel myself holding my breath now as I watched their heads bob up and down beneath me as they made their way back to camp. I hoped all of my squad was out of sight, and weren't going to try anything stupid. We waited a few minutes for them to pass, and once I was sure that I couldn't hear them any more, I spoke in a whisper to my squad.

"Does anyone have a good view of the camp from up here?" I asked, as I moved further up my tree to try and get a better look.

"Yeah," I heard Izzy whisper back. "Can see the whole camp."

"Me, too," whispered Loren and Charlie.

Mason and I climbed our way higher and found that our tree was standing a good few feet above the rest.

"We'll stay here for the night and try and get a handle on this camp," I said, quietly. "Stay quiet and only move if you have to."

Mason and I took it in turns to have the best spot for watching and taking notes on the camp. Every now and then I could hear one of my squad mates repositioning in the trees, but no more sounds came from below except for the rustle of the breeze through the forest. Dim lights glowed inside the small houses around the camp. The kids went to bed at the usual time we always did, at 2330hrs, and I had a feeling they would be up again at 0530hrs. Nothing had changed too much. There were still patrols that walked around every few minutes; their footsteps left glowing prints in the grass underneath the veins and then they would go and sit outside their booth before going back around again. From what we could see, the kids and the Raiders had all been split up into four quadrants. Guards stuck to their own zones, meeting up every half hour to handover information. Lights in HQ continued to glow all night and went out when the sun came up. Perhaps there were guards on the inside, too. At 0500hrs, a few Hornets rose from the Armoury and buzzed over the camp and surrounding areas. I held my breath as they flew over our trees, blowing the leaves apart. Mason and I decided we would climb down a little further just to be safe from them.

The Raider mothers – two of them left now – woke at 0525 and came walking over to the kids' dorms from a little house one street outside the courtyard. I looked at the house, etching it into my mind as best as I could, knowing that soon enough I would be standing before it. The children filed out from their dorms, but already had their gear and packs. Perhaps they wanted them prepared for a fight instead: they were standing around waiting for orders to go to the Armoury. The kids from each squad split off into two groups and marched in different directions, each heading for their own quadrant. They were all unaccompanied: most likely the Raiders weren't expecting another attack. With the children all leaving for their daily chores, I kept my eyes focused on HQ.

It was nearly midday when the doors to HQ opened and a few Raiders began to file out into the courtyard. One Raider caught my eye. He looked familiar but walked with a limp, and his pale face now bore the marks of burns and scars: Carterra.

I could hear the sharp intake of breath from some of my squad when they, too, had realised who he was.

"Maybe he got away…" I muttered, quietly. "I should've finished him, if there had been more time…" I trailed off, feeling my cheeks burn with anger as I looked at his terrible face.

"Don't worry, we'll get him this time," Wade said, through a clenched jaw.

We spent the rest of the day watching Carterra as he limped around the camp, watching the children carefully, but also checking in with all the guards at the watchtowers and patrol booths. He retired back into the Armoury mid-afternoon and the rest of the camp carried on with their normal day. A few Hornets emerged from the Armoury at around 1700hrs, buzzing low over the clearing and then over the forest.

The next two days carried on the same. We all took it in turns to sleep. I must admit, the Raiders were very efficient and had added a whole lot of houses in the western quadrant of the camp. It started to make me think about the Raider children, if there even were any… I guessed all the classes would have to start from somewhere, right? Perhaps they kept their young far underground, or maybe they would be arriving with the Sovereigns.

I listened carefully for any sounds and then whispered to my squad, "Let's get back to the ridge."

Quietly, we made our way back to the ridge of the valley, still in the cover of the forest, but well away from the camp and any prying eyes.

"I think we can do it tonight," I suggested, with a smile.

Charlie nodded in agreement. "Sounds good."

"Carterra hasn't moved from the Armoury since the first day… He looks really bad," Wade said, with a smile.

"Well, I think we'll definitely be blowing up the Armoury," I began. "And HQ. Warpers will need to be put at each patrol site in the four quadrants. They seem like the best places. One team will get the Raider mothers, then the children, and lead them back this way," I said, pointing along the ridge in the direction of our trucks. "Another team will set the Warpers at the patrol points, two will take Blitzers to HQ, and I will take my Blitzer to the Armoury."

"By yourself? Are you sure, Maddy?" Aiden asked, quietly, his brown eyes looking at me almost sadly.

"I'm sure. It'll probably be the easiest. Besides, I've seen the whole thing," I lied, knowing full well the Armoury was the one place that never sleeps.

"Wade, Skylar, Beau and Izzy – you guys can get the mothers and kids out of here. You don't turn back, you just keep moving. You understand?" I asked, sternly, looking each of them in the eye.

They nodded and I continued. "Charlie and Mason – you guys to HQ and get one Blitzer on every floor. Just try," I said, as Mason shot me an alarmed look. "You've just got to destroy it enough to get it to collapse in on itself. That okay?" I asked, concerned now, but they nodded.

"Aiden, Loren and Emily – you guys are putting the Warpers at each patrol booth. Aiden, can you take two?" I asked, knowing I was asking a lot of one guy.

"Yes, I can do that," he said, a little nervously but gave me a shaky smile.

"Good. We'll move out at midnight. Make sure your watches are all in sync. We'll first split off into four groups and take down the Raiders in the watchtowers because they never check in with anyone. On our way back, we'll take out the patrol guards when they reach their booths five minutes later and drag their bodies under the houses. We'll wait until we know we've got the kids out and then everyone will go to their places. You four go get the mothers and kids back to the ridge; you three set the Warpers at the booths; you two to HQ and I'll head off to the Armoury. I think that we'll aim for everything to go up in flames by half past midnight. How's that sound?" I asked, cautiously, looking back up at their faces.

"Good," was the general consensus. I only hoped that it would go to plan. If not, I may not be the only one to fall tonight, and that was something I was not comfortable with.

Chapter Seventeen

I shoved my heavy pack into Wade's arms, keeping only my swords on my back as I began to climb quietly up the watchtower. It was pretty high, but I kept my eyes focused on the two Raiders above. I reached the top and climbed around to get a better look at the Raiders inside. Both had their backs turned and I took my chance, swinging my legs over the side of the platform and climbing up over the rail. Quickly and quietly, I reached for my swords and lunged forwards, plunging them as hard as I could into the backs of their heads, watching as the life drained suddenly from their bodies and they slumped in a heap in the corner of the watchtower. Blood poured from their pale heads, their mouths hanging open, their eyes showing no signs of pain or surprise.

As quickly as I had before, I climbed back down the watchtower, giving Wade a wicked smile when I reached the ground with a soft thud.

"Easy-peasy," I whispered, as I put my pack back on.

He smiled back, then led the way towards the patrol booths. We stayed out of the dim light filtering into the small lanes. I was getting a little paranoid that our footprints left in the glowing grass wouldn't disappear, but thankfully they only stayed for a few seconds. Hundreds of Raiders slept quietly in their beds, unaware of the danger lurking just outside their windows. I looked at my watch when we reached the last lane before the patrol booth that sat just outside the courtyard. Like clockwork, the Raiders strolled around the corner along their well-worn path, oblivious. Wade turned to me, pointing from himself to the Raider on the left and then to me and back at the Raider on the right. I nodded in agreement and as soon as their backs were turned, we came rushing into the light and stabbed them through the head. We each caught the Raiders and dragged their bodies over to the nearest little house, shoving them under the wooden porch, leaving a trail of black blood in the darkness.

Wade and I waited in the darkness for the others to arrive. I kept an ear out for any movement in HQ or the houses, or even the kids, but there was nothing. As the minute-hand on my watch flicked over to five past midnight, I could hear the soft thuds of footsteps as my squad made their way to the courtyard. A moment later and I could see the faint glow of bright veins surrounding the courtyard.

One lanky figure made its way over to us, before ducking over to the booth and pulling a Warper from his back pack. Aiden.

"Mothers first," I whispered to the other glowing shadows, and Wade came to life beside me, joining the other three who were running silently over to the house across the lane.

It took a few minutes, but there were no screams; just small whispers and a kind of scuffle before the four of them returned, pulling the two Raider mothers into the courtyard, their pale skin shining in the bright moonlight. Their faces were very concerned, set with anxiety and fear.

"If you make a sound, or do anything other than what we tell you, your children will die," Wade whispered forcefully to the mothers, who both nodded in frightened agreement as they were dragged along.

They pulled the mothers to the western and southern dorms, pushing them up the few steps and through the door. A moment later and out came the children, all doe-eyed and obedient, keeping their eyes forwards as if this was a normal thing to be happening. Wade gave me a wave as he led the way out of the camp, the forty kids trailing behind, surrounded by Skylar, Beau and Izzy. It seemed strange that we were once in these kids' position, and it could have just as easily been them coming to rescue us.

"Set the Warpers and the Blitzers. Good luck. Radio for help," I whispered to the rest of my squad, who were left in the now-empty courtyard.

My tummy did an awkward kind of black flip as I pulled myself up off the grass and headed east, back towards the Armoury. I was definitely afraid, but I knew that the Armoury was something we had to destroy. I ran almost freely back through the camp as I had done when I used to live here, unafraid of the Raiders or the world outside. I made it to the Armoury within a couple of minutes and stopped on the edge of the darkness, calming myself and re-tightening the straps on my pack.

"Go on – you can do this," I egged myself on. I took a deep breath and ran to the doors, pushing them open slowly, bringing one of my swords from off my back.

As I knew there would be, two guards were on the other side of the door, and they jumped with surprise when they saw me, but I didn't get the reaction I had suspected.

"What? Why are you out of bed, child?" the one on the right asked, annoyed.

I didn't say anything but continued to move towards them, hiding my sword behind my back.

"Answer when you are being spoken to," the other one said, getting angry now, standing slowly before me.

"You have orders to be obedient," the first Raider said again.

I gave no sign of stopping or saying a word, but continued towards them. The Raider closest to me took in a deep breath, and lunged towards me, trying to slap me in the face, but I was quicker. With one smooth swing of my sword, I cut off his hand. His dark eyes looked straight into mine as he drew in a deep breath, but before letting him get out a scream, I shoved the sword straight into his throat. I didn't wait for him to fall to the ground, but weaved around him and lunged straight towards the other Raider who looked at me with surprise. He held up his gun, blocking my swing.

"How…" he stuttered, as he swung the back of his gun towards me, missing my face, as I dived.

I took the other sword from off my back and sliced him as hard as I could around the kneecaps. As he fell towards me with a howl, I drove my sword into his chest, cutting off his sound and his life.

Knowing that other Raiders could have heard that, I didn't waste any time trying to cover my tracks, but instead sprinted down the hallway and to the door to the stairs, with the sound of my boots hitting the concrete floors bouncing around the high ceilings. I listened hard when I reached the bottom of the stairs, but there seemed to be no one out on the terrace of Level one. I turned the handle slowly, and peered out into the bright light of the terrace. Just as I was about to step out, two Raiders glided past the door and off down the next stairwell. I calmed myself once more, listening hard to the floor and went for it.

I went through the door and ran over to the left side, keeping away from the balcony and from prying eyes. I did my best and stuck to the shadows, calming my breath and my heartbeat, otherwise the Raiders were going to get me before I got the chance to get them. I dashed down the stairs, keeping one sword tightly in my hand, the other back in its holster. The further down I went, the darker it got and the fewer Raiders I had to steer clear from. Finally, I made it to the bottom of the staircase and could see the open space through the red lights glowing like veins in the dark walls, where about ten golden-glowing Hornets sat on a raised platform. I looked down at my watch: ten minutes left.

'You're doing good, Maddy,' I said to myself firmly, in my head. 'Just a little further and then get out. Getting out will be easy...' I trailed on and on, encouraging myself, making it seem less lonely.

I saw the hatch, and my mind wandered back to the Tidesse. Before I knew it, I was marching over to it, opening the hatch and jumping down into the darkness. The red lights in the walls surged, brightening up the dark little world around me. The five dark spidery chairs sat eerily around the glowing Tidesse.

'Stupid, Maddy... Stupid!' I shouted in my head, angrily, as I peered through the red lights.

I took a look around and not seeing, or hearing, anyone, I ran forwards and took out the Blitzer from my pack, setting it up underneath the chairs, pulling out its other six pieces and placing them around the room. I smiled when I realised the Hornets sitting just outside the hatch door were going to go up in a spectacular explosion of their own. I set the timer to 0030hrs... Eight and a half minutes to go.

'Well done. So, let's go now,' I said happily, in my mind, but my eyes turned back to the Tidesse glowing white through the red lights.

'Well, I did say getting out would be easy. And I have eight minutes... I'm sure another couple of minutes here won't matter.' I was beginning to worm my way out of my own plan.

I walked over to the Tidesse, running my hand down its right side. It felt abnormally smooth, but the pictures and words and whispers came out of it. I cleared my throat awkwardly, and stepped back a little so I could see the whole Tidesse before saying. "Who are the Sovereigns?"

A cool voice, much like Eris Black's, emanated from the Tidesse, as pictures of tall pale figures in red and golden cloaks sat high upon chairs in a dark room.

"The Sovereigns: the last family of the original Gouteszi, charged with the responsibility of carrying the legacy of our people. Torin and Lior Sovereign, and their children, Malik, Padreery, Josctellen and Ronan, make up the family. For centuries, by the mercy of Lithuteum, they have ruled and overseen all Gouteszi life, renowned for their resolute principles and eternal life, this family lives forever and rules forever. The Gouteszi are nomads in nature, roaming the galaxy and settling only when they find a compatible world."

Big pictures of different coloured worlds, some with rings, some with four moons, flashed across the Tidesse.

"Many of the worlds found had already been populated by other species, but with the strength of the Gouteszi comparing to none, these worlds have been taken over. Nearly two centuries ago, the youngest son, Ronan, parted ways with his family in a bid to discover a new home: a home that will house the Gouteszi for centuries to come. However, there are some who believe he found such a place years ago and wishes never to share it. Currently, the Sovereigns journey to a planet in an almost secluded part of the universe. Reports have been told of how weak the human species is, and that already the planet has come under siege and will soon eradicate the humans. Some believe that the Gouteszi have already visited this planet millennia ago, and perhaps have had some impact on the species currently inhabiting the planet."

"Enjoying yourself, Maddy?" asked a raspy cold voice from behind me.

I nearly screamed with fright, but managed to hold it in. I had been so mesmerised in the story that I had completely forgotten I was on a mission.

"Nah," I said, almost playfully. "Bit boring, really." I turned around, giving Carterra a smile.

He did not smile back, but I nearly laughed when I saw how messed up he really was. Red burns and deep scars dug into the right side of his face, and he was now missing his right eye, as well. All that was left was a deep black hole. I shuddered a little and tried to not look at it.

"Of course, you would find this amusing..." he trailed on, as he limped over to the Tidesse.

I backed away from him around the chairs, pulling out one of my swords.

He sat down and watched the Tidesse, his right leg remaining straight and stuck out in front of him.

"Lost this one," he said, coldly, patting his right thigh. "You may think you're doing well, Maddy, but you are just one little maggot in a big wide world. I am just one general: there are many more like me. So keep going... Keep fighting for as long as you can, for it is futile. The Sovereigns will be here soon and they won't want to keep the last of you in pits. No, they'll put you to work, make you their play things, take all the children and turn this into the new Gouteszi planet."

"Whatever," I retorted, backing up a little further, checking my watch: five minutes.

"So, you've found new friends have you?" he began to ask. "Starr will be your downfall, but I know you'll be too foolish to see it."

I could tell by the way he was talking that he was smiling.

"Good old Ronan. Very old..." he trailed off.

"So he's a Sovereign? First class. You must be feeling quite out of his league..." I teased. "You know, I used to hate this girl in second grade. Her name was Katie-Lou. I mean, who even names their kid Katie Lou? My Dad was army and her dad was air force, and we'd always fight. She had the coolest lunchbox, and a pony and everyone loved her..."

I chucked my sword back in its holster, keeping one eye on Carterra as I looked up at the closed hatch door. I jumped up, trying to spin the handle clockwise to reopen it. It didn't help that I was so small. I kicked off the inside of the hatch, pulling the handle round and was relieved when I heard it click to unlock. I jumped down and took a quick break, listening for the sounds of any Raiders above me.

Carterra cut in to my little story. "Obviously, the Lithuteum kept your mouth shut. Don't bother trying to escape. I've already alerted my army and they are out searching for all you little brats. You are worth nothing, Maddy: not even your own kind can trust you, and yet whatever game you're playing, it doesn't seem to be working." He kept his eyes forwards, I couldn't believe he hadn't yet noticed the Blitzer just under his seat.

"Oh well, that's nice of you to say that," I said, condescendingly. "I can see you are one for motivational speaking…" I was trying to figure out how I was going to get out of this place.

"The Sovereigns are coming. They are so much bigger than you. Smarter. You can try and try and try… You'll always fail against the Gouteszi: they always do," Carterra began to sing quite madly towards the end, and suddenly he burst up from his chair, his one eye looking wildly at me. I think he'd just noticed the wires coming from the Blitzer.

I freaked out and jumped back up into the hatch, kicking off the wall and opening it up, scrambling out as fast as I could. I heard Carterra's uneven footsteps striding towards me, his breath ragged. As soon as I made it out of the hatch, I turned and push the door down, but Carterra's head and arms came reaching out towards me. He grabbed my leg, but I managed to twist out of his grip, kicking him away, hearing him bellow out in pain. I didn't even look back to see if he was following, because I knew I had even more problems now: I stood up and looked back up at the Armoury coming to life. Hundreds of pairs of eyes all looking down at me.

I kind of did an awkward wave, then ran for it, back up the staircase, my swords out, cutting down every Raider in my path. The sound of Hornets began to fill my ears as they began to take off from the bottom level. Raiders on the other side of the Armoury shot at me with everything they had. Golden balls of light shot towards me, and I managed to duck around them as they went for the walls, melting through the metal of the ship. I pushed harder and harder, ducking and weaving around the Raiders, stabbing them through the chest and legs and anywhere I could reach. A group of five Raiders came bursting down the staircase towards me, and I could hear more coming from just behind. As they came running straight for me, firing their guns, without even thinking I jumped over the side of the balcony, their shots firing the Raiders who were behind me. Cold air rushed past me as I fell back down, level after level. With relief, I hit the rising Hornet I had heard, the golden light radiating from beneath my feet. The Raider inside it panicked and began to accelerate faster, aiming for the ceiling. Realising what he was doing, I shoved my swords back in their holsters, and swung over the side of the Hornet, holding on tightly as we hit the ceiling. We hovered in mid-air for a moment, and I could see the terrace of Level 1 just in front of me. I pushed off as hard as I could from the Hornet and leapt out towards the rail.

'You're so not going to make it,' said a sarcastic voice in my head. But to my relief, my hands grabbed on tightly to the rail, my body falling down and hitting the wall below with a smack.

A little winded, but all right, I pulled myself up, climbed over the rail and ran straight for the staircase. More Hornets seemed to buzz loudly from the Armoury, but I didn't dare look back. I burst back into the dark hallway, taken aback by the fact it was still night-time. I dashed down the hallway and ran as hard as I could back through the dusty lanes, dodging the few Raiders who were walking, confused, around the camp.

"Maddy!" called the frightened voice of Emily over my walkie.

I skidded to a stop, checking my watch: two minutes, thirty-five seconds.

"You all right? What's wrong?" I asked, hastily, reaching for one of my swords as a Raider looked confused in my direction.

"I can't make it... I can't..." her voice crackled in and out, then there was a sudden scream.

I racked my brains. Emily was doing the eastern patrol booth. I looked out to the edge of camp, where I knew there was safety for me, but then turned back with a huff as I headed back towards the patrol booth.

I made it there pretty quickly, but I didn't know what I was going to find. Emily was surrounded by three Raiders: one was pinning her against the wall of a small house, and the other two were looking confusedly at the Warper set at the patrol booth.

I ran forwards, throwing my first sword straight into the Raider holding Emily up. It hit him square in the head and then into the house, keeping him in place. His grip loosened and Emily slumped to the ground with a thud. The other two Raiders looked angrily at me and grabbed their weapons as I made my way towards them. I pulled the sword from the Raider's head, lunging towards them with a powerful swing. I hit the one on the right, and he howled in pain as he fell. But I wasn't fast enough to get the second one. He reached his pale hands towards me, grabbing me by my shoulders and lifting me high into the air, before throwing me hard through the window of a house opposite. I burst through the glass, landing hard against the wooden floors. Knowing time wasn't on my side, I got back up, ignoring the pain, and jumped out of the hole I had created. The Raider was waiting and shot his weapon at me, firing one shot that disintegrated into hundreds of tiny pieces, hitting me all over my body. I shouted out in pain, falling forwards onto the ground. He laughed cruelly, striding towards me, raising his gun to fire once more. Taking my chance, I swung my legs around, knocking him onto his side, and before he could get back up, I punched him as hard as I could in the head. Over and over, until his face was a black bloody mess and he couldn't fight back. Tired now, I stopped and checked the Warper was still set for exploding… Yep, definitely going to explode in the next thirty-three seconds.

My stomach flipped anxiously, and I ran back to Emily. She was unconscious, but at least she was still alive – for now. I looked around desperately for the quickest way out but there was none. Feeling the panic now, I pulled Emily's body up, putting her arm over my shoulder, and ran as fast as I could back towards the forest. More Hornets began to buzz in the air above us, golden light filling the sky. Many Raiders began to fill the streets now, running to action. I pushed through them, glad that they mistook me as one of the other kids, but I held one of my swords tightly in my hand, ready. I weaved in and out, and pulled Emily further and further away from the patrol booth. I looked down at my watch, desperate for just a little more time, but I wasn't lucky enough: seven… six… I dashed forwards. It looked like we only had a few streets left, but there wasn't going to be time to get out. Five… four… I pushed Emily down onto the ground as I skidded to a stop, jumping behind one of the small houses. A Raider noticed me, and his dark eyes flashed with excitement as he began to run towards me. Three… two… one…

Bursts of light shot up around the camp. I could feel the ground vibrating as the Armoury began to explode. A great rumble was heard and then the flames shot high up into the sky. The Warper at the patrol booth went off, and I ducked my head down low, curled in a ball on the ground. The first ring of fire cut a foot above my head, and the Raider in front of me was sliced in two as the fire slashed through his chest. Another ring of fire went off, and then another and another. The camp around me began to shake and burn with fury. Raiders, still trying to get out, ran in all directions, unable to see through the thick rising smoke. The Warpers kept going and going: it felt like forever. Giant rings of fire slashed out at everything in their path, ripping their way through houses and buildings and Raiders.

After what seemed like hours, the Warpers' rings of fire got fewer and further between, decreasing in size and anger. Feeling that the worst was over, I rose slowly, shaking the ash from the top of my head. I turned back around to see the entire camp levelled and on fire: it was as if someone had set fire to twenty football fields. The house that I had hid behind was demolished, black and charred, and it had to be the highest thing left standing, at about a foot and a half tall. I turned back to Emily. She was covered in ash. I pulled her back over my shoulder. I noticed now that there was a big gash in her right leg, but it seemed to have stopped bleeding. She'd be all right soon enough. Slowly, we made our way back into the cool forest. Apart from the crackling and a few screams from the still burning remnants of Raiders in the camp, it was rather quiet in here, the trees swaying back and forth calmly, unaffected by the destruction.

Tired now, and feeling the ache from the hundred small bullet holes in my body, I trudged on along the path away from the Raiders. I could see many footsteps in the ground and I revelled in our achievement of getting the kids out. No matter what the humans were going to say when we got back, no matter how much trouble we'd be in, I knew that they'd be glad.

Chapter Eighteen

"Maddy?" crackled Aiden's voice over the walkie. "Where are you? Is Emily there? Over."

I put my sword back in its holster and reached for my walkie on my shoulder, still stumbling along with an unconscious Emily on my right side. "I've got Emily. We're coming back to you now," I said quietly. We were still kind of close to the camp, and I could hear a few quickened footsteps running around me. "Everyone else make it back? Over."

"No. Charlie and Mason aren't here yet. Wade took everyone else back towards Saigo, and Loren went with them. Did HQ go up? Over."

My heart sank and I turned back to look at the burning camp. "I can't be sure HQ was destroyed. Just wait for Emily and me and we'll talk then. Over and out."

I stopped then, listening to those footsteps in the forest around me. They didn't seem to be heading my way, so I could be sure it wasn't Charlie or Mason, and that the Raiders hadn't heard us yet. I huffed, and picked Emily up, her long body lying limp over my shoulders. It was hard to have her up there with my swords, but I managed. I ran back to the truck as fast as I could. It took me a few hours, but I knew that I had to first save the people I knew I could save.

Wearily, I jogged across the little break in the stream and back up the hill to the trucks.

"Maddy?" Aiden's voice called from out of the darkness.

"Yeah, it's us," I called back, softly. My body was really starting to hurt now.

I could hear his footsteps grow louder as he jogged down the hill to meet me. "You guys hurt?" he asked, when he reached my side. I could see the glowing chemicals in his veins light up his face. He had a big cut down the left side of his head. Blood trickled slowly from it, staining his shirt.

"Can you take her?" I asked, pushing Emily's body towards him.

"Sure," he said, quietly, as he lifted Emily from off my shoulders. I kind of fell forwards: the relief of having her back here safely was overwhelming, but the empty feeling of anxiety was just as powerful.

"Woah… Maddy, you good?" he asked, as he turned back to look at me.

"Fine. I'm fine," I said, exhausted, getting back to my feet. That was the only break I was going to have tonight, and I decided then and there that I wasn't going to stop again until I knew where Charlie and Mason were.

I followed him back up the hill and under the tarp covering the last remaining truck.

"Yeah. Wade thought it'd be best to put the mothers in the back of the truck, and make the kids run the rest of the way back to Saigo. Loren went with them, just in case," he said, with a cautious smile. Hornets could be heard buzzing overhead, but we were safe for now under the tarps.

"That's a good idea," I said, as I opened the door to the backseat and helped him get Emily inside. She looked pretty pale in the light, her brown hair falling out of its tight braid.

Aiden and I stood in silence for a moment, watching Emily breathe slowly in and out.

"It's nearly four o'clock in the morning," Aiden said, breaking the silence, looking down at his watch. "The sun will be up soon. I don't think we'll be able to do anything until tonight."

"No, I'm going back now," I said, defiantly, repositioning my swords on my back. "Now is the time to do anything we can for those boys. The camp will be a mess. You stay here with Emily. Radio in only if you have to," I declared, beginning to order him around again.

"Wait, wait. I'm coming with you. Emily will be fine and we'll write her a note for when she wakes up, telling her to stay put," he said, with a small smile. "You're not going back alone."

"Fine. Then let's get moving," I said, quietly.

Remembering the walkie Gabe gave me to warn Saigo, I searched for it in my pocket. I felt a sudden surge of energy flow through my hands, and then the walkie turned on, crackling away.

"Gabe? Gabe can you hear me? It's Maddy," I asked.

It took barely a second before I heard Gabe's eager voice reply. "Maddy? Maddy – you're all right? How'd it go?"

"It went all right. Wade and a few others are bringing those forty kids like us back. They've got the two Raider mothers with them, alive. Hornets are coming. Aiden and I will be following closely behind. We've just got to go back for Charlie and Mason."

"Okay. Are they all right?" His voice was less eager now.

"Don't know," I answered, truthfully. "I'll call in again when we do know. It'll take another day, at least, before those kids reach Saigo. Make sure everyone is ready. Everything good your end?"

"I'm confined to my workstation and my living quarters. I was in huge trouble with Majors Miller and Walker, but Black stepped in and got me out of the prison cells. They're terrible places. Less air, no light. And the food is worse than the stuff you guys are given–"

"Okay, Gabe. We've really got to go," I interrupted again. "Thanks again for everything you've done. I'll talk with you later. Over and out." I turned the walkie off, and put it back in my pocket.

"He's a good guy for a Rebel," Aiden joked as he popped the letter he'd just finished writing into Emily's jacket pocket.

"Ready?" I asked. With a nod of agreement, we made our way back out from under the tarp and ran as fast as we could, back towards the camp. Instead of running through the forest, we took a chance and ran straight across the clearing to get to the other side of the camp. It was strange, just the two of us, running through the forest on the other side, coming closer and closer to the still-burning camp – the place we were supposed to be well clear of by now. There were still quite a few Hornets in the air, circling over the wreck. Over in the distance, I could see the green lights of Crows coming our way… Reinforcements. I hoped they didn't spot Wade and the rest of the squad kids in the dim light. I wanted them to get as far away as they could before the Hornets found them.

Finally, we reached the last remaining tall daggers standing around what was left of HQ on the surface. There were still quite a few Raiders around, but they seemed too dazed or hurt to be doing anything. Hornets were the main activity, but I wasn't worried: they wouldn't be able to see us in the dark.

With Aiden following closely behind, I dashed out from the trees and ran across the charred ground, past what used to be streets of houses, now burnt ashes on the ground. We stopped when we reached the daggers, leaning against them to take a quick look around to see if we were good to go. With a nod from Aiden, we ducked low and made our way to the ruined HQ building. Three of the walls were still standing, but most of the roof and front of it had been blasted by the Warpers. We crawled through a small opening at the front and scrambled down what was left of the dark hallway to the staircase. The door to the staircase was jammed a little, but eventually, Aiden and I managed to get it open. Quietly, we stepped down the stairs. I listened for any signs of Raiders and couldn't hear any on the first floor. I had never been in HQ before and never known how many floors there really were or who worked here.

Aiden and I walked out of the staircase and into the first level. There were many long tables spread out on each wall of the large room. The tables were stacked with black boxes and funny-looking devices. One was shaped like a telescope but was pointing directly at the wall. Curious, I looked inside, and could see straight through the wall and the dirt, all the way to the next open level spot which seemed like miles away. It overlooked a valley in the darkness. Another device seemed to just be an ordinary black slab of glass, but when I ran my hand over it, a giant 3-D map jumped out, filling the corner of the room with the map of the camp, and all the valleys and mountains around it. There were heaps of red and green dots, all moving around – green ones zoomed over the mountains, and there was a whole collection of red dots sitting under the ground off in the distance: Saigo.

Remembering my mission, I pulled Aiden away from the table at the other side of the room. He seemed almost annoyed that he didn't get to fully explore a white box that had red little creatures crawling around inside it. We walked over to the next staircase, almost getting a fright when we saw a pile of Raiders dead in the corner, all heaped together, black blood dripping down the stairs. Mason and Charlie had been here all right. I pulled out one of my swords and could hear Aiden move his gun off his shoulder. I listened again at the door, before pulling it slightly open.

The world before us was bustling with Raiders, running this way and that; giant maps like the one I'd seen upstairs on the walls, with Raiders pointing and talking furiously. I could see more green dots zooming around the maps now; even larger green masses heaped together on what looked like cities to the east.

Aiden and I crunched down lower, watching the Raider world before us. I listened hard through the mayhem for Charlie or Mason, pushing past the Raiders' confused and angry voices and down the levels, as far as I could. I could hear a lot of shouting and then a door slammed loudly on the floor below, cutting out all sound inside the room. My heart sank. Of course, there'd be the same stuff that made it impossible for me to hear inside the room, just like with Carterra's tent.

I closed the door the rest of the way, very slowly, and turned to Aiden.

"They're below us. They have to be," I said, sadly, looking back out at the room full of Raiders.

"What?" he said, nearly too loudly. He controlled himself and muttered, "But, how do we get through all them?"

I thought for a moment, hoping something would come to me, but it didn't. The only way I could think of getting down the level was by killing every Raider in that room.

I shrugged my shoulders. "Kill them all," I suggested, quietly.

Aiden sighed and looked behind me, and then back down at how many rounds he had in his gun. "How many people are we willing to lose today?" he asked, kind of scared.

"We just have to try," I said, in a low voice, pulling my other sword from out of its holster. "They don't have weapons. We can catch them by surprise."

"All right, all right. I'll go first and open fire… You come out behind me and head around the side of the room?"

I nodded in agreement, and we changed places by the door. I could hear Aiden's heart begin to race as he reached for the handle.

It was all a blur. Aiden stormed out from the staircase and gunned down countless Raiders. I was right: they definitely were surprised. I dashed out behind him and raced around the room, cutting down every Raider in my path. Some tried to lunge towards me, but Aiden would shoot them down, or I'd be fast enough to stop them. When I finally made it to the other side of the room, I closed the door to the next stairwell, helping kill every last Raider in the room. It took a matter of moments before Aiden and I stood alone in the room, covered in scratches and bruises and black Raider blood, with about forty Raiders lying motionless on the ground. He gave me a kind of weird smile, as he reloaded his gun and made his way over to me. I opened the door without hesitating, cutting down the few Raiders who had been standing guard to the level below. I tried listening through the door, but couldn't hear anything.

I shook my head at Aiden. "Can't hear a thing," I said, quietly.

Before he could answer, our walkies began to crackle. A blood-curdling laugh rang out from them, echoing eerily through the hallway.

"Well done, well done!" said the terrifying voice of a man. "I can see you've made it past all of those fools! Now, how about you come inside and we can decide which half of your friend you'll get to keep."

I looked at Aiden, who turned instantly pale, a fear-stricken look on his face. I got angry, gripped my swords tighter and turned the handle open forcefully, ready for this to be over with.

We burst angrily through the room to find ourselves, instead, on a balcony overlooking a deep, dark pit. I looked around the open space and could see: hanging right above the pit was Mason, tied up around his arms and his legs, swinging in mid-air.

"Mason?" Aiden called, loudly, and we could see Mason's head roll back, blood dripping from the top of his head.

The laugh sounded again, echoing around the dark space, but this time I could see who it came from. There was a tall Raider, standing with guards either side of him, resting his hands along the rail, looking straight at the two of us. He had unnervingly bright eyes, his smile cruel, and was watching us excitedly, as if it were a game. He didn't look like any Raider I'd seen before.

"So his name is Mason, is it?" he asked, looking back up at Mason hanging in front of him. "Welcome, children. I'm sure you've never been allowed to see this wonderful masterpiece," he said, gesturing to the space around him. "I am Magnus Rovio."

I looked either side of Aiden and me. We were all alone; no guards coming. Before us was one small metal bridge going from one side to the other. I listened for anyone else and the sound of thousands of hearts beating reached my ears, coming from below. I looked down into the pit and saw, to my disbelief, the red veins stretching out through the darkness to countless red balls of light now covering the walls all the way down to the ground. I could just make out tiny black shapes inside each one, my heart sinking with fear.

"What is that?" Aiden asked, firmly, raising his gun a little higher.

"Those? Those are our children. Class Four coming into the world. They're sleeping at the moment, so do try not to wake them… They can get a little grumpy," he said, still smiling, gesturing to the red balls below. "This… Mason," he said, gesturing to Mason once more. "Tried to put one of these on the floor above." He raised a Blitzer by his side. "He wasn't alone, this one here was helping him." The Raider stepped out of the way, and I could see Charlie, hanging limp by the arms, being held up by two Raiders.

I looked at Aiden, and pushed his gun down lower.

"A wise decision, young lady." Rovio said happily, as he watched us.

"What do you want?" I asked, calmly, turning my eyes to him.

"What do I want, my dear? What do you want?" he replied, quietly.

"I want my home back. I'm taking it back," I said, staying as calm as I could.

"Oh… I understand. Perhaps you were never taught to share as a child, or maybe even you were the child who stole all the toys, and now you are having a taste of your own medicine. We all have things we must learn… So let me teach you just this one thing: this world is not yours any more. I suggest you get prepared to lose," he instructed, a smile still spread across his face.

"I'm sorry – did I stutter?" I asked, angrily, matching his smile. "I'm taking back my home, whether you like it or not… I suggest *you* get prepared to lose." I copied his last line.

He laughed once more. Even the four Raiders at his side laughed. "You think I fear children, such as yourselves? No. So full of yourselves… How could you do any wrong? You're invincible… Now back to my original question: which half of Mason do you want to keep?"

I dared not to think it, but I could see no possible way of getting Mason down. I stormed my mind with ways of saving them both, but Charlie was too far away and surrounded by Raiders, and I had a feeling that Mason's fate was already decided. I gave Aiden a look, trying to speak to him through it, trying to tell him to be ready. I looked from him to his gun, and back up again, hoping he'd understand.

"Well?" Rovio asked again, staring up at Mason's body.

I gave him a small smile, and took a deep breath, daring myself to be brave. "We'll take the lot, thanks," I exclaimed, as I jumped up onto the rail and dived for Mason.

With one swift swing of my swords, I cut the rope around his legs, and grabbed on tightly to the rope at his hands. I could hear the Raider yell, and a spray of bullets came from either side of the pit, from Aiden and the Raiders.

I swung Mason and myself just over to the bridge and cut the rope around his hands, both of us landing with a crash onto the bridge. It was pretty small and I nearly fell over, but managed to regain my balance. I untied the ropes around his hands, pulling him back towards Aiden. I could see a deep gash in the side of his torso, but he was coming back to consciousness now, muttering something I couldn't understand.

Aiden had killed three of the other Raiders, and I took my chance. I ran back along the bridge, straight for Rovio. He didn't move, didn't even blink, but instead, pulled out a long silver stake, twisted in the middle. I jumped towards him, but suddenly a deafeningly loud scream filled my ears, forcing me to lose my concentration and come crashing into the rail in front of him. He laughed happily and dropped the alien tech at his feet, stepping back towards another door behind him.

"I do hope you don't survive this," he called, happily, as he marched back out the door.

Charlie, who had now just come back to life, crawled forwards towards the silver stake and twisted it back into place, cutting the sound off. I rocked back and forth in agony, feeling warm blood drip from my ears.

"Come on," Aiden said, too loudly. "We've got to go!" he yelled, climbing over the rail onto the bridge to get Mason.

I reached forwards and pulled Charlie towards me, helping him over the rail. He cried out in pain several times: I could see deep cuts across his back, and his face was badly beaten.

"Did you think we'd leave you here?" I asked, slowly, with a small smile, as I gave him a big hug.

"Maddy…" he trailed off, sadly.

I stepped back and looked at Charlie, his wavy hair matted with blood, his blue eyes tired and sad. He wasn't looking at me, but instead at Mason, who was still muttering something incomprehensible.

"What is it?" I asked, slowly, looking from Charlie and back to Mason.

I walked over to Aiden, Charlie following slowly behind, and helped Charlie back over the rail.

"Come on, Mason." I said, encouragingly, trying to help lift him to his feet, but he stopped me, shaking his head and muttering "No…" over and over.

Below us, I could hear a sound that sent shivers down my spine — the sound of Raiders clawing their way out of their red sacs, the sound of fluid washing over the floor and Raiders taking their first breath.

"We need to destroy this place," Aiden said, angrily, looking back over at the Blitzer left on the ground on the other side of the rail. "But why would he leave?" he asked, shaking his head.

Feeling pretty confused, I still tried my hardest to bring Mason to his feet, but he managed to push me back. "Because I can't leave," he muttered, quietly.

I stepped forwards but he shook his head once more. "I can't leave…" Tears began to run down his face now.

"Why?" I asked, beginning to feel less like a winner.

"Because he's got twenty-four seconds left," Charlie said, looking sadly down at his watch.

"What does that mean?" Aiden said, angrily now.

"I'm sorry. Thank you for coming back for us," Mason said, sadly, getting to his feet, holding the open wound that was still gushing blood from his side. He rested his hand on my shoulder, looking sadly into my eyes. "I know we'll win. Thank you for showing us how to be human again, Maddy... Even if you are defective." He smiled, but before I knew what was happening, he turned and stepped off the side of the bridge.

I screamed out in panic and tried to grab him, but couldn't. I watched his body fall through the darkness, towards the red glow and the Raiders below. Suddenly, his body exploded... He was there, and then he was gone. The explosion set off even more loud bangs from the bottom of the pit, and the bridge began to shake, as did the whole ship around me.

"They shoved a bomb inside him..." Charlie muttered, sadly, watching the fiery explosion begin to erupt at the pit below us. The sounds of Raiders screaming began to fill our ears.

"He's gone, Maddy," Aiden said, quietly, as I continued to stare desperately down at the fiery pit.

Feeling the tears run freely down my face now, I stood up slowly and ran back to get the Blitzer from the other side of the bridge.

"Well... Let's do this right, then," I said angrily, setting the Blitzer to go off in two minutes, before throwing it over the side of the bridge, down into the depths of the Raiders being born. "Let's go!"

I turned back and helped Aiden pull Charlie back up the stairs, past all the dead Raiders, lying motionless on the floor. For some reason, I decided I'd bring the black slab of glass that was the map with me, tucking it under my spare arm. Aiden even filled his pack with a few of the other things he could see, giving me a small smile.

"Gabe will love this," he said, quietly.

Aiden went first, out through the small opening to the ground. I went after Charlie, helping push him through the hole. We didn't check whether the coast was clear, but instead just walked straight back into the forest. A few moments later and the ground beneath us began to rumble, and a great big fiery ball of flames shot out through HQ, sending the remaining Raiders running to the opposite end of the camp.

Aiden and I carried Charlie all the way back, not saying a word. I was glad that we had, at least, rescued one of our friends, but it still wasn't enough. Mason could have been any of us, and yet I felt completely responsible for him dying. I was the leader, he had trusted me, and now he was dead. My heart felt so heavy, and I couldn't bother stopping the tears run down my face. Loss was one human emotion I wish I could never feel.

Chapter Nineteen

We made it back to Saigo with only four Hornets on our tails. Luckily, Gabe had warned everyone and there were Hangjets waiting, ready to fight. There seemed to have already been a fight, with downed Hornets and Raiders still burning on the ground around the force field. Aiden drove quickly back through it, giving Steve, in the checkpoint, a sheepish wave. I sat in the back seat, holding Emily's hand, and having Charlie hug me tightly. They were both pretty shaken up, but neither would speak of what had happened to them, so I just sat there in the middle.

Aiden drove the truck around to our hangar and we were greeted by some soldiers' angry faces, but mostly by happy faces from civilians who'd come up to the ground to have a look at us. We parked in the shade of the hangar, and Aiden got out of the truck, running round to Emily's door and helping her out.

"We're home now, Charlie," I said, quietly.

He kept his head on my shoulder, holding my other hand and sniffed. "You probably think I'm such a loser."

"No. I sent you in there, and I'm sorry, Charlie. You were so brave… both of you."

He looked up at me now, his blue eyes wearily searching my face. "How do you do it?"

"Do what?" I asked back, watching Aiden help Emily over to Dr Shaw, who was waiting by the door of the hangar at the front of the truck.

"Keep moving? Keep fighting…"

"Because that's my job. Now come on, let's go see the others," I said, quickly, shuffling out of Emily's door and walking around the back of the truck to help Charlie out.

There seemed to be a lot of yelling from Major Miller, and also a lot of confusion as to how we had heard they weren't going to let us out. My dad wasn't angry, but his eyes filled with tears when he saw me. He gave me a big hug, and I hugged him back, knowing I wasn't going to tell him how I felt, but his hug made things feel a little better. At least he understood what it felt like to lose one of your own, a friend. That quiet knowledge helped carry me through. Eris Black congratulated me as the squad leader for carrying out such a 'dangerous and daring' mission, as she worded it. According to her, Ronan Starr was making arrangements for us kids to have the best equipment he could manage: that way we could keep sticking it to the Raiders the best we could. Dr Shaw hugged me as well. He seemed even more concerned about me than my dad.

After a round in the machine, I woke up in my bed in the dark dorm, hearing many more hearts beating all around me. Each of the four dorms was now filled with girls on our level, and I felt proud that we'd rescued them all from the Raiders. One life for forty seemed like an all-right deal at the end of the day. It was strange to see all the new additions at breakfast the next morning, the four dining tables filled with many more faces. The empty space Mason left at our table was a little more distracting though.

"So…" Wade began slowly, looking at Aiden, Charlie and me. We hadn't spoken much about what had happened, except to Majors Miller and Walker, Dr Shaw and Black.

I could feel Aiden look at me out of the corner of his eye, but none of us answered.

"Well done on getting everyone back," I said, quietly. "At least that part went to plan." I added, with a small smile, looking down at my drink.

"We're a pretty good team, aren't we?" Aiden said with a smile, looking up at us all now.

We all nodded, and agreed.

"We just have to keep on being brave," Beau said, cheerily, from his place next to his sister.

"Yes, definitely. And working together seems to be the way to go," Izzy said, with an even bigger smile.

"Wade? I think those girls are looking at you…" Loren said quietly, pointing over to the table on the far end of the dining room. She had a hint of excitement in her voice. "You may have some admirers already."

I looked up at Wade, whose face seemed to turn a bright shade of red, and laughed at his reaction. He seemed to sit up a little straighter, flexing his muscles just a little more.

"Maybe they can teach you how to count?" Charlie said, provokingly, from my side, with a smile.

"Hey, I can count…" Wade insisted, defensively.

"Oh, really? And when I asked you to do a head-count on those kids and you told me we have 43? You call that counting?" Skylar said, happily.

We all laughed together, at Wade's expense, but he laughed along, too. Gabe arrived at that moment, coming to sit with us at our table, a big smile spread across his face.

"That alien tech you got me is amazing!" he shouted, happily, pulling one of the drinks towards him.

We all listened as he went on and on, barely stopping for breath. Aiden was right: he was a good guy.

I looked around at all these happy faces, realising how far we'd come from being mindless soldiers for the Raiders. People are what is important. And yeah, maybe we're just kids, but we'll be ready, we'll be waiting to fight. We're going to take back our world piece by piece, even if it takes the rest of our lives.

My name is Maddy Walker, and I'm not alone anymore. I have a family, I have friends, and I have a place in this world. I'm going to lead from the front, to be brave and strong, and prove my worth every step of the way. Those Raiders are going to rue the day they decided to take my home, and I'm ready. This war has only just begun.